I'd been a sailor for a y[...]
not had sex since my s[...]
only a wank. But, now, as a sailor, I was obliged to
go ashore with mates and play the hettie game,
watching them box off with the birds. I often got
strange looks because I wouldn't. And I could never
let on to those sexy baby-sailors, who's sailor suits
made their buttocks look even more horny, trapped
in bum-hugging bell-bottoms, that it was only their
pants I wanted to dive inside. Thus frustrated, I
tossed myself regularly - in the heads, in my
hammock, in my office. Constantly I tossed myself,
but always alone.

Below decks, those of us granted a pass were
preparing to go ashore - pressing uniforms; the
older sailors, civvies. As always, Paul was close by;
his locker being next to mine. His pert white butt,
trapped between tanned brown torso and thighs,
was closer to my cock than was comfortable. In
fact, I believe I felt my dick glide, semi stiff, over
his right buttock cheek as I squeezed past, in order
to reach the ironing table.
   "I hope that was your finger," he giggled.
   "You'd need something fatter than a finger to
satisfy you," I teased.

▶ virgin sailors

KEN SMITH

an *erotic* anthology

PROWLER BOOKS

Virgin Sailors by Ken Smith

Copyright © 1998 PROWLER PRESS
3 Broadbent Close London N6 5GG. All rights reserved.

First printing September 1998
Cover photography © 1998 Prowler Press

web-site: prowler.co.uk
• ISBN 1-902644-03-4

Printed in Finland by Werner Soderstrom Oy.

British Library Cataloguing in Publication Data.
A catalogue record for this book is available from the British Library.

▶ contents

Dedicated to the many gay sailors who have been discharged from the navy, and the many more who are still in it!

BOILER ROOM BOY

Boxer was bent over some machinery, head stuffed deep inside, boiler suit folded to his navel, the arms tied around his waist, butt drawn in tight by the blue material. If I could have handcuffed him there and ripped that boiler suit from him and stuffed him stupid, then I would have, but Boxer's sexual preferences was still a mystery to me.

I had no idea where he got his nickname from. He didn't look like a boxer and definitely didn't wear them, especially under that boiler suit. Beneath that, I was only too aware, was naked flesh, a thick short dick and a small pussy of jet black pubes. Every silken sweaty part of his upper torso was solid muscle; two years of torturing tight nuts and bolts. And speaking of nuts, his were hairless and hung, coconut sized, beneath that bone.

"Boxer!" I shouted above the noise of the ship's generators, "Have you seen the Engineering Officer?" Boxer didn't reply, elbow working up and down, a kind of wanking action, an action I was sure he was familiar with!

"Boxer!" I yelled, even louder, and placed my palm onto his greasy, sweaty back, running it down to the crack into which his body fluid was draining.

"Fuck!" he screamed, banging his head when I startled him and spinning around to face me. His pretty face beamed on seeing me; baby soft, it looked so cute covered in parts by grease make-up.

I stroked my finger on a blob above his thin black eyebrow. "Commander Cruft?" I asked, waving a wad of signals.

"Not here," he bellowed, "I'll take them if you want," offering a sticky black hand. My face gave my reply when I grimaced but I wouldn't have been allowed to give them him anyway - secret stuff and all that. "Scared of a bit of shit!" he shouted, pulling five fingers down my cheek, printing an Indian war-paint mark from temple to chin.

At that moment, old Crufty clattered down the ladder and came over. "Signals, Sir," I saluted.

Crufty grasped them in thick fingers then glimpsed my face, "Clean yourself up, Signalman. How dare you come into my engine room looking like that!"

Boxer stuffed his head back into the machinery, hiding his giggles as I shouted, "Sir!" As soon as Cruft had disappeared into his office, I stuffed my hand between Boxer's thighs and goosed him, squeezing that delicious dick hard in my palm.

A second bump on Boxer's head, when he jumped in surprise, saw me legging it up the ladder and him gripping his sausage and shouting something. Lip reading, I think he said, "Suck this!" If that was the case, then I would have gladly done so right there and then; feasting on his sweat and grime and spunk.

We were both on the middle watch with about an hour to go. The Signal Office was pretty quiet but the weather wasn't and the ship was bouncing around like a tit in a tantrum. The teleprinter fired up an began clattering away - a signal reminding us that there were force eight gales in the area spewed out. Marconi, a nickname given to the baby signalman because he was a whiz kid, was on duty with me. I pushed myself up against him as he read the incoming message, "Anything interesting?" I asked, kissing his neck.

"Piss off!" he rebuffed, pushing his arse against my stiff cock. "I don't know, Knocker. I hate this middle watch. You always get horny around three." That was the truth, for all of us in fact. Dead on three, up popped our peckers whether we wanted them to or not. And when your at sea and the only thing shaggable is a pretty youth, whether you fancy boys or not, instinct tells you that your cock should find a hole, and a boy's bum or mouth becomes very inviting indeed, or, in my case, the most inviting place!

"Wanna crash out early?" I asked, giving him the opportunity of an extra hour's kip - sleep, rum and fags having the currency of gold on a ship.

Marconi swung around, his cock was as stiff as mine. "And what do I have to do for that?" he smiled.

"On your knees!"

"Half your tot and twenty smokes as well," he bargained, even though he was already pulling his prick from his pants and going down, knowing only too well that I would say yes.

Marconi had been doing this sort of thing well before the navy and was a master at mouthing cock. I pulled my prick into the open. His lips parted and his mouth went straight to the base. No messing about for Marconi. He loved sucking cock!

"Just the head," I demanded, knowing I would shoot quickly; thoughts of Boxer still lingering in my mind. "That's good, around the ridge."

Marconi slurped and savoured, jerking himself off, but in his eagerness he couldn't remain at the head for long and was soon back to the base, allowing his throat muscles to do the work. I rubbed his prickly head and grabbed the back of his neck, pushing harder and deeper. There was no need, he couldn't have gotten anymore of me.

"You want my cum, don't you? You're gagging for it!" I teased, pulling out as he fought to get the lot back down his throat.

"Uhm! Uhm!" he moaned, his throat contracting tightly on my thickening cock.

He grabbed my arse and squeezed tightly, his right hand pumping as fast as one of Boxer's engine pistons. I knew he was almost there, we'd done this so many times before And as thoughts of screwing my Boiler Room boy, naked, greasy, and draped over throbbing machinery swamped my mind, I let go the whole whack in one thick squirt.

Marconi went mad, his throat massaging every droplet from my dick. With a muffled squeal, he sent his own stream sailing over my serge bell-bottoms, the remainder seeping in strands from his cock. Quickly I pulled him up and fell to my knees, taking what was left into my mouth and milking him dry.

The office was strangely silent with Marconi absent. I still had an hour to kill until my morning watch relief. I pulled my dick out again and ran visions of Boxer and Marconi's bobbing head through my mind. Ringing bells, indicating and important incoming signal, put paid to a second shooting. Reluctantly, I got on with my job.

A ship in distress was the news I didn't wish to read. It would mean that I would remain on watch until things got sorted. It wasn't good for those relieving me either, and I dispatched the Bosun's Mate to wake them early.

Drowsy, eye rubbing boys greeted me when I answered the buzzer and let them in. The coffee canteen was the first thing they headed for, getting their early caffeine fix; the second fix, nicotine, pulling fags from my packet and drawing heavily upon them. Meanwhile, I felt the ship shudder as more revs were stuck on the engines. I thought of Boxer in the boiler room, half naked and sweating as he beefed them up, or put more gas in them, or whatever he did down there.

"Where's Marconi?" asked my opposite number who was of equal rank and in charge of his shift.

"Sent him below early. It was dead as a Dodo until ten minutes ago." I detected a wry smile on his face when I told him, wondering if he knew why I was always letting Marconi have time off. It didn't really matter, there was nothing he could do about it. Not only that, his blond baby signalman had been early to bed on more occasion than I could mention, and I'd caught them pressed together several times.

"Going up top for a breath of air," I said, after explaining the situation. "I'll be on the flag deck if you need me."

The bridge was buzzing as I passed through, the navigator plotting a course toward the distressed ship, the duty Bunting trying to gain contact by voice transmissions and swapping information with other craft bearing down on the damaged vessel.

I nodded "morning" to the Bunting and walked out onto the port side of the flag deck. The wind was howling, hammering rain and salt spray into me. I'd donned an oil-skin so I was protected from the foul weather, but the problem with oil-skins, the rain usually ran down the neck.

Several seaman were positioned around the flag deck, binoculars in hand, scanning seaward in search of the vessel. I noticed Spud leant against the twenty- inch signalling lamp as I stuffed my head between funnel and bulkhead and attempted to light a fag.

Spud was a scrumptious sailor, eighteen, jet black hair and queer. I recalled the day when the whole ship discovered that news.

We were mustered aft. Spud was being Court Martialled for screwing a young sailor. He got ninety days detention. And that was no joke - a navy prison was far removed from any civilian one. I felt sorry for him as he stood there, red faced, his private life paraded before grinning men and boys. He'd made that major mistake. He'd not made sure that the lad knew what he wanted, and as a consequence, the boy reported him. Had Spud been doing my kind of job - secrets and all that stuff - he would have been discharged. But, sadly for him, his preference for boys was made public knowledge and he went to prison. I could not imagine what horrors he went through during those ninety days.

But it wasn't all bad for him because when he got back on board, I was one of the first to search him out and ask for a blow job. He was pretty nervous at first - once bitten - but soon he was munching on my meat on a regular basis. Not only that, I discovered from him who the lad was who had shopped him. It was Ben, a campish boy sailor. I had no hesitation about dragging him into a secluded compartment and discussing his sexuality. He soon realised that he'd made a mistake and did indeed like sucking cock and being screwed. We met up several times after that. Locked in total darkness of our secret hideaway, I pumped his little arse with prick whilst playing with his cock. He just loved it and often I had to place my hand over his mouth to stifle his squeals of delight when we both detonated our dicks.

I moved over to Spud, who was crouched down, resting his binoculars on the bulkhead surrounding the twenty-inch lamp. "Mornin' Spud," I whispered, running my hand beneath his waterproofs and gripping his dick. It was solid, as would most cocks be at 5am.

Spud flinched slightly, still aware of his past mistake. "Oh, it's you, Knocker!"

In the darkness, I bit on his earlobe then unbuttoned his fly and pulled his prick into the wind and rain. Spud kept his left hand on the binoculars and dropped his right into the opening of my oil skin and sprang my dick free. Together we gently tugged on our cocks, Spud continuing to scan seaward as if nothing were happening. "That feels great, Knocker. Go a bit faster!" he breathed heavily.

I increased my pace. Spud followed suit. I felt a dribble of cum roll down my finger, then the whole load. A call from the bridge door, requesting I return to my office, caused me to quickly lick Spud's juices from my hand and put my cock away. "Sorry," said Spud, apologising for being unable to finish the job, even though it wasn't his fault.

I pecked his cheek. "Next time. Catch you later," I said and headed into the bridge. I overheard the Captain ordering a decrease in revs and a new heading for the Coxswain as I entered. I guessed that the incident was over and we were returning to relative normality. That was confirmed in the Communications Office and I was officially relieved. I left my relief and his lad to their own devices and headed for my hammock.

The Mess was dark, only the red night light above the hatch bathing it in a warm seductive glow. Men and boys snored and shuffled and talked in their sleep. The scent of sweaty sailors swam in the air, siphoning in and out of sleeping nostrils. It was a heady smell, yet somehow extremely sexy and arousing. Once again my cock stiffened. I brushed beneath a couple of boy-sailors' hammocks, listening for signs of wanking, ready to assist if required, but all were asleep.

Normally, after finishing a night watch, we'd jump straight into our beds without washing, eager to get to sleep. Washing disturbed the built up drowsiness and made it harder to get off. Maybe it was the extra hour I had done, or maybe I was feeling a little grubby. Quietly opening my locker, I removed my towel and washing gear, stripped naked, wrapped the towel around my waist and headed for the aft heads.

The hiss of shower spray greeted me as I entered the heads. Pissing in the urinal as I passed, I moved around to the shower cubicles. My eyes danced delightfully in my head and my cock went delirious with desire. Boxer was smothered from head to toe in soap, humming happily. Again I caused him to jump when I called his name; this time the sound of the shower and his concentration on the task at hand occupying his thoughts.

"Not you again, Knocker?"

"'Fraid so!"

"Just finished?"

I spun the tap and hoped for hotter water than yesterday. "Yep."

"What was all the panic for?"

I ducked beneath the spray but, as always, with each roll of the ship the temperature changed form freezing to boiling as the shower was fed with a greater quantity of either hot or cold water. "Sinking ship."

"Should have been this one," he gurgled as he allowed his mouth to fill with water.

I could see Boxer was about to complete his bathing and head to bed. I didn't want him to leave so soon. I wanted to get that sexy vision planted firmly in my mind for the wank I intended to have once inside my hammock. "You've got a whack of grease on your back," I informed as he spun around and my eyes fell on his lazy, soapy dick.

"Shit! Have I?" I saw his gaze drop to my cock which wasn't as lazy as his. "Wanna wash it off for me?" he suggested. My cock began to rise to half mast.

I tried not to appear over eager to get into his cubicle but my cock was doing the opposite, giving me away. "Sure."

I took my soap with me, lathering my hands as I walked toward him.

Boxer placed a palm either side of the shower head, standing spread eagled like a criminal waiting to be frisked. His arse looked inviting beyond belief and it took every effort to concentrate on his back rather than those solid fleshy cheeks and the crack into which the bubbles were travelling.

There was no way I could keep my cock down as my hands worked over his neck and shoulders, then around his waist, then back to his neck via his spine. The grease had long gone but I continued to rotate my palms around his solid body. At one point bringing them up under his armpits and over his pecs. All-the-while, my cock grew and grew and eventually stabbed between his arse cheeks when the ship rolled to port.

"That feels great, Knocker!" he whispered. "Has the grease gone yet?"

I prodded his right shoulder, drawing my finger down to his butt. "Nah. There's a stubborn bit just here,"

Boxer didn't reply and let his palms fall to his side. He picked up his own bar of soap and began lathering, I was sure it was his cock which he was working on but I daren't explore to confirm this. Boxer moved his soap held palm to his butt and began moving the bar between the cheeks, parting them and pushing. My heart quickened as I began to contemplate if sex was on, if my Boiler Room boy was about to give me what I had so longed for since our first meeting.

I moved slightly forward so's my cock was against his knuckles as he rotated his hands around his buttock cheeks and between them. Another roll of the ship and my chest pressed hard against his back. My hands went about his waist as we both slipped on the soapy floor.

It was there, happy and proud, bigger than I expected it to be. I could resist no longer and grasped it tightly. Boxer flinched and sighed, a sizzling sigh, as I drew my soapy hand down to the base, pulling his foreskin back, then cupped the other palm under his balls and gently caressed.

My cock was bursting now and pressed, by the pressure of blood within, up against my navel. Boxer grasped it cautiously, soaping it with his soap. It felt so fantastic I could have easily come with that rubbing action. I allowed my mouth to fall onto his neck, taking things a step further. Boxer continued to soap, quicker and quicker. I did likewise, rubbing in a circular motion around the head of his delicious dick. Boxer pulled my cock down, directing it toward his slippery crack. I was not expecting that and on the next roll of the ship it slid, in one movement, all the way in. He didn't flinch when my dick sank as deep as it could possibly go. Instead, he released a gush of breath as if he'd been waiting for this moment for a very long time.

I moved my palms from his prick, up around his tits and began to squeeze. Boxer pushed his buttocks hard against my pubes. "Knocker," he gushed, "I've waited so long for you to do this to me."

Spray fell like confetti over our soapy bodies, running between chest and back, buttocks and cock. Firmly but gently, I thrust deep, then withdrew, then thrust deep again. Boxer gripped my butt, bending down and pushing himself hard upon my sex. His body became supple and submissive as he sighed my name over and over, willing me to work his insides, willing my cock to grow larger than it had ever grown.

I gripped his cock again, biting hard into his neck. Desperately I wanted to suck a love bite onto that tender, smooth skin but I knew that that would spell trouble. Boxer's cock head expanded, the ridge bulging out from the shaft. As I rubbed and thrust faster and faster, he arched into me, almost tearing my arse apart with his strong hands, then yelped as he sent his cum splashing against the Formica bulkhead. I ran my palm over his dripping cock a final time as I watched his cum and soap run to the deck - cum that I would dearly loved to have swallowed. Gasping, "Oh, Boxer!" I began filling, filling, filling him with the entire contents of my tightening balls.

Someone struggling with the metal door clamps, which I'd pulled tightly shut, caused us to break away. Sadly, there was no time for that last savouring of skin. But, just before the door barged open, I pulled our faces together, sucked Boxer's lips and tongue, then fell to my knees, to get the last remnants of his cum.

Boxer scooped up his towel, drying himself as the young sailor entered, then hastily departed.

In marched Ben, his slim suntanned sexiness wrapped in a brilliant white towel. "Hi Knocker," he grinned. "Taking a shower?"

I slung my towel back on the hook. "Yep. Wanna join me?"

"Sure!" grinned Ben, tossing his towel intimately on top of mine, his cock already rising.

CAMPING OUT

The ship docked at Portsmouth. I was more than relieved for that. It had been a bitch of a week, force eight gales. Continuously riding the big ones can piss you off in the end, constantly being tossed from bulkhead to bulkhead, or into sailors you'd rather be shagging than saying sorry to. Paul was one of those I'd loved to have been riding, rather than fifty foot waves. I think he knew that but never let on. I'd been close enough to his cock to give it a cautious brush with my palm and slapped his bum in a playful manner many times, but a smile and wink was all he'd ever offered. I often wondered, when he jumped from his hammock in the morning with his stiff cock poking through the fly of his Hong Kong, floral boxers, dribbling cum, whether or not he was offering me that mouthwatering massive meat - which somehow appeared far too big for his small frame - or just teasing. I hoped one day I'd find out. That one day I'd pluck up the courage and tell him I fancied him stupid.

I'd been a sailor for a year but, unbelievably, had not had sex since my school days, and then it was only a wank. But, now, as a sailor, I was obliged to go ashore with mates and play the hettie game, watching them box off with the birds. I often got strange looks because I wouldn't. And I could never let on to those sexy baby-sailors, who's sailor suits made their buttocks look even more horny, trapped in bum-hugging bell-bottoms, that it was only their pants I wanted to dive inside. Thus frustrated, I tossed myself regularly - in the heads, in my hammock, in my office. Constantly I tossed myself, but always alone.

Below decks, those of us granted a pass were preparing to go ashore - pressing uniforms; the older sailors, civvies. As always, Paul was close by; his locker being next to mine. His pert white butt, trapped between tanned brown torso and thighs, was closer to my cock than was comfortable. In fact, I believe I felt my dick glide, semi stiff, over his right buttock cheek as I squeezed past, in order to reach the ironing table.

"I hope that was your finger," he giggled.

"You'd need something fatter than a finger to satisfy you," I teased.

"Bum bandit," parried Paul, then to the whole mess, "Smiffy's a bum bandit."

"Shut up and take it like a man!" a butch sailor bellowed.

I poked my tongue out when Paul turned to face me. "Yea, take it like a man," I repeated.

"You got lovely, sucking lips, Smiffy," smiled Paul, grasping his cock, which looked stiffer than it should have. "If you get a couple blowjobs this weekend, come back and give me one."

"Anytime!" I winked.

Paul tucked his prick away and grinned a knowing grin.

"I'll have the other one," a cute, naked seamen called, jumping from behind the lockers, wiggling his dishy butt and swinging his cock in a clockwise motion.

"I want a meal, not a morsel," I replied, deflating his ego and his four inches.

Paul scooped up his hold-all and scurried up the ladder, "Have a good one, Smiffy," he shouted, accompanied by an extremely sexy wink.

I waited until his butt was out of view before continuing to dress, contemplating whether sex with Paul was only a couple of days away. I'd already decided when I returned that I would offer him one or both of those blowjobs, whether I got them or not.

Not long after Paul had left, I hoisted my hold-all up the ladder and after I'd been inspected by the Officer of the Day, was trotting over the gangway. The first pub beyond the dockyard wall was my initial port of call. It was the usual thing us sailors did - a quick pint and chat before catching our respective trains. The place was buzzing with sailors from various ships. I had a quick glance around for Paul but he wasn't about. After chucking a couple of coins in the fruit machine, I chose a windowed corner to sit and watch sailor boys and men get sloshed. I'd always found it fascinating how close men and boys could be, without there being any sex involved; manly arms slung affectionately over youth's shoulders or wrapped around waists or draped over cute buttocks. Men and boys can be really loving toward each other when women are absent.

I noticed a boy sailor - a little worse for drink - draped over a burly Bunting Tosser. Their cheeks were touching, and I do believe I glimpsed a peck on the boy's cheek. They wandered out not long after that, the older sailor supporting the younger. To where, I do not know. To bed, I hoped. Something I longed to do with a boy, one day. When I was more sure. When I was more brave. When......

The bar was beginning to clear, sailors leaving for their trains. Mine wasn't far off, and as I drained my glass, I began to think of the weekend break - what it would hold, whether I would get that thing called a blowjob, whether I would meet that boy I longed for.

That may well happen, I thought, because we'd been at sea for three months and during that time my family had moved to a village close to Portsmouth - Wickham. What Wickham would do for my frustrated sex life, I had no idea, but a sailor suit in places where they were not usually seen, often brought attention on oneself. Hopefully, that attention would be the kind I was searching for.

The train journey was uneventful, apart from being in the company of scruffy, loud schoolboys, two of which had cum stains on their black trousers. I guessed I knew what they'd been up to during lunch break, or in my case, during lessons.

Alighting at a deader than dead railway station, my heart sank. Why on earth had my family moved here? I wondered. A short walk brought me to a large, empty square surrounded by several shops, a pub, and tumble-down cottages. What was noticeable was the people, that was, their absence. Not a soul in sight to greet this youthful, would-be sailor-boy-lover. A solitary sports car did speed by, honking its horn, but it seemed the pilot was only too pleased to pass through this peaceful hamlet in the shortest time possible. Had he known how I was feeling he might have offered me a lift back to my ship, to his home, even his bed!

I found a living person in the rickety Post Office. At least I thought she was living. She looked older than the building itself. My parents new home, I was informed, was 'up yonder hill, about a mile'. Thanking her and purchasing a Coke for the extra energy I would need, I began my ascent of the tree lined road.

Houses were few, I noted, as I climbed ever skyward; only fields of corn, grasses, and other crops spread for miles around. Thoughts of a new improved sex life, my first sex life, faded fast. And, then, like a God given grace, I heard joyous sounds. In amongst the twittering birds and farmyard noises, I heard the voices of boys. I think I almost ran to the five bar, wooden gate of the field they were coming from.

Cracking open my can of Coke I rested my body, arms slung over the top bar, and absorbed the beauty of boys bouncing merrily around the field, kicking the usual bag of wind. Football crazy boys, spurred on by World Cup mania, pretended to be their heroes. It was a wondrous sight!

Lads, from youth to boy, chased each other, in pursuit of the ball, often using foul play - I did see a pair of shorts brought to ankle height - attempting to score that winning goal, in a goal without keeper. Shorts clad boys, naked above the waist, kept my eyes and mind occupied for a good half hour. Dearly I wanted to trip across the field and join in, but being at least two years older than the eldest boy, I somehow felt too old.

For the last five minutes of playing spectator, I perched myself on the top bar of the gate for a better view. A misdirected kick sent the ball sailing in my direction. I stumbled slightly forward wondering whether to retrieve it with a kick and send it sailing back, but with my footballing skills I guessed I'd only make matters worse. But that decision was made for me by a youth who came charging after it.

Silver-stranded, wavy hair caught in the breeze above his reddened, puffing cheeks as he galloped toward me, his sunburnt chest glistening in the sunlight as it teasingly rose and fell as he sucked in air. Instinctively my eyes went from face to crotch, and even from my distance I could easily make out a fine bulge in his grass- stained shorts.

I have no idea why he did it, and even the shouts from mates couldn't hurry him, but, after scooping up the ball, he turned and looked directly at me. A broad, sunshine smile erupted from his bright face, engulfing me in rays of warmth, sending tingling sensations throughout my entire body. His second glance, even more seductive - halfway back to the other players - caused me to stumble from the gate and him to laugh; a laugh more golden than the yellow corn surrounding me. In that instant, I believe I fell in love!

I think I caught his name in those lad's shouts - Chuck or Chip - or perhaps they were footballing terms. Whatever it was, my final ascent toward home was going to be brighter than any part of the day so far.

I left the boys to their football and their summer camp, and moved off. A further quarter mile - it was certainly the longest mile I'd ever walked, I would inform the Post Mistress - I turned left into North Lane; a road I can only describe as a dirt track. My family, it seemed, had moved into the outback.

A further sweaty mile along North Lane and I was in front of my home, if I could call it that. A shack of a building, built from wood -wood that looked as if it had been washed up upon a beach - stood before my dejected face. Had my parents gone mad, or what?

The usual, excited, "Kenny! Kenny!" greetings came form brothers and sisters and parents. I accepted their cuddles in the usual way but somehow refrained from asking why they had moved from a lovely cottage into a cow shed.

Evening couldn't come quick enough, having answered a barrage of questions about my navy life, but avoiding those, "I bet you've found a girlfriend in every port!" interrogations. And as soon as the opportunity came - one of those silent gaps after every question had been repeated and answered twice - I found an excuse to leave.

I freshened myself with a quick shower then re-dressed into my uniform. It was about 7pm and the pubs were open. I decided I would do the three day camel ride back to the village, beat up the Post Mistress for lying about the distance, then meet the local lager drinking lads; although, in a place such as this, they probably drank Real Ale or brain damaging Cider.

Thankfully, neither of my folks drank and my brothers was too young. So, left to my own devices, I headed back along the dirt track; the pleasant evening sunshine beating on my back.

More relaxed now, I took in more of my surroundings - cows, horses, squirrels, cottages - I hadn't noticed them before - and a variety of birds. Sadly, not a burly farm-hand, stripped naked to the navel, in sight. Turning right at the end of the track, my mind instantly flashed back to my 'sunshine smile' lad. I opened my ears, eager to hear the sounds of playful boys, but all was still. I was being silly, anyway. What chance was there of me picking up a youth who I didn't know? Picking up anybody, to be honest. And if I did meet him again, what would I say? After all, I was extremely shy and pretty thick in the chatting-up cuties department.

Moving down hill, I approached the five bar gate, set slightly back from the road. Passing the old oak which shielded it from my view, my stomach tightened in a knot from my groin to my throat. 'Sunshine' was sat upon the top bar, bare legs straddled either side, crotch in his shorts pushed up, silver hair sparkling in the evening sunshine, suntanned shoulders and back glistening boy sweat.

My body froze, surges of sexual desire stunning me like some scared animal!

Sensing my presence, Sunshine spun around. "Hi!" he beamed, tanning my face red with a single smile.

My stomach ached with desire, so much so, I even felt sick. "Hi!" I replied, not knowing whether to continue walking or stop and torture myself.

"You're not from around here?" he beamed again, breaking my body into panic ridden particles with his soul stirring smile.

"No." I felt awkward. Was one word answers all I could come up with? I was older than him. More knowledgeable. More travelled. More most things. But his beauty and my desperate desire to engulf him in arms and legs, left me speechless.

Sunshine spun his other leg over the gate to face me, opening his legs and offering a clearer view of his boy-bulge. "Like being a sailor?" he questioned, perhaps to draw me into a more meaningful conversation.

"Sure." Another one word reply. God, how cowardly!

Sunshine continued to bombard me with smiles and erotic strokes of his brown thighs. "Off to the village?"

This was getting me nowhere and the pain in my eyes from absorbing bulges and beauty was unbearable. I had to say something more substantial or leave before I dived on him and devoured him whole.

Daringly, I moved closer, almost standing between his parted knees, my eyes wandering from face to chest to crotch and back. "Know where all the girls go in the village?" I inquired defensively, taking on a straight role.

Sunshine brought his hands to his hips. "Girls? What's wrong with me. I can do anything they can!"

I'd never been hit by a ten ton truck before, but that confession had an equal force. And when I next moved my gaze back to his crotch, no longer was it a neat round bump but a straight and solid sex, scrumptiously stiffened down his left thigh.

Though I desperately wanted to reply, I just couldn't. Sunshine laughed, a real boy-laugh, leant forward, took my cap and plonked it upon his silvery hair, the wavy strands protruding sexily over his ears and forehead. "Come on," he encouraged, holding out his slender palm.

I took his hand nervously as he jumped from the gate. My cock crowded my bell-bottoms when he squeezed my palm intimately. He looked stunningly beautiful wearing my cap and I could easily visualise him in the complete outfit. Should he join the Royal Navy, I mused, he wouldn't be a virgin for very long, but , somehow, guessed that perhaps he wasn't; even that he had had far more sexual encounters than I'd ever had. Indeed, it was Sunshine who was seducing me!

"What's your name?" he asked, dragging me across the road and toward the cornfield.

"Kenny."

"Ken. I've got a mate called Ken. We looked our names up in a dictionary one day. Did you know it means comely?"

I liked the way he emphasised cum of comely and had no doubt that coming was foremost in his mind. "What's yours?" I asked.

"Chip."

"And what does that mean?"

"Got lots of meanings but one of them has something to do with chickens," he winked.

I had no idea what he meant by that but guessed it was sexual in some way. "It's a lovely name and you look as cute and cuddly as a little chick, but I've given you a nickname of my own - Sunshine. It's that smile of yours. As big and beautiful as the sun."

"Sunshine, eh! I like that." And giving another broad grin, he pushed me into the hedgerow and planted his smiling mouth onto mine. For that long, oh so succulent smacker, I stopped breathing. Never before had I been kissed by a boy, and I almost passed out from the euphoria of it. And during that magnificent mouth to mouth manoeuvre, I took the opportunity to grasp Sunshine's stiffened sex, holding it, so tightly, I never wanted to let it go - ever!

"Can't wait, eh, Kenny Cum-ly. Still want to go to the village and find a girl?" he teased.

"Nah!"

Sunshine pushed me through a gap in the hedge, into the cornfield. Hand in hand we cut a swathe through the tall golden stems, the ears slapping against my uniform and his naked chest. Twenty yards into the sea of gold I scuttled my ship, bringing Sunshine down with me; our bodies rolling playfully over and over as we flattened the corn around ourselves - a bed for boys to learn about boys.

It was Sunshine's eager hand which was first to move between thighs, levering my dick into the warm evening air; and how incredibly good and refreshing that felt. But not as incredible as the hot mouth which unexpectedly swallowed my sex. Only three movements down to my black pubes and back, and I filled his mouth with cum; gripping his head tightly for fear he might pull away. He gulped down the fluid, fiercely flashing his tongue over my cock-head and into the eye. My brain spun and my eyes rolled back, my legs quivering and stomach knotting as the sensation became so wonderfully painful that I needed to pull away.

Sunshine's lips met mine, cum and saliva dribbling down his chin as he kissed me passionately. "I guess you needed that!" he delighted, and kissed my nose and forehead.

"Shit! That was... out of this world!"

"You're first time?" Sunshine smiled, knowingly.

I felt like an amateur by admitting that it was but Sunshine was pleased by that news, giving me a loving hug and saying that he was glad that it was his mouth to be the first to savour my virgin cum.

"I suppose cos you like girls, you won't want to suck mine?" he questioned, but still smiling. "S'ok. I don't mind. But can I do it to you again, please?"

I didn't tell him that I didn't fancy girls but pushed him down into the corn and climbed on top of him, pressing my mouth onto his cherry coloured lips. Sitting upright, I could feel his young sex pressing into my bum as I rode my palms over his silken chest and up under his hairless armpits. Sunshine giggled as my fingers stroked the sweat in the hollows.

"Take your top off," he begged, stroking my cock and bringing it firm, then pulling the zipper down on my uniform jacket and wrenching my white front and collar from my body.

My smooth stomach skin and navel revealed, he began to rub and kiss my nakedness, licking excitedly around the tiny indented knot. His nimble fingers swiftly unbuttoned my waistband and pulled my bell-bottoms over my buttocks.

I was excited now, more relaxed and confident, and soon had his shorts unfastened and drawn down to his knees; the cutest of cocks with only a wisp of cock hair, revealed. He was younger than I had suspected.

I grasped the thick but short sex and began to play, pulling the foreskin down over the plump red head. I noticed pre-cum slipping down one side and slid my thumb over the eye and brought it to my mouth. The taste surprised me, not at all unpleasant. Indeed, it was so nice, I couldn't wait for the creamer stuff and hoped he was old enough to produce it, but didn't ask.

Perhaps a little shyly, being such a novice, I moved my head down and began to suck. Sunshine whimpered and sighed as my mouth worked, rubbing frantically at my black cropped hair, pushing my face deep; making me take it all. And that I did, pushing my palate hard and deep, delighting that at last I was pleasing a boy. At last I was doing that thing I had so longed to do.

"Oooh! Stop!" Sunshine surprised me, and I wondered if I was sucking it wrong, or my teeth were digging, or something. "I nearly came!" he gushed, drawing my face back to his for more kissing and slurping of tongues.

"Don't you want to come, then?"

"Course! But together. You know? 69's."

I did know of 69's but didn't think it was a boy on boy thing. But Sunshine seemed to know everything. Instantly, we were head to tail.

"Gosh, what a lot of hair," he delighted, burrowing his dainty nose into my pubes. "I love boy's cock hair. Can't wait to get more of my own."

"I love yours just as it is. Your dick is just wonderful," I praised, and devoured it to the base.

The heady euphoria swamped me once again as Sunshine's mouth engulfed me -hot, soft and wet. This time I would hold back for as long as possible, if I could; until his gush of boy-juice jettisoned and filled my wanting mouth. And, for some strange reason, I hoped, desperately hoped, that those youthful juices would come from him in torrents. Come from him in a frenzy of excited release.

Our palms worked wonderfully over each other's young flesh, foraging and enhancing the sensation of working mouths. Mine, over arms and legs - with their dusting of fair hair - and, more frequently, over his satin chest and tiny tits. His, concentrating on the abundance of bushy pubes above my cock and the sprinkling beneath my armpits.

Passions rising, no longer were heads bobbing, just rounded, flexing buttocks, thrusting and pulling back; ramming frantically into wide open mouths. It was Sunshine's gasp of delight which exploded my cock deep down his throat, so deep I thought he might choke. But it was I who choked when, simultaneously, he siphoned the contents of his small balls in swirls of sweet spunk, filling my mouth to capacity and beyond, my lips dribbling the excess over my chin. How could such a minuscule ballsac contain twice their volume? I considered - gulping gratefully and gluttonously; gorging on his enlarged plum for the final remnants.

The dull dongs of a gong drifting over the cornfield caused Sunshine to jump to his feet and quickly dress. "Hell. Got to get back to camp. Supper gong," he informed, but not before kissing my cock and face for a final time. "Meet me here tomorrow. About ten. Bring some Nivea, or something!" he shouted as his cute butt disappeared, bunny-rabbit-like, through the hedgerow.

"Nivea!" I called after him. "Why?"

"You'll see!" he waved and grinned again.

I glided down the hill toward Wickham village, sparks of love igniting my insides like miniature firecrackers. My excitement was electric. I had made love to a BOY! I wanted to tell the whole world. I wanted to climb to the highest hilltop and shout it out loud. I wanted to do it again, and again. I wanted my euphoric state to stay with me forever!

The village pub looked drab from the outside but before entering I glimpsed a 7 -11 across the square and trotted over. A youth stood behind the counter. Because of my flushed cheeks and dizzy state, I wondered whether he knew I had just made love for the first time in my life. I wondered, also, whether he knew it had been with a boy. I plucked a blue tin of Nivea from the medical section. Suddenly, becoming self-conscious of purchasing what I thought to be a feminine product, I replaced it and pulled a small pot of Brylcream from the shelf above. But even as I paid for that more legitimate item, my self-consciousness grew, aware that I had no hair, at least not hair that required lacquering down.

Hastily, I exited the 7 - 11, to the wide grin of cherub cheeks, positive he knew that I'd been sucking boy-cock in the cornfield only minutes previously.

The pub was better in than out and contained the usual pub furniture: juke box, dart board, beer stained tables with wooden chairs beneath. Customers were few - two farm-hands playing dominoes, an elderly couple, a group of posh, wealthy types, and a back-packing lad beside the unlit, log fire.

I slotted myself close by the back-packer - I could never resist being beside good-looking guys. But little happened during my pub session, apart from me getting slightly sozzled; and not once did the back-packing youth get speared by the Cupid arrows I was constantly firing at him. Come eleven, I did the return camel ride back home, in a kind of zig-zag fashion, and was soon snuggled up in bed, wanking furiously over visions of Sunshine sucking and savouring my sex.

I must say, 9am was a more civilised time to leave my bed than the usual 6am. I felt wonderfully relaxed and happy as I showered, and was pleased to see the sun beaming through the bathroom window as I soaped my body, bringing my sex solid with sweet smelling Camay bubbles and lather. I refrained from jerking myself off; saving it for Sunshine.

I dressed in shorts and tatty T-shirt for my meeting with my Boy Wonder-ful. Sadly, my navy issue short were far from tantalising or titillating, but I hoped Sunshine wouldn't mind. After all, what was beneath them was more important.

Excited, almost beyond control, I was soon heading along the dirt track and toward the cornfield - Brylcream bulging in pocket. Actually, it made me look like a very big boy indeed. Anyhow, I wasn't too bothered about being a big boy and was amply gifted, and when it came to other boy's cocks, I did prefer smaller ones. Sunshine's was just about right. Just perfect, in fact.

The cornfield was soon upon me, having almost marched the distance. Sunshine wasn't about and I was suddenly saddened but I made my way through the hedgerow gap and to our corn bed. My eyes lit and my face flushed bright when they were greeted by the vision of Sunshine sunning himself in the shelter of the tall corn.

"Did you bring it?" were his first eager words.

I rubbed the bulge beside my cock and smiled. "Yep!"

"Oh. I thought that was your cock," he beamed, bowling me over and on top of him with one of those smouldering smiles.

Swiftly we were licking faces, chests and nipples, then sucking tongues and lips and eventually cocks. And, somehow, that felt even more exciting than yesterday's passionate embraces.

"Get it out, then," Sunshine ordered.

He couldn't have meant my dick, that had already been rolling around his mouth for the past ten minutes, so I retrieved my shorts, whilst he continued to suck my balls and bursting bell-end, and passed him the Brylcream.

Sunshine laughed, a deep, boyish, roar of a laugh. "Taking up hairdressing, are we?"

"What's it for?" I ignorantly inquired, my face slightly flushed from my naivete.

"You're going to fuck me," he laughed again, unscrewing the cap and dipping a finger into the white cream, then sniffing it. "But I didn't expect to get a new hair-do at the same time," he giggled again.

I'd heard all the banter on board about bottoms getting knobbed and the Golden Rivet stories, but I never ever thought that boys had actually did it to boys - shoved their cocks up bums.

Desperate to hide my ignorance, but knowing Sunshine instinctively knew I was a novice, I humoured him by saying, "Well, I thought I'd give you a descent parting at the same time!" Spreading the cheeks of his slightly hairy butt wide apart and darting my tongue into the hole.

Sunshine just loved that and pulled on the back of my head, slinging his legs over my shoulder and wriggling delightedly against my stiff tongue.

Next, dollops of white cream were delicately drawn over my stiff shaft and bulging cock head, and a larger quantity up into his dainty hole. "Don't do a thing," he commanded. "Just lie there."

'And take it like a man!' suddenly flashed through my mind, and I laughed inwardly.

Sunshine placed his knees either side of me, one hand pressing on my tight tummy, the other holding tightly onto my lathered cock. Gently, he eased his cute, tight buttocks backward, guiding my cock head between them. I felt giddy with excitement, desperately wishing to push forward, to sink inside this boy and bury my cock into depths I had never dreamt of disappearing into.

A deep sigh slipped from Sunshine's mouth and his face grimaced, but only slightly. I felt my bulging cock-head pop into his tight hole. Like that first blowjob, I thought I would come instantly. Desperately, I wanted to drive my dick home but I could see that it was painful for him, and even thought that it might be the first time he'd been screwed.

Sunshine stopped briefly, then, with a slow backward movement, he sat right down, palms pressed firmly on my rising chest. My head exploded! I could no longer hold back my desire to thrust and withdraw. Gripping his buttocks in both palms, I pulled my cock out to the tip then rammed it back home. Sunshine yelped and fell onto my chest. Our mouths met and he sucked furiously upon my tongue, gasping, oohing and aahing, and demanding I fuck him hard. There was no need. My hips and buttocks were rising from the flattened corn and pushing all that I had into his relaxing butt.

Squealing now and shaking with excitement, Sunshine sat up and began driving down on my upward thrusts, all-the-while jerking his cute cock in rapid movements. His pretty boyish face brightened with pleasure. His fingers working furiously over his own sex, the other diving inside my mouth and playing with my tongue and lips. A sensational feeling engulfed my cock. I was ecstatic!

"Sunshine!" I shouted, shooting several salvos of semen inside of him. "I've come! God, have I come!"

Sunshine leapt from my cock, cum dribbling from his bum-hole and my slippery solid sex, and scrambled quickly over my face. Still jerking off, he rammed his young tool into my mouth. Cum gushed, gushed, and gushed - it seemed it would never stop - down my throat, with so much force, the first jet didn't even touch the sides; shooting straight into my stomach.

Body quivering, Sunshine sat back up, grabbed my still stiff sex and sent it back up his hole. Again he slammed into me and I could feel my own cum swirling inside of him. Moments later it was a repeat performance. I emptied my cock a second time into his delicious dark hole and he emptied his onto my lapping tongue.

We continued screwing until early afternoon, until the Brylcream tub was dry, and had Sunshine not had to leave for a scouting trek, I think I'd have bought another pot and we'd have continued well into the night.

We said our goodbye's with more kisses and cuddles, sadly knowing that we would not see each other again - Sunshine returning home, me to my ship. And with a final hug, kiss and wave, he returned to camp.

The taste of Sunshine's cum was still fresh in my mouth and the sensation of screwing him singing in my dick as I slung both mine and Paul's hammocks. Having further to travel, he would not be back on board till early morning.

I lay back in my hammock, pleased and proud I was no longer a virgin. Delighted that my virginity was lost to the most beautiful boy on earth. Slowly, I drifted into sexual fantasies of Sunshine and I screwing, and soon I was asleep and dreaming.

Ken Smith

My dream was so real, I could feel Sunshine's hot mouth working my cock down to the base and back. As often with wet dreams, just as I was about to shoot, I awoke. But the sensation of rising cum was still prominent and getting better. I moved my hand to my cock to finish myself off. A cropped head was bobbing frantically up and down my shaft. "Paul!" I gasped, coming before I'd finished my sentence, "What are you doing!"

Paul gulped my cum, slurping his tongue around the dribbling head for a few moments before raising himself level. "Got a couple of blowjobs ashore. Thought you might want one, Smiffy," he smiled. Then, giving me a secretive kiss, whispered, "Got one for me?"

My head disappeared into his hammock!

THE KEEPER

My eyes opened wide. It was just a wonderful sight. Tall and slim, pinkish white with a thicker reddish top. It was just magnificent. Never before had I purchased something as delightful as this. In fact, never before had I purchased something so expensive. Something which was bound to give me endless pleasure. Endless fun. Yes, I couldn't wait to open the door to that lovely lighthouse - my lighthouse.

A circular staircase wound me giddily through the living quarters then to the computer controlled, million-candle-power lamp at the top. Opening the weather-beaten door, I climbed onto the rail-guarded platform. A gust of wind caught my blond, wavy hair and swept it over my face. Hugging the rail beneath the re-enforced glass, I did a slow circuit of the perimeter, taking in the awesome sight of sea, cliffs, fields and countryside village. The whole scene was bliss to my hungry eyes. A sheer joy to behold.

"Peace and quiet, at last," I sighed.

A heavy black cloud, far off in the distance, released a bolt of lightening and moments later a thunder clap shuddered through my body. Hail pellets appeared from nowhere and began to bombard me. Hastily, I completed my circuit and returned below, unwinding myself in an anti-clockwise direction until I reached the living quarters.

Already I felt at home, the lounge having been decorated almost to my taste - modern, yet not overly so. And the fact that I need not bring any furniture at present meant that I wasn't waiting on any removal lorries, which helped keep me relaxed on this special day.

I pulled the last cigarette from its pack, crunched up the box and tossed it toward the bin. Lying back on a large sofa, which begged you to fall asleep in its lumpy arms, I lit the cigarette and inhaled deeply. A second, more vigorous clap of thunder caused me to jump as the storm came even closer, and I leapt from the sofa and threw open the curtains of the recently installed, bay window.

As black as night, now, I stared into that threatening sky as it loomed overhead like the Angel of Death, flashing is daggered white teeth and snarling as it spat iced bullets into the double-glazed panes. It was an unbelievable sight, frightening and threatening, as the Angel roared in howls, eager to penetrate through the Lighthouse's very skin and consume all within. And then, the sun, in a single solid shaft, parted the heavens, and all was still once more.

Moving to the lighthouse base, I began to bring up my belongings from the Range Rover - pictures, pots and pans, bedding and the like. After a sweaty hours work each of my worldly possessions had found a place to live - my picture of a muscular, handsome, hunk of a black boy over the ornate gas fire. My pair of marble, Greek, boy statues either side of the bay window. And the bronze, boy statue beside the fireplace. Other items, such as books, CD's, booze etc., all stowed into fitted cupboards.

And after that strenuous task, I poured myself a stiff scotch and wished myself good luck, because I might need it; for, if falling from the lighthouse top some dark and dismal night didn't kill me, then a regular clockwise and anti-clockwise winding and unwinding of my tired body as I struggled to the top and back, most surely would.

The sedating scotch soon had me relaxed and pleased with my purchase, and my efforts. Dragging a deck-chair from a storage cupboard to the lighthouse top, I plonked myself sun-facing and relaxed for the remainder of the day.

My first night in the lighthouse was the quietest I'd ever spent, far from the hustle and bustle of London's city streets, only the wind and soft waves lapping over the jagged rocks far below, and the squeals of seagulls as they bobbed and weaved above the ocean.

Dawn broke with a rush of sunshine as the October sun lifted itself clear from a flat calm sea and begun it skyward climb. I'd slept like a baby in a Mother's comforting arms, snugly wrapped in feather-down duvet.

Before even descending through the dining room and then into the kitchen below, I headed toward the lighthouse top and threw open the door. Yes, it was chilly, Winter just over the horizon, but I couldn't resist breathing in that salty sea air. Breathing new life into my City poisoned body. Again I circumnavigated the lighthouse.

"This is the life," I thought, filling my lungs with clean fresh air as I scanned seaward.   Several ships, one of which was Royal Navy, sped from east to west and the reverse; although from this distance they hardly appeared to move. Closer to shore a couple of fishing boats were laying lobster pots or pulling in nets; bombarded continually by colonies of gulls. Over the cliff top a jogger was doing a roller-coaster run as he climbed and descended hillocks. Also, a couple more sane people casually strolled, circled continually by a yapping dog - its barks rising in the breeze.

Toward the red-roofed village, blue smoke rose in twisted spirals from early morning fires, whilst the church clock could be clearly heard as it struck the hours; reminding workers and school-children it was time to leave.

Breakfast was a simple affair - light, I suppose, was the correct term. Orange juice and two toast. Not marmalade. I hated that. It was the peel. I'd have eaten something more substantial had I had it, but bringing food wasn't foremost in my mind upon moving here. My first task, then, would be a stroll into the village to replenish the food cupboard. I also needed stationary and some computer stuff. That was most important. After all, the reason I had moved here was to write my novel.

Coffee consumed, weak, barely enough granules for a decent cup, I wrapped up warm, unwound myself to the front door, and headed toward Tarring village.

There was no warmth in the sun's rays. Well if there was, it was cooled by a decent sea breeze which wrapped continually about me. A grassy and hedgerow-hugged footpath kindly took a mile off my journey as it meandered past fields and farms; and inside an hour I'd travelled the two miles and was entering the sleepy, though not dead, village.

Three pubs with sea-faring names, The Floundering Frigate, The Cabin Boy and The Lighthouse, were the first of the buildings which stood out. I guess, being a Real Ale person, they could have hardly gone unnoticed. Buggy pushing Mothers were out early, heading no doubt to the Supermarket or Post Office. The Post Office, I recalled, that constant home for Pensioners. Why did they queue for a postage stamp? I often wondered. Especially as they were available in so many newspaper shops.

Thankfully, the Stationary Shop-come-Newsagents-come-Music Shop-come much much more, was practically empty. Two reams of cheap photocopy paper, a couple of ink cartridges and a box of disks were soon collected and paid for, then it was off for groceries.

The Supermarket I gave a miss. I'd always disliked them. Unfortunately, in the City there was no way to avoid buying your food in them. Here, however, in a cozy village, small shops were still the norm. Places you could buy decent grub - home baked bread and pies; real sausages; free range eggs and the like. Not to mention places to give or get the good gossip.

The Butcher boy was bright and young, and continually bombarded me with heart-warming smiles. And I must confess, I was somewhat more interested in the bulge rising beneath the blue and white stripped pinny, than I was with the pound of extremely thick bacon he was wrapping for me. I think at that point, whether or not I was the only Gay person in the village, did cross my mind.

"You the new owner of the lighthouse?" was a surprise question which fell from the red-lipped mouth between the continually cheerful Butcher boy's cheeks.

"That's right," I confirmed, wondering how on earth he knew.

"It's a lovely building. I often walk up that way. I am strangely drawn to it, and love it when it's windy and the sea's rough. I've always wanted to stand on the very top."

That was a lot of information for a boy to impart to a stranger, I thought. And his possible request for an invite into my home, caused me to re-examine his blue and white stripped bulge, before replying, "Yes, it's a beautiful building, and the view is breathtaking."

"I'm Spike," he smiled. "You know, I can always deliver my meat if you don't fancy walking down when the weather's bad." and passing me a business card. "Just ring your order in."

"Thanks, Spike. I shall remember that. I'm Luke, by the way."

Spike gave me a groin disturbing grin as I lifted my shopping and headed toward the door. "Don't forget, Luke. We're here to please our customers," he grinned again.

The walk back along the footpath, mostly uphill, certainly took the puff out of me as I strode into the southerly wind. Indeed, I wished that I'd come by car. London living had definitely taken the fitness from my body.

As I rested against a moss covered style, Spike re-entered my mind. Did I look that Gay? I wondered. That available? And were his words evocative and sexually provoking, or were they just friendly chat? Possibly I was reading too much into them. Also, the fact that it had been almost two years since I had any sort of relationship, any sex to speak of, might have had something to do with my excitement.

I didn't really want to remember Jeff's death, yet again. Or the deep and loving relationship with which we were blessed before he was killed. But Spike had certainly done that, reminding me that I would dearly love another. And I have to admit, he was my type - cute, cuddly, polite and petit. Pretty, in the boyish use of the word.

A Telephone Engineer's van awaited my arrival. Already, in my euphoric state of mind, being in such a serene setting, I was forgetting the things I'd organised for the day. He wasn't overly upset at my lateness and after serving him coffee, black and no sugar, the beefy youth began running wires for a telephone in every room - no way was I going to do spiral circuits each time the phone rang.

His task complete, commenting on what a wonderful way to live, he left - informing me that the line would be connected within the hour. A two tone ringing from the phone, his deep accented voice on the other end as I picked it up, confirmed his promise. Instantly my mind travelled back to the butcher boy and his bulging pinny. Had I forgotten the Sunday joint? I asked myself. Of course I hadn't. I didn't eat beef; didn't eat a great deal of meat at all. But I was sure contemplating buying some!

I began preparing myself a late, proper breakfast, and the smell of bacon carved by cute fingers was soon wafting into my nostrils and causing hungry gurgles in my empty stomach. Two large eggs were added to the pan and spat in protest.

I always preferred to eat in the lounge and I was soon tucking into my lapped meal. Whether it was fact or fantasy, that meal was the best bacon and eggs I'd eaten in a long while; but that may have had more to do with the walking building up a healthy appetite. Once again my mind re-entered the Butchers. Did I really want a Sunday joint? Not really. What I really wanted was the Butcher boy!

The phone was in my palm - a shaking palm. Unlike me, I'd even memorised the phone number on the Business Card. I quickly replaced the receiver, my palm now sticky with sweat. How could I do this? I'd only been in the lighthouse a day and I was ready to proposition a village youth. Whatever next! More importantly, Spike had said he would be pleased to deliver if the weather was foul, and it was hardly that. The only thing that was foul was my mind.

I took a very cold shower!

My next task was to unpack the Apple Mac and set it on the desk beneath the bay window; a constant sea view to keep my mind tranquil whilst I worked. Everything in its proper place, I fired it up. It was always a difficult moment, that blank screen staring back at me, awaiting the first word, first sentence; hopefully, paragraph. I'd sort of remedied that by setting up a template which did at least have 'Title by Luke Smart' staring back at me. But today, even a title for my long awaited novel eluded me. But then 'The Butcher Boy' sprang to mind and I typed it in.

That was as far as I got and, beckoned once more to the top of my lighthouse, I climbed upward and out onto the circular patio, this time bringing with me my binoculars. I scanned seaward first, bringing distant ships and smaller craft close up. They were a powerful pair for their lightness and I could easily make out the crew on yachts; even the name on a large, foreign, oil tanker.

Bored with viewing tankers and tacking crew, I brought my attention to the cliff tops. Way off were a group of ramblers, wrapped up well against the possible inclement weather. I brought my attention closer by, to a solitary figure sat on the edge of the cliff, knees huddled close to his chest, arms wrapped about them, cigarette in hand. A couple of tweaks on the focus knob as I centred on the lad's face, my heart gave a disturbing leap when it was greeted by Spike's. He was looking directly at me! I was suddenly struck with a self-consciousness, thinking that I was some perverted Peeping Tom.

Spike's right hand raised and placed the cigarette into his mouth, and he took a drag. Then, to my total shock, his left hand raised and waved in my direction. I let the binoculars fall to my chest. My breathing increased. "What must he be thinking?" I tortured myself. And answered, "He's thinking that I am a pervert!"

I wanted to dash below as an undeserved shame came over me but, instead, brought the glasses back to my eyes and peered back in his direction. Spike had stood and was heading toward the lighthouse, his face grinning and flushed red from the southerly wind. My heart went into rapid pulsing and my breathing took on a manic pace. Spike was coming to see me. "Oh, shit!" I cursed.

Although I wanted to move, I just couldn't. But what was keeping my feet fixed firmly on the deck and my eyes on him, wasn't my fear of the possibility that my doorbell would soon ring, but, that he no longer wore his pinny. Below a brown, waist-length bomber-jacket, he was dressed in a pair of tight Levis, outlining, so beautifully, what was hidden in the shop; what I had so desperately wished to set my eyes upon, and now was! It was delightful, and as much as I thought I dare not, I continued to focus on that fabulous swelling, fetching it imaginatively into the sea air.

A second wave from Spike, and my heart skipped another beat, but he didn't continue toward the lighthouse and turned toward the village. And with that change of direction came a second treat - firm rounded buttocks, drawn in by the tight denim and divided neatly by the seam.

Frantically I waved, even called his name, I have no idea why, but Spike never heard and continued in a surprisingly manly stride toward the village and out of view.

Below decks, for some reason my lighthouse had taken on a ship's terminology, I once more fired up my Apple and this time did write; detailing my first meeting with the boy butcher; describing his coal-coloured hair and matching thin eyebrows and eyelashes; his dark sexy eyes which seduced with the softness of a kid's fluffy toy; his slim arms with a dusting of black hair on each forearm; but more than this, those lips; those lush, thickish, red lips.

I made coffee, a spoonful of sugar for energy, and continued at the computer, moving onto Spike's body. I wanted to write immediately about the large bulge of boy-sex hidden teasingly beneath the Denim dungeon, but wrote about his frame - fit and fine; crafted by country living; biceps and chest firmly built by chopping joints and carrying carcasses, but not overly so; and thighs, stout and strong, supporting that scrumptious upper torso, slim waist and sturdy robust buttocks. That was as far as I got.

My cock crammed tightly against my leg, desperate for attention, I dashed into the bedroom, disrobed, and drew my palm delicately along the length; delighting in my descriptive writing whilst moving forward several pages and pumping hard as those, as yet, unwritten paragraphs paraded Spike naked before me.

At the point of pelting my pelvis with torrents of cum, the telephone rang. Spike's voice, deep and delightful, drove deep into my dick. I couldn't stop pumping as he told me that he'd seen me at the top of the lighthouse and asking had I noticed him. He'd wanted to come over but had to return to work. It was the way he said come which ran my hand rapidly over my throbbing cock-head, and that's exactly what I did when thoughts of him coming over me seeped through my body and sent spunk sailing in a single stream onto my chest.

I cannot recall the rest of our conversation.

I was exhausted and shaking nervously. What the hell was I up to? More importantly. What the hell was Spike up to?

I'd been living in the lighthouse for two weeks now. Regularly, I visited the village and pubs, and had got to chat with the over friendly, perhaps nosy, locals. Spike had become my main conversation companion but I still had not plucked up the courage to invite him over or get him to deliver his meat, even though he'd hinted at it often enough. He remained fantasy sex for my creative mind, and more paragraphs of my book than I dared to admit had both of us in every conceivable sexual situation. But I was in no doubt that the time for me to make that move was fast approaching. And watching him doing his lonely vigil on the cliff top brought my attention upon him most days; sometimes observing him, unseen, behind curtained windows.

It was the end of October, Halloween, which was to bring unforeseen excitement and mystery into my, mostly, quiet life. I shall never forget that night. The violent storm. The pounding sea over rocks, and that ceaseless whining wind.

It was about eight in the evening and I was being serenaded by strings from four speakers as I lay snug in my lumpy settee. A frantic banging from below caused me to lower the volume of the stereo. I wasn't mistaken, somebody was hammering on the lighthouse door; a desperate kind of banging. My first thought: what was wrong with my doorbell?

I spiralled down the staircase, all the while calling that I was on my way. The wind almost laid me flat when I opened the door, and the sight which greeted me, certainly did! At first I thought it was Spike when my eyes fell upon the bedraggled youth; he was certainly the spitting image of him, though younger. Next, remembering it was Halloween, I assumed it was a 'trick or treater' come to call, but having thought that, his outfit certainly puzzled me, and again I wasn't sure.

The boy burst by me and bolted up the stairs. He appeared frightened.

By the time I'd reached the lounge, he was already heading higher; eventually standing on the lighthouse patio, scanning seaward, wind buffeting his frail body.

Grabbing his shoulder, I dragged him inside and slammed the door against the storm. "What's all this, then?" I questioned, somewhat annoyed.

"She's gone fa sure. Sunked. Ta bottom of ocean. All ans, an all."

I hadn't a clue what this ruffian was on about but he was certainly distressed about something. "Who are you? What are you doing here? Where are you from?" I suppose it was too many questions but they just fell from my mouth.

"Smyke's me name," he sobbed. "From Thunderer," pointing seaward. "Sunked now. All ans," he sobbed again.

If this was a Halloween trick, it was the best I'd ever seen! But try as I did to contain my annoyance, I still was; believing I was on the receiving end of some kid's prank. "Thunderer. What's that?" I interrogated.

"Frigate, Thunderer," he continued to sob.

"Right, Smyke. It's a good trick. I'll get some chocolate for you and then you'd better go. Your folks might be worried. It's pretty late to be trick and treating."

Smyke looked totally bewildered. "Please let me stay, Sir. Til mornin. I ain't got no folks. I'm the Capin's boy. Rescued me fromt workhouse, 'e did. Ain't got nowhere to go nah. E's sunked wid er. Drownded!"

Smyke moved across to the sofa and slumped down, head bowed between his knees, arms wrapped around them, continuing to sob. Situations seldom fazed me but this one did. I hadn't the faintest notion of what Smyke was on about but something was happening which was beyond me.

I hadn't really taken a good look at the lad but when he moved onto the sofa, I took in his attire. The boy was wearing white breeches, knee high, dirty breeches at that. His T-shirt, if it was that, was also dirty-white and torn to tatters; his frail white chest revealed. Shoeless and very grubby footed, he stood about five-one. I'd also glimpsed the arse of his breeches had been partly ripped out, his bare buttocks peeping through. Like his feet and legs, his arms too were grubby and grimy; a dirty bare shoulder revealed through the torn material.

Smyke continued to sob and now shake. He was cold and wet and, by the looks of him, starving. I swung the fire up an extra notch and called him over. "Would you like a hot drink, Smyke, and some food?"

"Thank e kindly, Sir. I'll av a toddy or a tot. Me bones is freezin!"

"Toddy or a tot?" I queried, disbelieving a boy was requesting alcohol.

"Please. Capin always gis me a hot toddy or a tot of rum before we beds down."

I had rum, most drinks, but giving a scraggy youth such a strong beverage left me in a moral dilemma. I glanced across at Smyke and was about to say that that wasn't on, but seeing how hopeless he looked, snuggled close by the fire, I fetched a bottle of Navy Neaters - the proof of which could kill a horse - and poured him a good measure.

Smyke grasped the glass in trembling fingers, upturned the vessel and sent the whole measure down his throat. "Ah! That's nice stuff. Thank e Sir," he smiled, like a man who'd been drinking rum all his life.

I have no idea why, maybe the shock of seeing it disappear so readily, but I asked if he wanted another. Two hefty glugs and the tumbler was re-filled, and one single gulp and it was emptied again. "Thank e, Sir. I feels much betta nah."

"I'm sure you do," I mused, and poured myself an even larger one but, unlike him, coughed severely as it tore my throat apart. Smyke roared a childish laugh. I laughed with him. In fact we both laughed loudly. And what a joy it was to see that young boy's face light up.

I dropped beside him, the two of us huddled by the fire. Steam was rising from his wet clothing and black hair. "Would you like a bath, Smyke? It'll thaw you out and make you feel better."

The shock to him of that offer was unexpected. Indeed, it was practically one of horror, and he shouted, "Nah. Don't make us do that, Sir! Bosun sticks me in the tub if I stas to smell igh. Don't like it though. Anyways, I ad one a fortnight back. And ize just swum the ocean, an all."

It was a natural reaction, placing my arm over his shoulder. But I was surprised when Smyke leant into my body, placing an arm around my back and the other around my front, hugging me lovingly. "OK," I smiled. "No wash, but tell me more about yourself."

Smyke cuddled me tighter. "As I says, I'ze from Thunderer. It the rocks, it did. Sunked." Smyke gripped me tightly and I moved my palm into his black hair and gave him comforting strokes. "I'ze the Capin's boy. I looks afer im. No more. Dead e is. Treated me kindly did the Capin."

Smyke glanced at me with deep, dark, tear-filled eyes. I brought a finger beneath them and gently brushed away the sorrowful droplets. Smyke smiled as I stroked my palm over his flushed cheek, then, stunning me, kissed me full on the lips.

I would have to confess that that solitary kiss sent such a sensation throughout my body that I would have gladly whisked him up in my arms and taken him to my bed; to love and hold, cuddle and caress, comfort; but, still unsure of exactly who or what I was dealing with, returned his kiss with one upon his cheek. He cuddled me tighter yet.

Smyke looked exhausted, his eyelids constantly fluttering those big black eyelashes over his eyes; his body rocking gently as he came close to slumber. Cupping his lightweight frame in my arms, I cradled him toward the sofa and laid him down. It had been so long since I'd held another person in my arms, that the warmth of his youthful body brought such a sexual surge, I could have devoured him on the spot. Made love to him all night long.

With a single tender kiss upon those lush red lips and another upon his forehead, I bade him good night and covered him with a blanket.

It was early morning, close to three, when I was disturbed by soft bare arms wrapping around my nakedness. "Didn't mean to wake e, Sir. Can't sleep on me own. I always sleeps wiv the Capin."

"Smyke," I whispered, my lips caressing his ear. "You OK?"

"Am now. You gonna av me now, Sir?"

"Have you, Smyke? What do you mean?"

"Av me like the Capin do. I likes that. As I says, I'm is boy. Is Moll."

My mind raced excitedly as Smyke's words filtered into my sleepy mind. He was the Captain's boy. His Moll. Smyke was the Captain's prostitute, no that wasn't fair, he was his boy-lover!

"Oh, Smyke," I sighed and pulled him comfortingly close to my body, for he was surely feeling lonely and vulnerable.

"Take me, Sir. Please let me be your Moll tonight," Smyke pleaded, arching his bottom into me.

I hadn't noticed until that moment that he was now naked, his silk smooth skin fitting snugly into my shape. I felt somewhat guilty that my sex was stiff with excitement, with the joy of having another's nakedness touching mine.

I breathed deeply, excitedly, brushing my lips over his neck and bare shoulders, my palms caressing his smooth buttocks. He smelt of the sea, gun-powder, ropes, even tar and oak wood. He smelt delicious!

My palm moved around to his young sex and I cupped it gently, stroking the small spheres then along the young sturdy shaft. Smyke whimpered as I caressed, cuddled, climbed on top of him and slid into the darkness of his buttock cheeks.

Oh-so-gently, I glided into the depths of his bottom. Smyke wriggled excitedly. Turning his head to one side, he whispered for me to kiss him. Our mouths met as my body pushed him gently deeper into the mattress, all the while our tongues licking and my buttocks thrusting, deep, deep, and deeper between the Cabin Boy's covetous cheeks.

"Oh, Sir!" Smyke whimpered, sending semen squirting beneath his flat and tender tummy and into my working palm,

"Smyke! Beautiful Smyke!" I sighed, shivering sensationally as I sent my own stream sailing inside of him.

We kissed and caressed, cuddled and stroked for an hour after that most wondrous and welcome loving making. Never in my life can I recall such tenderness from anyone with whom I had made love, compared to that of Smyke's which swamped me in waves and overwhelmed me that night.

We made love again and again and each time it was more powerful, more loving, more wonderful. Smyke was the youth I had been searching for for two lonely years. Now I had found him I would never let him go. He could be my Cabin Boy. My Moll. Forever!

It was the slamming of the lighthouse's heavy oak door which caused me to wake to a vacant space beside me. Jumping naked from the bed I started to dash below, but guessing I would have a better view of where he was headed, ran to the lighthouse top.

Throwing open the door and dashing onto the patio, the howling wind shrinking my privates and erupting goose pimples over my nakedness, I ran around to the lighthouse front. Smyke was racing toward the shore, fighting hard against the wind and rain. "Smyke!" I screamed, then screamed his name again even louder. But my calls were to no avail, my words caught in gusts and carried windward.

In total shock and horror I watched as he ran to the water's edge, then continued into the sea, his body engulfed by crashing waves.

"I'm coming, Capin! I'm coming!" were his last words to sail up on the stormy wind.

"Smyke!" I yelled. "You'll drown!" Then, out of the corner of my eye I caught sight of something white. Squinting into the howling wind, my eyes watering with its ferocity but also in despair, I saw flapping sails and broken masts - a ship's battered rigging. I squinted again and they were gone - so was Smyke.

I was in stunned shock and sadness for the remainder of the morning. I decided I needed some answers. There had to be an explanation of what had happened, if indeed it had happened, and headed into Tarring.

Braving the foul weather, I cut along the footpath to the village. Bypassing the Butchers, even though Spike had acknowledged me with a grin and a wave, I headed directly to the Library. With the help of another youthful assistant, I was handed the old records detailing the Village's history. I set the thick, heavily bound book upon a table and, in the solitude of a quiet room, began my search - for what, I wasn't sure. Deep within its dusty pages, Thunderer, leapt out at me.

Beautifully handwritten, beside the date in the margin, it told of His Majesty's Frigate, Thunderer, which floundered and sunk in stormy seas. Although a Cabin Boy had raised the alarm, all hands were lost; and despite his brave efforts to rescue his Captain, the boy had drowned. His name was Smyke.

My body shivered cold and hot as I read his name. I could not believe it. Smyke was a ghost!

I slammed the book shut and shakily returned it to the assistant then hastily left the Library. A shout from Spike, as I passed the Butchers, reminded me that I needed meat.

"You OK, Luke? You look pale."

I nodded I was fine and Spike made up my order whilst I remained in deep thought.

"Tell you what, Luke," Spike began, startling me from my thoughts, "why don't you let me bring these up this afternoon. It's early closing, so it's no trouble. No point in struggling all the way home in this weather."

Without even realising that I'd agreed and even forgetting to pay for my goods, I walked dazed from the shop and headed home.

I'd slept most of the rest of the day and was now being woken by the doorbell. Spike apologised for being late. In fact it was very late and the sky had already darkened.

After placing my meat into the fridge, I invited him up to the lounge, allowing him to climb the spiral staircase before me. Until that moment I had not seen Spike's body close up, apart from when hidden beneath a pinny or through magnifying lenses. And how adorable that was, his tightly clad buttocks divided by that seam, beckoning me to bite them tenderly, to burrow between them, to .....

And again, Spike sitting on the sofa on which Smyke had slept, his parted legs offering his boyish bulge to be caressed by hungry eyes, or by eager hands, or by.......

I sat beside him, desperately wanting to touch him, touch any part of him. I was amazed by his resemblance to Smyke. He was almost identical. Merely older. And having made love to Smyke, I guessed that Spike's naked body might well look as beautiful, if not better. May well be as tender. As willing?

We chatted for a while about this and that - the village, music, food, TV - just getting to know one another kind of talk. After an hour of swapping information, coffee was replaced with Cognac, the fire lit, and a more relaxed position, upon cozy cushions, taken beside it.

Had I done this last night? I immediately thought, glimpsing those familiar features of black hair, rosy cheeks, and soulful eyes.

"You might think this strange, Luke. But I feel that I've been here before. It all seems so familiar. And, I think I've told you before, for some strange reason I seem to be drawn here."

Spike couldn't have put my own thoughts any better. I too was convinced I was doing a re-run of yesterday. And if that was what was happening, did this mean that within a few hours we would be in bed together, making love? I could hardly control my excitement as that thought surfaced, and I could definitely not control my erection as that did likewise.

Touching Spike was no longer resistible, and, reaching toward his thigh, I placed my palm upon it. "You know, Spike, I have the strangest of feelings as well."

Spike's movement, somehow, was and wasn't unexpected, and, cupping my fire flushed face in his hands, he bent toward me and kissed my mouth firmly, yet gently.

My heart skipped two beats and my sex stiffened painfully. "Oh, Spike," I whispered. "You are so beautiful."

Spike didn't speak and slid my body backward, weighting me down with his as he began a more passionate embrace. Hands instinctively sought out sexes and began slipping over them. Breathing increased as we rubbed our bodies together; rubbed our cocks.

T-shirts were discarded and tossed toward the sofa and soon flesh smoothed against flesh as our chest rubbed together.

It was with such a start, the way in which Spike sat up then stood, which caused me to think I had made a terrible mistake and question him concerningly, but Spike appeared not to hear my words and headed toward the window.

"Spike. What's up?" Spike still didn't reply and appeared to be shaking, staring intently into the darkness outside.

"Spike!" I called again, raising myself and joining him.

"Look! Oh Lord!" His voice had a frightening tremble to it.

"What?" My own voice taking on an unnatural higher pitch.

"The ship. Its rigging's breaking up! God, it's sinking!" Spikes voice was filled with panic as he shouted those words.

My whole body shivered as it absorbed Spike's fear. I stared hard into the darkness but could see nothing except white topped waves crashing over the rocks in the distance.

BANG! BANG! BANG!

BANG! BANG!

BANG! BANG! BANG!

My head swung toward the spiral staircase and the hammering coming from the lighthouse door far below. My body froze and my face whitened as the boy rushed toward us. "Smyke," I murmured, then loudly, "SMYKE!"

"Yes?" Spike answered, in a strangely calm voice.

My mind raced - confused, frightened!

Smyke continued heading for me, he appeared desperate to reach us, he was moving very fast. "Ugh!" I yelped, jumping to one side, fearing that he would collide with me. But he didn't and ran straight into Spike.

It was at that precise moment of impact with Spike that Smyke glanced toward me and beamed the broadest of smiles, whispered something, then vanished.

"Yes?" repeated Spike. "You were going to say something?"

I sucked in a deep breath for I'd not breathed for those startling seconds. "Did you see that!"

"Oh, the ship. I think I was just imagining it. Storms can play tricks on your eyes."

"No, the bo........." I stopped my sentence short. Spike appeared to have calmed and there seemed no point in continuing or making myself into a fool.

"Let's carry on where we left off," suggested Spike, hugging me tightly. "I feel Ok now. But I had the strangest of feelings back there."

Spike shivered.

We let the matter alone whilst we resumed our cuddling and kissing, comforting ourselves with caresses. It was Spike's suggestion that he spend the night and soon we were snuggled beneath blankets, exploring our complete nakedness for the first time.

Lying on our sides, Spike's soft bottom sitting in my lap, my palm caressing his cute cock, he arched his willing cheeks into me and softly whispered, "You going to take me, Luke? Let me be your Moll?"

NAVY DAYS

MONDAY

How did they expect us to eat this crap at 6am. Jim, the Junior Chef, was brilliant at blow-jobs but frying a fucking egg was beyond him. I offered him a seductive smile and scooped a couple of the limp, liquid cackleberries onto my plate. They looked about as appetising as Twiggy's tits, and I sleepily led them to a table where a stocky, butch stoker was sat scoffing a bowl of cornflakes. The greasy rashers of bacon I'd collected en-route helped cheer the sorry sight and I arranged them into a happy face before slamming the lot between rounds of bread in an attempt to create something that looked edible.

The stocky Stoker's eyes never left his bowl but he was aware I was searching his every expression; searching for sexual clues. It was a must for me.

Sex on board a Royal Navy ship was usually hard to come by and you couldn't afford to be wrong if you were going to proposition someone. As far as I was concerned, everyone dropped their pants until proven otherwise!

Beneath the table, I let my leg brush against the Stoker's but he pulled quickly away and remained transfixed by his wheaty-pop breakfast. Shame really because he was quite a wheaty-pop himself. Anyway, the day was just developing and he looked like he'd just come off watch and was heading for his bunk. I hung around until he'd finished eating, just to glimpse his bum and absorb the rest of his features as he left the Dinning Room.

I liked Stokers, they were a bit of a turn on for me and had the reputation of being 'goers' if you got one. I reckoned it was their boiler-suits, usually unbuttoned to the navel, and the inevitable line of sweat trickling down a smooth, bare chest. And knowing that they were completely naked beneath the greasy blue material.

I'd been below decks into the Boiler Room many times - to deliver signals to the Commander of Engineering - and watched the young lads dipping oily rags beneath those boiler-suits and into their crotches; mopping up the liquid as they exuded sweat in the 100 degree temperatures. I often wondered how that would smell - steamy, sweaty crotch and oil. I reckoned it would smell just fine, especially if the legs were parted over my feasting face. But, as yet, I had never poked a stoker.

I thanked Jim for his wonderful creation and gave him a wink, signalling I'd see him during the week for one of his Haute Cuisine blow-jobs.

The Communications Office was somewhat silent for a change, just a printer chattering away in the corner and the telephone buzzing. Tim was bent over the printer reading an incoming signal. We were alone, so I trotted over and pinched his bum.

Tim was a great fuck and a fun guy, and I was privileged to know he liked being screwed and obliged him whenever he was on heat. But with his butch manner and manly voice, which didn't suit his young age and features, nobody knew of his tendency to swing - unless he was two timing me.

One peculiar aspect of Navy life, guys seldom told each other if they were having it away with other guys. It was added protection. The least amount of people who knew of one's sexual leanings, the better. The guys who usually got rumbled - for rumbling each other - were those who formed threesomes or more. Two was the safest number and there were ample hideouts in which to perform. Also, a couple of guys knocking around together was less suspicious.

Tim spun around and I grabbed his cock. It was semi-hard and protruded just enough to make it look appetising. I grabbed his golden-haired head and planted my lips onto his, giving him a good morning kiss, or good night in his case as he was going off watch. He pushed me away but managed half-a-smile. I guessed it had been an hectic night and he was tired.

He called me a 'Tart' in that masculine manner and I wondered how he could make such a feminine word sound so butch. I wrapped my arms around his waist and squeezed his cock, but he butted me away with his backside. Well, I had to try! I even offered to return to his mess-deck and tuck him in, but he grabbed his cock and muttered something about sitting on it. That's precisely what I had in mind. Well, him sitting on mine. I guessed we didn't have a date.

I didn't know if it was just me but I was constantly thinking about sex. I didn't join the Navy with 'getting laid' in mind, but there were so many good-looking guys it was impossible not to constantly think about it. Also, there was so much groping or guys strutting around naked. And in the mornings, so many stiff cocks on parade it was difficult not to dribble and drool at the delight of them - many of which were still dribbling from an early morning handshake. Had there been a post of Early Morning Cocksucker, mine would have been the first application on the Captain's table. That said, not every guy was edible. Some were gross, grotty and even gut-heaving. But a good few of the Baby Skins possessed beautiful bouncy bollocks, buttocks and bonnie boners - all requiring a friend. And by God, I was in the befriending business!

Tim went to bed - alone. I went to work on the incoming signals. Within half-an-hour the office had filled with its complement of watch-keepers, so I shot off to my own office on the deck above.

This was a real hush hush place and only two of us were allowed access, which was a real bonus as some of the things I did there were pretty hush hush as well. The thought that one day I'd get caught filled my mind many times, but when you have a mouthful of Marine it's difficult to let it materialise into a real fear. In fact, often the size of the Marine's cock manifesting in my mouth was more frightening. No wonder they were such good fighters. No need the threaten the enemy with a bayonet. Just show them your dick, darling!

It felt like it was going to be a dull day. No War Games. No enemy to investigate. Nothing much to do except fire up my equipment and check that it was in working order. (Sorry, wrong equipment. You're disgusting!) Which is what I did.

Well, what would you know? Blank screens. Not a green dot in sight. Just like the contents of East 17's underpants, or was it their heads!

Surprised? I'll say I was. For a million quid you'd at least expect the batteries to work. It appeared my day wasn't going to be spent alone.

I needed an Electrician. To be honest, I needed a shag! But an Electrician would be a start. My favourite Sparks answered the phone - one that I hadn't shagged - and informed me they were snowed under with problems and could only spare a Baby Sparks - a Sparkler, I suppose. Desperate - and I was - I agreed. In a flash, he was thumping my door.

To say 'My lights came on' when I opened the door. Christ, my hormones could have powered a concert at Wembley. And as they sped around my body, my Main Attraction was soon on show!

It was the sweetest voice that asked, "Do you have a problem?"

Well, I did. But now I had an even bigger one. That was no one-and-a-half-volt-battery bulging in my briefs, but a pylon of power promising to protrude!

Christ! Boys could not be that beautiful. It was criminal. Cruel. And I cried, "Come inside," in a dribbling drool.

My super Sparkler set about stripping down the machinery whilst I set about doing a mental version of the same thing to him. Usually naval working clothes did little to enhance a body - even a beautiful one - but this Power Pack must have had a buddy or lustful admirer in the stores, because he'd set a pair of working trousers upon him, so tight, they might have been painted on.

Together we searched for the goblin in the works, but there was only one goblin I was interested in. And my mind worked overtime thinking of a way I could use some paint-stripper on those pants!

"I think it's up," he cheerfully chirped, giving me a grin the length of his flies. Did he mean what I thought he meant or was he referring to my dick? - which certainly was!

"Up?" I repeated, looking lustfully straight at his crotch, then at my own.

"Yes. The mast," he clarified.

"Oh!" I sighed, disappointed, and tried to produce a grin of similar length.

He'd have to go aloft to sort it out but couldn't do it alone - safety and all that. Now, when it came to heights, climbing over a locked toilet door was about my limit. But my mixed up mind told me that at some point, up there, there would come a moment when I might have to grab this little Sparkler - for safety reasons, you understand - so I agreed to assist. Trouble was, this Sparkler looked too hot to handle and I could see myself getting burnt.

A fair swell rocked the mast back and forth as we climbed the hollow centre. There was a ladder on the outside but even if he told me I could fuck him when we reached the top, I don't think I could have climbed it.

Sparkler opened the hatch to the the blue sky above, and as I delighted in his buttocks when he climbed through, I somehow managed not to bite them. But when we stepped out onto the platform, the only thing I was biting was my lip. Sixty foot doesn't look high from ground-level, but up there in the breeze and four way sway of the mast that notion soon vanished. And so did my erection!

Sparkler soon found the offending aerial and the cable that had freed itself but it was just beyond his reach. He was a brave, little bugger and without hesitation began to climb the guardrails in order to reach the broken cable. Then it happened. My premonition came true and he asked me to hold him. I don't think I leapt on him over quickly but it was Panther-like.

I stuffed my eager hand down the back of his pants, so far, my fingers delved between the crease of his buttocks. He looked over his shoulder, quizzingly. I guessed I'd gone too deep. Reluctantly, I withdrew and grasped the back of his belt. He gave me a 'That's better' look and resumed his climb. But it was no good, I was stopping him reaching the final inches.

"It's no use. You'll have to put your arms around my thighs and hold onto me tightly," he ordered, rather masterfully for a youngster.

I don't recall saying, "Oh, thank you. Yes please. Thank you, God." But I sure as hell thought it.

He resumed his climb. When he reached the danger point, precariously balancing on the top handrail, I threw my arms around his young muscles. With both arms wrapped tightly around my treasure, he eased himself the final inches. Miraculously, he made it. His nimble fingers began their task of teasing wires together. However, my nasty little digits unexpectedly but delightedly had discovered his dick. I could just make out the shape of his bell-end against the tip of my index finger.

Gently I moved my dexterous digit from beneath the supple sausage and slid it over the top. My strokes were minuscule, micro-dot movements, making out the shape of the bell-end's ridge. Amazingly, it began to move. I continued to manipulate in miniature. Slowly a manifestation began to take shape. It felt magnificent and manly as it matured into a monster!

His pert little buttocks were in my face, so I daringly let my teeth take the slightest nip. His meat jarred beneath my fondling friend.

I was in fear of dropping him as my excitement increased and was just about to strengthen my hold, when down he jumped. "Finished," he gleefully announced.

Well, I wasn't! And I looked hard at the masterpiece I'd created with one finger, and like the tart that I was, questioned, "Don't you think you'd better make sure?"

He gave me another grin - the length of both our flies this time - and planted his sexy eyes right onto my stiff prick. Then he told me he'd have pop down to my office and check if my equipment was working - he'd be right back.

Well, no lad looks at my dick like that and gets away with it!

I watched him bolt down the hatch like some sexy rabbit, but what this bunny didn't know - I had a plan.

I waited until I heard the clink clank of him ascending the inside of the mast. I popped down the hatch, pulling it shut above me. In total darkness I waited to snare him. It was a gamble, I might be wrong.

The sounds became louder as he approached and my crotch expanded in sympathy. Perched on a rung, legs wide apart, feet pressed against the bulkhead for support, I continued to wait.

His head came between my thighs and into my crotch. He released a surprised yelp. Placing my palm on the back of his head, I gently teased his face into my bulging crotch. He didn't pull away but edged slightly higher and simply told me my equipment was working. He was right, it certainly was!

He sounded nervous and I wondered if I'd finally made that fatal mistake, but I eased his head further onto my cock and slipped my other hand between my crotch and his face. Sliding my fingers over his moist lips, I pushed them into his wet mouth. He didn't pull away or warn me off. Ejecting my erect dick, I pushed it against his mouth.

He began to move his head from side to side, as if trying to avoid contact but his movements were not convincing. I persisted, not forcefully, just teasingly - indicating my cock was up for grabs if he wanted it. Moments later, his lips parted and his mouth carefully covered the head. It was sensationally hot and I wanted to push deep but knew he had not done this before. I let him work the head at his own pace. Slowly but surely, little by little, more of my meat began to penetrate his soft palate.

As I caressed his face with loving strokes, his movements became more eager, more lusting, more deep. His pretty face began to work frantically, sucking my cock from the tip to the base. I lifted the hatch, allowing the light to shine down on his black hair, and excitedly watched as he lavished my length.

Stopping him before I came, I raised his body until his boyish bulge was level with my face. Greedily, I pulled his shirt from his pants and lifted it to his pin-sized nipples. My tongue licked his soft flesh and firming studs, then around his navel. Reaching inside his pants, I released his prick from his pants. An extremely consumable cock with a foreskin sprang into view and I rolled the loose flesh back and forth over the head several times before consuming the whole length with the passion of a starving child.

Whilst we crazily kissed and darted tongues into mouths, we finished each other with our hands. Him coming first, his white cum splattering all over me, mine falling to the depths of the deck below.

It was a brilliant start to my week. And what a place to have sex. I couldn't say that I now belonged to the Mile High Club, but sixty foot was a start.

One thing was certain, I was a mile high all day!

TUESDAY

I knew something big was going down, besides my erection. It wasn't often I was dragged from my bunk at 3am. At least not by a big butch Bootneck - unfortunately.

I felt the ship shudder as the Skipper rolled-on-the-revs, sticking 35 knots onto the speedometer. I climbed topside into the gale-force winds in an attempt to blast the cobwebs from my bewildered brain, before it was bombarded with ultra-sonic sounds. Electronic Warfare was my game.

The stern churned a funnel of white foam. It shone in the moonlight like a train on a wedding dress as the props dug deep into the ocean, slicing our bows through the stormy sea. I thought of Wheaty-pop dipping his oily rag into his crotch as he beefed the engines up. Before I had time to let that voluptuous vision reach my dick, a mountain of Marine tugged at my arm, insisting I hurry.

When something like this happened, I was entrusted with an armed Marine as protector, who would guard me in my office whilst I worked. In these situations, everyone was the enemy.

We had half-a-dozen Marines on board. All straight? Except one, who relished being sucked. And he was with me now as we ran to my office, me following him, naturally. I wouldn't have missed a view of that backside for anything.

Zak was my Marine's name. Well it would be wouldn't it? It was the kind of name you would give an Android, and Zak fitted that description admirably. His muscles were like metal. And if you had any notion of parting his solid steel buttocks, forget it. You'd need a dick like a can-opener because Zak did not get fucked! But he did get sucked and had a Pit-bull in his pants. If everything went to plan, it would be parting my lips over it when things calmed down.

I got the jist of what was going down from the Communications Officer. No need to go into details, save to say one of our boys was in trouble.

Zak and I entered my office and I began firing up various pieces of electronic wizardry. Zak bolted the door and stood solid in its entrance. I told him there was no need, he could sit if he wished. But I got the feeling he loved the butch pose - legs apart, arms behind his back, rigid as a post, pistol swinging from his hip.

Jesus. He looked gorgeous!

Soon the office was buzzing and lights were flashing - an ergonomist's paradise. I sat before my console, headphones on head, miniature mike at my mouth, and began twiddling various knobs - scanning the relevant frequencies. Meanwhile, the jammers were warming up in case they were needed.

Zak stood like a chiselled, stone statue behind me. I could see his reflection in one of my screens and was able to distinguish the outline of his Pit-bull. I'm sure I saw it move, growing and growling in his pants, and glance over my shoulder, giving him a brief smile. He acknowledged with one of his own but didn't speak. You'd have thought we were total strangers rather than Suck Buddies, but duty was duty to this Marine.

"For Christ sake, Zak. Take your bloody cap off!" I suggested, giving him another smile.

He thought for a moment. It seemed like a big decision, so I let him ponder it over. I suppose it was more of a sexual request, really. Well, if I couldn't see his dick just yet, at least I could relish his shaven head. Jesus, I just loved running my hands over the sharp spikes, and thoughts of shaving it whilst he gave me a blow-job filled my mind many times. Alas, Zak didn't do that either. He only received sex - the bitch!

I made contact with our boy in trouble and set the tape deck rolling in case of cock-ups and to refer back to at a later date. Then informed the Captain on the hot-line. I heard a clunk beside me and jumped. I suppose I was a little tense. These situations certainly sent the adrenaline surging. It was Zak's cap not a terrorist attack, and I shot a quick glance at his shaven head. Zak grinned. He knew what I was thinking and gave me a look which suggested I get on with my job.

I grinned back and muttered, "You tormenting bitch," beneath my breath.

Zak shouldn't have distracted me so because I lost contact with our boy whilst playing with my hormones instead of my hardware. I had five minutes of pulse racing panic trying to regain it.

Concentration back on course, I resumed my job with the skill of an artist - delving into code-books, decoding, recoding, switching frequencies, jamming and unjamming. It was frantic but I loved it. All-the-while, Zak stood silently watching me. Sometimes I wondered whether he was overwhelmed by the technicality of it all.

Without warning two pieces of equipment went pop and their screens blanked. "Fuck!" I screamed, thumping the console, frantically flying around the office, desperately trying to regain contact and retain the information I already had.

"Zak," I yelled. "Get an Electrician!" Zak, pleased to be involved in a crisis, jumped to the task and was on the phone in a flash.

"He's coming," he grinned, excited by the trauma I found myself in.

"You slut, Zak!" I shouted. "Did you have to say 'coming' like that?"

Minutes later a couple of heavy thuds echoed through the door. Zak released his pistol, placing his meaty hand around the butt. I knew it wasn't a terrorist. Zak must have know also, but he had a job to do and was more than likely doing it to the best of his ability.

He threw the iron bolts, pulling his pistol from its leather holster, and opened the door. He was greeted by the smiling face of my Baby Sparkler. Well, if you could have seen Zak's face, and mine to be honest, I reckon ten gallons of cum filled his balls in that instant.

I was right, he was a slut and I wanted to slap him but I simply asked if he was going to let my Sparkler in. Then whispered, "And whilst you're at it. Stop dribbling!"

Brad, that was Sparkler's name, gave me one of his fly-length grins, totally ignoring Zak. That pleased me immensely and I gave Zak a look which said, "Serves you right, you bitch." But Zak was totally besotted and began telling Brad my problem.

I was just about to say, "Who's bloody office is this?" when Brad charged straight through Zak and asked about my predicament. Which at the moment appeared to be Zak.

Speedily, Brad worked his nimble fingers at the wiring, temporarily regaining contact with our lost buddy long enough for me to complete my task. Panic over, I made coffee whilst Brad began a more permanent job.

Zak had seated himself - at last! I think he was in a state of sexual shock. I had to ask him, several times, if he wanted a cup.

Zak and I drank our coffee in virtual silence, both observing Brad's tight buns as he bent over, soldering wires. It was an awesome sight and I began to bulge in my bell-bottoms. A quick glance between Zak's legs confirmed his thoughts were on a similar wavelength.

Now. Remember what I said about threesomes? Well, I could see that that rule was just about to fly through the port hole. I wanted sex. Zak wanted sex. And Brad? I doubted if he'd refuse. My dilemma. Should I have sex with Zak, or Brad, or both? Or should I let them both go? In which case I was sure they would end up shagging somewhere. And that thought didn't bare thought. I can be a jealous bitch!

Decision made, I delved into Zak's pants and pulled out his Pit-bull, parting my lips over the enormous head. Zak was speechless but was so engrossed with Brad's backside, he didn't bat an eyelid and simply stood, releasing more of his manhood and enabling me to get most of his meat into my mouth. As I moved down its length, I kept one eye on Brad, waiting for him to turn around.

Brad spun to face us and was just about to inform me everything was back on line, when he saw what I was up too. His mouth dropped open and not a word left it. His eyes began to sparkle. I gazed between his thighs as he subconsciously caressed his cock and watched as the volume between them increased in size. I stopped sucking Zak and nodded for him to join us. Zak's dick gained an inch as Brad moved forward, unzipping his pants and pushing his terrific tool tantalisingly through the fly. Eagerly I went down on his mouthwatering morsel when he reached us.

It was such a perfect prick and I pushed my mouth hard into the base, bringing it fully erect. All the while, my left hand rolled Zak's foreskin back and forth over the head of his cock, keeping it firm.

Bringing their dicks head to head, I licked along both then devoured each in turn - first Brad's, then Zak's. I continued the sequence whilst they kissed and tongued each other's throats. In my lustful state, I wanted to lavish both cocks simultaneously and made an attempt to get them into my mouth. But Zak had enough dick for the three of us and I couldn't manage it. Pulling my prick from my pants, I began to work on myself.

Zak was awe struck by Brad's boyish body and began stripping clothes from his smooth skin. When Brad's trousers and briefs came down, I almost came at the sight of the black moustache above his dick and totally forgot about Zak. I began to mouth greedily at the uncut cock, my mouth consuming all of him, lips pushing hard against the soft black hair, eager to tease his teenage juices onto my lavishing tongue.

Standing up, I pushed Brad down. Instantly his young mouth began working on our cocks, repeating what I had been doing. He was a fast learner. An ecstatic Zak sank his tongue deep into my throat. It was almost as big as his dick and I sucked on it with just as much passion. Meanwhile, Brad went so deep on me my balls disappeared and I nearly shot my load.

A sudden urge to screw Brad surged through my groin. He was a virgin for sure and might not be ready for it. But with my brain being bombarded by hormones and testosterone, I left Brad sucking on Zak's massive monster and went to my safe. Excitedly I spun the combination, 69 69 69 - Well, it was easy number to remember - and returned with condoms and lube.

Standing behind Brad, I glanced briefly at Zak, who looked as if he were about to come, and watched them perform. I'd seen porn before but this was electrifying and exotic beyond belief. I could see how threesomes could easily become the norm for me.

Raising Brad's buttocks, I tore open a sachet of lube - my fingers trembling with excitement - and smeared the slippery liquid into his hairless crevice. Slowly I began to tease my fingers into the tight opening. Brad moaned with pleasure and mouthed ever faster on Zak's dick. I guessed I'd got the green light and teased a condom over my dick and lubed it with two sachets. I reckoned it was going to be pretty painful for him.

Ever so gently, I eased myself between Brad's muscular, young buttocks. He released a yelp and they flexed tightly. Once he'd relaxed,

I teased a little more of my prick into his tight passage. The head of my cock vanished!

I'd gone deep enough to make movement and began to ride him more robustly. And with each forward thrust, more and more of my dick disappeared into the dark depths of Brad's trembling buttocks. Suddenly, I was all the way.

Desperately I began to thrust and withdraw, Brad responding by pushing hard against my pelvis. Soon we were in unison. Brad was loving it! Almost immediately, Zak released an manly gasp and he shot his load. Brad pulled his head away. The jet of creamy white cum sailed through the air in a single stream and landed on his bare back, sliding towards his parted cheeks and my thrusting cock. I guessed the sight of me fucking Brad was too much for Zak.

To say I was shocked. I was absolutely stunned! It was unthinkable. Brad must have pushed some sexual button of Zak's because he raised Brad from the kneeling position - me still attached - and went down on him, sucking the teenager furiously and pumping himself hard. There was no doubt Zak could come again, he had an automatic weapon. There was always another round in his barrel.

Whilst Zak worked on Brad's big bone, I pushed deep and hard into his rear, the spunk sliding between our naked bodies as my chest rubbed over Brad's bare back. Moving my hands around Brad, I grasped Zak's shaven head and rubbed the spiky hair. At the crucial moment, I pulled Zak's head deep onto Brad's cock, forcing him to swallow the whole length. With a trio of gasps, the three of us came.

I made another round of coffee and we sat silently drinking it, each pondering our own thoughts. Me wondering if Zak and Brad would get it off at a later date, or if the three of us would repeat this some day. Or if Brad and I would make out.

The telephone buzzed. Brad and Zak were called back to their respective bases. With a kiss for each, I reluctantly released them.

The afternoon dragged and I was bored. All I could think about was Brad. I fired up my equipment, giving it a final check before going below decks.

Opening one of the panels, I began to study the multi-coloured wiring. Taking a pair of wire cutters, I selected a green one.

SNIP!

The telephone was in my hand. "Hello, Brad. It's Matt. Yes, number

two's gone on the blink again. Okay. See you in a few minutes, then."
WEDNESDAY

Tuesday finished on such a good note I thought I must mention it. Brad returned to my office and I told him straightaway what I had done, pointing out the wire I had deliberately cut. He laughed, and played 'Pretend I don't know why you did it'. In no time the fold-away bunk I had in my office was sprung open and we were humping furiously. We sucked and fucked, fucked and sucked until our balls were desert dry. I didn't ask whether he fancied Zak and if he was going to hump him. I'd rather not know.

Today, because we had all been good boys - if only the Captain knew! - we were granted a Make and Mend. In layman's language, time to repair kit and catch up with washing clothes etc.. Or to put it more bluntly, have a bloody good rest!

I wasn't feeling at all horny and cruised to the canteen for some grub. Jim was there slopping slop onto plates. He gave me one of his 'Do you want to play with my sausage?' looks. I tried desperately not to appear interested but somehow he got the opposite vibes, running his tongue and lips erotically over the wooden spoon he was using - so much for hygiene! I walked beside the counter searching for something which resembled food, Jim cruising me on the other side, continuing to suck suggestively on the spoon. He could see I wasn't impressed by what was on offer - discounting him - and giving me a broad smile, delved into a hot cupboard. The hugest of rump steaks was quickly produced and plopped onto my plate, accompanied by a sexy smile and a wink from those swooning eyes. I returned his smile with a blown kiss of thanks. I guessed it was his own dinner, the love.

Our brief bout of flirting was soon halted by the entrance of the Head Chef. He was a horrible, fat bastard with a face that only a Mother could love. I quickly shuffled away, tossing potatoes and veg around the steak, then soaked the lot with gruesome gooey gravy.

I chose Spotted Dick for sweet. No, not for that reason. I happened to like it. Then searched for someone more edible than my dinner to sit beside. My rump steak was prettier than most things filling their faces, so I took it to an empty table and began to attack it, hoping it wouldn't fight back. It was only then that I remembered something Jim had told me, some time back, and I wished I hadn't.

"It was not uncommon," Jim had said, "to get really horny at 4am when preparing breakfasts. And as most of the Chefs were big, fat, overfed farts, who he wouldn't stick my prick inside, let alone his, he needed a way of releasing his frustration."

"Now, a wank is fine," he had said, "but it was a long way down the line from a blow-job or a fuck." So, what was the next best thing? Well, he told me, he got his dick nice and hard, then, selecting a couple of juicy, uncooked, blood-red steaks, he wrapped them around his prick and pumped away like hell.

"It was nearly as good as the real thing," he had said.

And with that thought fixed firmly in my head, rump steak took on a new dimension. If I could have been sure that Jim was the only chef who had fucked my dinner, I reckoned I could have handled it - I expect he washed it afterwards. But the thought of the Head Chef sliding his meat around my meal was not mouthwatering.

The Spotted dick, I ate. It was scrumptious. But try as I did, I could not stop wondering what they stirred the mixture with and, indeed, if those little black bits were truly currants.

I had a real soft spot, or should I say 'hard spot' for Jim. He was excellent sex. His main forte was blow-jobs. As yet he hadn't dropped his pants and let me screw that main meal of a bum, but I expect the time would come. I was in no hurry. But what I liked most about him was his sense of humour. It was wicked.

I remember one time when we were trolling around a floral park, pissed as Penguins on pot, we came across a notice pinned to a tree. It read: Lost duck. Blue and green. Family pet. Dearly loved and sorely missed. Jim produced a pen and wrote: Thanks. It was delicious! It was something only a Chef could write. Further along we came across a similar notice about a cat. I stopped him writing: Made a lovely pair of slippers. Well, I love cats.

I continued to sit in the Dinning Room, drinking coffee and contemplating whether I really did want Jim's mouth around my meat, when in walked Wheaty-pop. I felt that unmistakable tingle in my togger as I observed him cruise the counter, placing grub on his plate. Eventually having so much of the stuff, I thought he planned on climbing it rather than eating it. Well, he was a growing lad. A quick glance between my legs told me, so was I!

His boiler-suit was unbuttoned lower than before and I could make out a line of fine hair creeping from his navel to whatever treat lay hidden below and no doubt soaked in oil. I shot him a penetrating glance which he held for a moment then averted his eyes. Yes, he knew what I was up to. Suddenly, the campest, slimline, black number came rushing up behind him and pinched his bum. Wheaty-pop gave him a wide grin and winked.

"So, Wheaty-pop was into Shirley Bassey look-a-likes," I thought and made a mental note to buy some brown boot polish.

Jim caught my eye, distracting me from thoughts of Wheaty-pop with a big black dick sliding into his bottom. Yes I know it was stereotyping but all black youths appeared to have dicks as big as Doberman's these days. I nodded to Jim, confirming our session was on.

Deliberately walking past the Black and White Minstrels as I left the canteen, I gave the them a 'threesomes are fun' flirting glance. Shirley giggled. Wheaty-pop changed colour. It was definitely a possibility, I guessed.

I had a shower before venturing to the Cable Locker which is where Jim and I had our humps. It was in the bows of the ship, deep in its depths and would only be busy when we were anchoring. Jim would always change into working clothes before coming there, otherwise it would look suspicious to see a Chef in his whites in that part of the ship.

Lifting the circular hatch, I descended into the dank smelling room with its huge rusting cables. It was the kind of place guys into a little slap and slap might love, with its various sized cables, ropes and wires hanging about. That wasn't really my scene but I expect I'd have a dabble with someone I could trust.

The familiar sound of someone descending an iron ladder echoed around the vast room. My heart began to pound. It was always a nervous moment because if it happened to be a Seaman, I'd no reason to be there.

I recognised Jim's bum as it came into view and grabbed his hips, lifting his lightweight body from the rungs. Back in the canteen I didn't think I was horny but the sight of that boy bum and the smell of his young body soon had me fired up. In a flash, I was nibbling the nape of his neck and eating his ears.

Jim remained still, allowing me to work on his neck and forage beneath his fly, fondling his furry forest. I found the fleshy feast and freed it from his pants. His was a cut cock, the only one I knew -

intimately. I found that disappointing at first because I loved a foreskin - if it worked properly - but I soon got used to it. I mean, the dick was attached to a really ravishable guy.

I released my own cock whilst his hands groped me from behind his back. He swiftly spun around, dropped to his knees and began sucking. In a flash my pants and nickers were down and both my balls were rolling around his massive mouth. I cannot say I enjoyed having them sucked, it was far too sensitive, but I seldom stopped him. I also had huge nuts and marvelled how he managed to get both them and my cock in there. I suspected he practised on a couple of new potatoes and a courgette.

Very little Jim did surprised me. So when he asked if he could tie me to the anchor cable, I simply said, "Why not?"

Jim tied my hands and then my ankles against the metal links. Already I became excited by this new experience. But, hell, if someone should discover us, this was going to take some explaining.

The cable was bloody cold against my bare bum and my white cheeks were soon brown with rust. I prayed that the anchor wasn't suddenly released and I went shooting through the hole in the deck-head and out onto the upper-deck.

Well, what can I say. Not having any control whatsoever whilst Jim did the business - like he'd done it all his life - soon had me begging him to finish the job. He teased me to coming, then stopped, then teased again. And when I did come, it was with such force it nearly knocked his bloody head off. Being sucked and restrained was some experience I can tell you.

Jim had dropped his pants and had been tossing his own dick whilst he worked on mine, but hadn't come yet. He released me from my bondage and I was just about to return the favour when he unexpectedly said, "Look what I've got!" And produced a massive carrot.

I looked at him quizzically.

"Shove it up my bum," he begged, handing me some lube.

Well this time he did surprise me. What with the bondage stuff and now this, I guessed he'd been reading some naughty books. Naturally, I obliged. I mean, if he was prepared to let a carrot fuck him, then at some stage he would let me.

I bent his beautiful buttocks before my face, pulling the cheeks wide apart, then sank my tongue deep into the hole. I reckoned he was stunned by how electrifying that was, because he yelped with pleasure as I worked his cock with one hand and tongued his rear. Soon he was writhing in ecstasy, begging for the vegetable.

I lubed the edible dildo and began to ease it between his parted cheeks. He'd chosen rather a large one for a beginner, but I controlled the entry so as not to hurt him. Moments later, I was pumping it powerfully into his passage, fearful not to lose my grip and lose it. That would have taken some explaining!

With squeals of pleasure, so loud I thought the whole ship must have heard his orgasm, he shot a wealth of cum clean across the cables and through one of the links.

"Bullseye!" I laughed.

Our session over, the best we'd ever had, Jim left the Cable Locker. Watching his biteable bum bounce up the ladder, I thought, "I'll soon be shagging that!"

Five minutes later, I followed, happily strolling along the main passage and humming a tune. When I reached Jim's galley, I stopped and suddenly thought, "I must remember not to have carrots for supper!"

THURSDAY

It was a pig of a day. Gale force winds and high seas. The ship was going up and down more times than my knickers. But I didn't mind the rough weather - rough anything, really! Perhaps the worst thing that could happen when it was rough was some sailor throw-up over your dinner, but even that could look more appetising than what was on your plate.

I'd never know a week like this. I was getting so much sex my dick was in danger of dropping off, and I think my foreskin was wearing out fast. I thought of going to the Doc with my red raw knob but that would only have raised his eyebrows. Unless I told him I'd been tossing every minute of the day. Which wasn't far from the truth because after I'd had a session, I liked to run it through my mind again before I slept. God, my sheets were disgusting!

A good few of the sailors were heaving their hearts up - poor dears. But I was one of the lucky ones. Not many things would make me heave. Well, seeing a couple of hetties humping probably would.

It was on days like this that I wouldn't have minded being a Medic mysel. Up in the Sick Bay nursing all those pretty Baby Sailors who hadn't found their sea legs. But I look crap in a nurses outfit! In fact, drag was something I never could get my head around. I mean, if you are a guy and you want to attract guy who like guys, then dressing as a bird defeats the object, doesn't it? It gets so complicated. Like, you're a guy who likes guys who likes birds but doesn't mind guys, so you dress as a bird so he can screw you, knowing you're really a guy. Give me a break. I mean, does it work the other way? Birds dress up as guys cos the guy fancies a guy who is really a bird. AAAAAAAH!

The weather was getting nasty now and we had more water inside the ship than out. And every few yards some spew to slide around in. The Captain ordered Nuclear State Zulu, which is a little tricky to explain but basically meant, 'Shut all the bloody doors, before we sink!'

Oh, I forgot to tell you. I'm living in a bath tub built from old Coke cans, Pollyfilla and discarded plastic bottles. It was a shagged out ship with a little gun on the front in case of air attacks. Tell the truth, we'd have had more success filling condoms with petrol and throwing them at the aircraft.

Molotov condoms. They sound like fun.

"Here darling, slip one of these on."

BANG!

"Wow. That was fantastic. Can you take my balls off the ceiling!"

But seriously. This foul weather was screwing up my screwing. All the trade was either mopping gallons of water from the decks or dying in some darkened corner. I did find a Cherub on the upper-deck having the contents of his stomach thrown back into his face as he bent his body - beautiful and beckoning - over the guardrails. I did the decent thing and left his bum alone, easing him below decks and into the Sick Bay. I helped undress him and put him to bed - well you would, wouldn't you? But even in his sickened state, he had enough wits about him to stop me nicking his knickers - polka-dot boxers. Not really my favourite, but they outlined his youthful leg muscles and love muscle pretty nicely.

I left the Sick Bay before a Baby Sailor got knocked up and I got locked up, then did a tour of the ship, searching for a shag. Tim was at work in the Communications Office. I departed swiftly before I was asked to help but managed a word with him, asking when he got off watch and if he was on heat. I think he muttered something about me getting a vasectomy. I guessed we still didn't have a date!

Jim was in the Galley turning perfectly good food into crap. I noticed a pot of carrots bubbling away on the stove and wondered which one was his lover from yesterday. He glimpsed me and gave a girlish giggle, dangling a jumbo sausage from his fly.

"Oh, Jim. You haven't been practising with that," I mouthed, but departed when he received a bollocking from the Head Chef. At least Jim was on the right track, using something closer to my dick. No, I'm not bragging. I meant the texture, not the length!

I thought of searching out Wheaty-pop in the Boiler Room but had no reason to go down there. Visions of embracing him tightly. Sucking in that smell of sweat, grease and oil, whilst my tongue slid down his throat, and my hands dived inside his boiler suit and feasted on his youthful cock and firm buttocks were, quite frankly, disgusting. But oh for the opportunity.

After those disgusting thoughts, tossing myself looked more than a probability, so I made for the forward Heads.

About halfway through the ship, who should appear? Shirley Bassey. Jesus, she wasn't camp. She was CAMP! How the hell did she manage to get recruited? Swish, swish, swish, she floated by, screeching, "HI!" in a pitch any choirboy would have been proud of.

Well if she wasn't a shag then I was a butch dyke. Watch it!

I watched her buttocks swing from side to side as she did her cat-walk number down the corridor, each cheek almost striking both bulkheads in turn. She glanced over her shoulder, giving me a smile. If ever there was a look which said, "I bet you would love to shag me!" then that was certainly one.

Adjusting my crotch, I increased my pace toward the Heads before I started tossing on the spot. I had almost reached them when Zak popped up from the deck below. My eyes lit up. "My shag!" I delighted.

Zak was in a hurry, and marched straight through my body blurting something about the Boss looking for me. Reluctantly, I ventured to the Signal Office to enquire what was up. Just my luck. The forward Heads were wrecked and I had become the chosen skivvy to clean them. What was a professional guy like me doing with his head down a toilet? You may well ask? Not that it was the first time my head had been in such a place.

Well, it so happens that in this lovely navy of ours, we were not only obliged to do our professional jobs but also mundane tasks like teasing turds around a U-bend. Thus detailed, Marigolds on hand, I began exploring the unsavoury contents of each bowl - unblocking and scrubbing. No doubt a few bad-mouthers on board would say I was exactly where I belonged. But, joy! And I hummed happily away, ramming my rod into every orifice and sprinkling Vim and bleach with joyful abandon.

I had almost finished fist-fucking the final bowl when the door burst open, almost pushing me down the pan. "We're closed!" I yelled. Not wanting another Baby Sailor bombarding me with bits of regurgitated carrot.

"Oops. Sorreeeeee!" came the triple soprano voice which I recognised instantly.

I spun about. There stood Shirley Bassey, panting, pouting and pinching her prick. Looking brown, beautiful and by God I think my banana just burst!

What could I say? For once in my life I was almost speechless but managed to mouth, "Use the end urinal."

Now then, I'm not a nosy bitch or a Cottage Queen but if the opportunities there......

Shirley unzipped her fly and began pissing. In a flash I was kneeling beside her, Marigold fist foraging around the adjoining urinal, head level with her line of fire. Her hand was cupped around her cock, hiding it from view. Don't you just hate that? What a tart!

Without warning, she pulled her hand away, turned toward me, grabbed my head and pulled my face onto her cock, spraying droplets of pee around parted lips. What a bitch! Didn't she know I wasn't into yellow. YET!

Talk about Fast Black. This girl was well above the speed limit and by the look of it eager to take me on a ride of a lifetime! In seconds she was flinging her wardrobe across the deck and standing naked except for a skimpy, leather jock. Well, that wasn't Navy issue!

I managed to stick my sensible head on and reached for a notice warning the crew that this place was out-of-bounds - on Captain's orders - and hung it on the outer door. Sucking in a breath of bleachy air - part excitement, part relief that no one had entered whilst she did her strip - I moved toward her. I began sweating excitedly. I was going into Melt Down.

Protected by the notice, I allowed the panther to paw me. And what paws! She was..... Well, what wasn't she?

I managed to erase the image of her dressed in a slinky outfit and wearing an Afro wig. But who was I to criticise? I still had my Marigolds on.

We chose No 3 cubicle to perform - my lucky number. My mouth was soon biting into her leather pouch, tongue sliding between her brown thighs and into the expanding material. In an instant it was off and my second 'cut' cock sprang into view and slid into my palate. It was a delightfully delicate dick with smooth balls the size of grapes hanging beneath. Like a Roman Emperor, I devoured the succulent pair as they hung over me.

Shirley moaned and groaned, squealed and sighed, yanking at my head and ears. I bit hard into those tight, wiry curls. She pulled me up and ripped my shirt clean from my back, her nails furrowing eight deep channels into my shoulders.

'Shit!" I shrieked. How was I going to explain that to my mates? Yes, we did have a cat on board but I didn't want to be accused of shagging it. I shrieked again as she knelt and her large luscious tongue lassoed my dick and balls.

Shirley began devouring me to an unbelievable depth, her ravishing passion sending cum pumping from my cock in uncontrollable bursts. Shaking and exhausted, I plonked my bum onto the bowl. She straddled me in seconds, her rounded brown buttocks pressing onto my cock, her thighs gripping my around my waist.

"Fuck me! Fuck me! Fuck me!" she begged and pleaded, rubbing her buttocks into my crotch, bringing me firm again.

"Calm down, dear," I said. "You only have to ask me once."

Sadly, I had no condoms. But this cat was wild and was looking for a taxidermist. My raunchy mind raced, desperately trying to think of an alternative. I glanced at my Marigolds. I could cut one of the rubber fingers off, but would it fit over my cock? Watch it! I'm not that small.

I resigned myself to the fact that I'd missed a shag. No protection, no poking. But I worked hard and fast on Shirley's dick, sucking on her miniature brown nipples and licking all over her skin. I shoved a couple of Marigold finger deep into her bum.

"I love you. Marry me! Marry me!" she squealed, sucking a love bite the size of an orange onto my neck.

"Oh, you dizzy Queen," I thought. Yes, we did have a cat on board but I was damn sure it didn't do love bites as well.

With an ear-splitting scream, as I shoved three fingers deep inside her, she came. Sending cum over my cheeks and cascading down my chest. But as much as she begged and pleaded, I didn't didn't fuck her. I was also sure that I wouldn't have sex with her again because she was the type of girl who would want my babies, and I was no good with kids.

I mean, after you've washed the little buggers, do you hang them up to dry by their fingers or their toes?

FRIDAY

Last evening we popped briefly into port to collect one of our Communications Staff who had got married, then popped out again.

The weather had changed, to the relief of many a Baby Sailor, but the task of clearing up continued. It was one of the worst storms I'd know and, unfortunately, one poor Seaman had suffered a broken leg. He was dropped off when we were in port. Rumour had it, next week we were going to troll across to Amsterdam. But it was only a rumour and we would most likely end up in Scotland - shagging sheep.

My Sparkler, Brad, hadn't ventured to my office since his last visit and Zak, too, had not be required, there being no traumatic incidents to investigate. I wondered if they'd managed to get together for a bonk, but doubted it. Although Zak was big and butch, he was a big girl's blouse when it came to propositioning guys. Brad, however, was a brash bugger and wouldn't be backward in coming forward with his boner. Anyway, I hadn't had sex since yesterday. What the heck, I wasn't trying for the Penis Book of Records. And my dick was still as sore as hell. Germolene really stings. I'll kill the sod who suggested it. It's like sticking your cock in a kettle of boiling water. One of my mates suggested Iodine. Yea, right. Walk around with a purple cock for a week.

I wondered why Tim had stopped spreading his legs. He used to be up for it at least once a month, but he did swing. Perhaps it was breasts and not balls at present. Wheaty-pop, too, was still a mystery but I'd bet a pound to a pinch of puff he was stuffing Shirley. And should I be lucky enough to get that boiler suit from his sexy skin, I bet his back would resemble a ploughed field. Mine was still pretty painful.

We spent several hours of today scanning the sea for a sailor who was lost overboard from another ship. A good many of the crew were on the upper-deck looking out for him. We had no luck. It was a sad time but life went on. The sea, like sailors, can be a real bitch!

I'd nearly gone overboard once - in a mini-hurricane - but luckily I managed to get my legs around something and save myself. Well, I'd had a lot of practice. After that incident, I'd learnt my lesson and stayed away from topside when it was too rough. But the only place I was in danger of falling into now was some sailor's backside. I mean, a carrot was nothing to some sailors. You could get a fruit and veg stall up some arses! My arse? Passing a pip was painful. Hey, I'm one hundred per cent butch I'll have you know. Okay, that's a lie.

Well, I was in love, you see. And when you get into that dizzy state, a lot of self-made rules fly out the port hole.

He was a scrumptious Thai youth - about the same age as myself. A civilian I'd met whilst ashore in Singapore. 'Beautiful' would not be a complement in his case.

I'd got well-bevvied on shore one night - sins of being a sailor - and had got chatting to him in a straight bar. Sometimes, in this strange life of ours, you can become besotted in a nanosecond. This happened to me.

I'd never seduced an Oriental boy before and my whole being tingled with excitement at the prospect. Back at his hotel, we entwined on his bed, fully clothed, kissing and caressing for what seemed an eternity before he finally allowed me to disrobe him. In childlike wonderment I removed each item of clothing from his satin smooth skin, kissing and licking every inch of his flesh before removing the next.

He lay before me in all his splendid nakedness. An adorable, edible brown beauty. He had the blackest hair I'd ever seen. Even his eyes were rich and dark and big. But so soft and gentle. I lost my soul into their depths. His name was Min. I would have done anything for him!

Min had been a virgin in every respect and I had been one, in one. Our bodies and souls meshed as he glided his body over me - that oh so tiny body. Moving his head between my thighs, he slid his mouth so tenderly around my balls and over my cock and sucked me like he was savouring his favourite fruit. Then, quite unexpectedly, he raised my legs, kneeling between. His chest met mine as our tongues searched mouths. Without me realising, he had lubed his short cock and entered my body, sliding it fully into my buttocks. His movements were slow and sensational. My head swam in a sea of sublime bliss as he seduced me. Gripping his boy buttocks, I pulled him him even deeper. Pulled him into a part of my being I never knew existed.

When I made love to him, it was even more meaningful. His youthful thighs gripped me like a vice, pulling every last centimetre of my young cock into the darkest depths of his body.

He came. Not with squeals and screams but with a sigh of deep satisfaction, as if I had given him the universe! And the sensation when I came was similar, none like I have ever experienced before. A zillion nerves erupting in ecstatic empathy. To be honest, I doubt I could ever find the words to describe those hours. And for the brief time that we were together, I thought I'd gone to heaven. It was the only time I could honestly say that I had truly made love.

The following day our ship sailed. I never saw or heard from him again.

At 1am I was called to my office. Routine stuff so Zak wasn't required - shame. But I did need assistance and another Communicator was loaned to me. It was Paul, the Baby Sailor who had just got married - silly boy!

Paul was a smashing lad, very quiet, and good looking. Whilst working at my console next to him, I shot a few glances in his direction. Nothing sexual or seductive. But because Paul did have a decent packet, I couldn't resist running my eyes over it. Whether or not he noticed, I wasn't sure. But one thing I was sure about and what Paul probably didn't know. I had watched him skylark with another sailor one afternoon. They were well into one another. But what was apparent to me and must have been to both, each had hard cocks as they grappled.

Now then, a stiff prick said to me that this kind of frolic had slightly more meaning than a friendly wrestle. Naturally, I began to wonder at the possibility of a wrestle of my own.

Can I first tell you about straight lads? The don't exist! Only if you have lived on a ship with five hundred sex starved sailors will you be able to understand this. You see, when you have been at sea for months and you're straight, and you need a shag. Then 'hide the sausage in a female' becomes hide it in any hole that will accept it. Now I'm not saying that all straight sailors run around shagging all the gay sailors - dream on! But a good old face fuck is that grey area which straight lads are able to cope with without thinking they've turned queer. With this in mind, what was hidden inside Paul's pants looked a pleasing possibility. After all, he only had time to get married - no honeymoon. Consequently - no shag. How sad.

Our mission accomplished, I set about my mission. First I did some serious chat about his wife and sex. Then in true navy skylark fashion, I began to arm-wrestle, tickle and hug this humpable hettie. And as sure as there are no gay virgins in Brighton, up popped his pecker.

I allowed Paul to wrestle me to the deck and get his thighs around my head; the rough, surge material of his bell-bottoms rubbing my face. When I felt that he was beyond the fun stage, I bit hard into his erect cock. He made the slightest attempt to pull away and giggled something which sounded like stop it. But I needed 'Stop it' in writing before I'd let go of a succulent, stiff dick.

Anyway, I did a quick anagram of 'Stop it' and it came out as 'Suck me' - I suffer from sexual dyslexia, you see. I prized his prick from his pants. His was one of those strange cocks, about as thick as it was long. For a mini-second I was worried about stretch marks around my mouth. But, shit, I swallowed it anyway.

Sex starved or sex crazy, I don't know. But Paul rammed away at my mouth, so powerfully, I hardly had time to breathe. All lights green, I popped out my own prick and offered it up for consumption. And consume he did!

For me, blow-jobs were the best sex acts to perform, and we had the rhythm in no time. A sexual metronome. No head movements, just buttock thrusting. Him then me. Him then me. Him and him. Me and me. Together we created Symphony 69 - Mozart, eat your heart out. And with those sexual symbols slamming in my head, cum went simultaneously from him to me and me to him.

I reckoned it was the best wedding present he'd received and I was really pleased for his wife. She'd obviously married a right little fuck bunny. I was delighted for her.

Paul left my office at 3am. I decided I would stay and crash for the night. I ventured to the forward Heads to bathe before turning in. At this time of day the ship was quiet, only sailors on watch floating about.

On reaching the Heads, I was baffled to see a notice saying they were out of bounds. I was just about to troll down aft, when I thought, "Sod it." As I entered, I heard a shower running. I gently closed the door behind myself and tiptoed toward it. Well, you could have knocked me out with a strawberry condom! The beauty being shagged was unmistakable, but who was shagging him? I moved closer, not wanting to disturb them but eager to gain a good vantage point. Brad was in total bliss, bless him. And the butch boy that was bonking him was beyond the bounds of beauty. The pair of white buttocks looked delicious against Brad as he bumped and ground, thrust and withdrew. All the while the lad pumping Brad's dick with one hand and stroking his balls with the other.

I was stiff in seconds. Withdrawing my cock I playfully pumped it.

The beefy boy bounced vigorously against Brad's buttocks, pushing him hard into the wet bulkhead, his mouth eating eagerly on Brad's unblemished back and neck. A fine spray of water cascaded over them like confetti. Brad was releasing gasps of delight as the boy's dick delved deep into his delicious flesh.

These two lads were in love. Of that I was certain. I knew. I'd been there.

I continued my surveillance, mesmerised by the sheer pleasure passing between them. Delightedly, I watched as the lad pumped Brad's youthful prick, rolling his foreskin back and forth and filling his buttocks with what I guessed would be a mountain of meat. I put my dick away. Somehow it seemed wrong.

Brad caught my eye and moved forward, bringing all of the lad's body into view. I felt embarrassed, like I had intruded on some sacred ceremony. But Brad was in another blissful world and simply smiled, knowing he was in no danger.

His seducer spun around, able to pick up on every expression, but couldn't stop shafting Brad because both were close to climax.

I was right about Wheaty-pop's back. It resembled a ploughed field. Shirley had definitely been there. So it was Brad and Wheaty-pop. I felt slightly sad because I had now lost Brad. I also felt envious that he was the one to suck in that oily odour and wash the grease and grime from Wheaty-pop's crotch.

Both came in bursts of frenzied excitement, holding back the screams of delight they dearly wished to release. I closed the door silently behind me and walked toward the aft Heads.

Come morning we would be back in port and I had the weekend off. I thought I should give sex a miss for a couple of days and allow my dick to repair. Then again, I desperately need a haircut. I guess I would have to pop ashore to Vince the cute barber. I'd heard he was brilliant at Cut and Blow-jobs!

TORPEDOED

"What you got in your hand, lad?"

"Balls!" the lad laughed, then spun around instantly realizing I wasn't one of his work-mates and noticing the hook on my arm indicating my rank.

"Charming," I said, before he had a chance to re-phrase his reply. "Let me see!"

With flushed cheeks, he held out his palm offering two large, silver ball-bearings. "Sorry, Hooky. I thought you was Buster," he apologised.

"Where do they go, then?" I asked but before he had a chance to reply, scooped them from his palm and dropped them into his trousers. Clunk! they knocked together as they disappeared through his trousers waistband and then into his white pants beneath, creating a bulge twice the size of the one already hidden beneath his blue bell-bottoms which I'd already noticed was ample for a lad his size.

"Don't know, Hooky!" he gasped as the cold spheres met his own.

I glimpsed his name tag - D. HEAVEN - and guessed straight away that his nickname would be Angel or some heavenly equivalent. And how appropriate that was - golden hair, striking blue eyes, rosy cheeks and lips to match. Body, so slim; waist, about the circumference of the torpedo he was leant against; chest, not much wider; and his height, about three quarters the length of the long weapon.

"S'ok, Angel. Relax. I'm not going to bite you." I think that was a lie! "I came down looking for Buster. Know where he is?"

Angel stuffed his hand into his pants, nervously foraging around for the silver spheres. "Buster went down the canteen, Hooky. Should be back soon."

"I might as well wait, then," I said, moving forward and stuffing my hand into his pants and retrieving a sphere. The other fell from his bell-bottoms and hit the metal deck with a clang, spinning away to port with the roll of the ship. "I think you've lost one of your balls!" I winked, handing him a crutch warmed sphere.

Angel's large mouth opened in a wonderful wide grin, revealing a row of perfect teeth and a large pink tongue which lapped nervously at each corner, then bent over to retrieve the rolling ball. "OK, Hooky."

I licked my own lips, thinking how good it would be to suck on that fleshy member or have it lapping around my cock. Then licked again as his cute arse bent and tightened in his bell-bottoms, offering a deep tight crack for my own tongue to sink into. "There's no need to call me Hooky," I said, relieving him of the burden of using my rank and allowing the possibility of a more friendly, less formal liaison.

"OK, Hooky."

"Smudge!" I corrected.

"OK, Smudge," he repeated and although he smiled, I could sense his uneasiness at calling a higher rank by a nickname.

"How long you been on board, Angel? They do call you Angel, don't they?"

"They call me lots of things!" he laughed. "Especially the P.O. But, yeah, a lot of the guys call me Angel or Stardust. I've been on the ship for a couple of months."

Angel continued to rub a rag over the torpedo, an action I found very evocative and erotic. I wondered, like me, if he too was imagining that huge length as something erotic as he lovingly caressed its solid shiny surface.

"That's a big weapon," I teased, moving closer to his bending body.

Another wide grin flashed a row of white teeth at me. "Yeah, I wouldn't like to be bent over when this beast came bounding through the bulkhead."

"How about being bent over in front of this beast?" I teased, gripping my semi-stiff dick, then winked.

Angel's face flushed brighter than the red head of the torpedo as he glanced innocently at my stiffening cock. "I bet the birds love that, Hooky," he shyly smiled, reverting back to using my rank and diverting the conversation away from boy on boy sex, although banter like this was common.

"You bet!" I confirmed, guiding the conversation in his chosen direction but watching closely for hints to keep it going the way I wanted.

Angel pulled his white front over his head, a line of sweat visible on the back. "Whew! Hot work this," he said, tossing it over the workbench behind him.

I glimpsed a twinkle in his eye as he did that but also studied more closely his well-defined muscles on both arms, chest and abdomen. My cock went even stiffer as I watched that solid flesh ripple as he continued to rub and caress, tease and torture stubborn grease stains from the smooth, cold metal.

I visualised nibbling on his nipple buds, browner than his tanned torso, and darting my tongue into his navel knot. I caught a glimpse of his white underpants as they rode up from his bell-bottoms waistband, and that excited me even more. "Got a girl?" I asked, venturing back into his sexuality.

Angel continued to rub robustly on the stubborn stains, whether intentionally or not, his hips gyrating his crotch into the solid shaft, each buttock cheek flexing as he moved right to left, left to right. "Nah!" he said, twisting toward me, revealing a short ladder of cock hair climbing just above his underpants waistband; below that, a cock which had risen slightly.

I could sense a hint of a green light but wasn't really sure. "Me neither."

Angel swung to face me, resting an arm on his weapon, his own weapon having risen yet another inch. "Good looking guy like you. Thought you'd be married with a dozen sproggs by now."

I still wasn't sure if we were having a mind game, teasing and testing each other. I moved closer, close enough to inhale his fresh sweat. And how sensational that smelt, although partly masked by a cheap deodorant. "I like my nookie too much," I told him.

"Any port in a storm, eh!"

"Any hole!" I winked.

Angel flashed his long eyelashes over his blazing blue eyes. "Fuck! I'm getting my kit dirty," he said, glimpsing some grease around the crotch of his bell-bottoms, his palms rubbing around the area.

"Take them off," I casually suggested. "Evening rounds have finished, so you'll be OK."

"Think that'll be all right, Smudge? Buster won't mind, will he? I won't get in the shit, will I?"

"Course not!" I encouraged, knowing for a fact that Buster wouldn't mind in the least. Given half the chance he'd rip them from this boy with his bare teeth. Swim through crocodile-infested waters just to sniff his knickers.

Ken Smith

I watched in eager anticipation as Angel nervously unbuckled his belt. And the slowness with which he completed that task almost caused me to rush forward and do it for him. Down dropped his bell-bottoms. I wasn't sure where to look at first but chose his firm calves, then moved up to his solid youthful thighs - thighs that had sped him over sports-fields, for sure. Thighs that had wrapped around a youth, I wasn't! Thighs which would wrap around me, I hoped. God, did I hope!

There was a shyness in his look but also a kind of naughtiness as he stood before me and smiled, wearing only a pair of whiter than white tight briefs. My mouth went dry with desire. Was his cock stiff, or wasn't it? This was my first thought as I mentally wrenched those underpants over his hips and buttocks. I could see the outline of his hidden weapon, thick and long, stretched toward his right leg, almost to the point of becoming visible. "Is that a gun, or are you pleased to see me?" I joked.

Angel blushed again and began to search his locker. "Shit! Left my overalls in the mess."

"Doesn't matter. You'll only get them dirty as well and have to wash them." I suggested, not wanting him to cover that delightful body. In fact, wishing he'd remove the remaining item which was sending my head spinning from imagining its contents.

"Suppose so," he grunted and continued his circular cleaning motion, moving closer to the torpedoes pointed, red tip.

I moved closer to Angel, almost to the point of touching him. "This your first ship?"

"Yep. Joined up six months ago."

"A baby, eh?"

"Yeah!" Angel smiled again, still quite nervous. "It's a bit strange and scary. Everyone seems so sure of themselves. Get the piss taken out of me as well. But the guys are mostly OK."

I sensed an opportunity to comfort him and stroked my palm down his moist back, then patted his bum. "Don't worry, you'll get used to it. Everyone goes through the mill on their first draft. Trick is, give as good as you get!"

Angel grinned a more relaxed grin. I patted his bum another comforting pat. "Anyway, Buster will look after you. He's a nice bloke and big enough to sort out any trouble."

"He is that..." Angel hesitated for a moment then laughed. "His cock, I mean."

That observation of his took me completely off-guard, even though sexual statements were commonplace on board and taken in one's stride. However, such a direct one warranted a reply, a reply to test the water, a question to discover if Angel held more than a casual interest in cocks other than his own firm offering rubbing seductively against the torpedoes head.

"Been peeking?" I laughed.

The familiar flush filled Angel's face. "Can't help it. Buster bunks above me. When he gets up in the morning it's almost stuck in my face. Jesus, it's nearly as big as this thing!" he exclaimed, wrapping his arms around the torpedo and giving it an affectionate hug.

For me that was a pleasant mental picture, and I could easily visualise Angel's luscious lips slobbering up and down Buster's enormous slippery shaft. And although I doubted Angel could manage the whole of Buster's dick, the thought of watching twelve inches of cock vanish into Angel's pretty face sent my own cock cramming against my thigh.

"I bet the birds love it!" Angel speculated, again bringing the conversation straight

I sensed the possibility of Angel's own desire for Buster's big one when he said that and chose the opportunity to enlighten him. "Probably. But if I were you, I wouldn't bend down in front of him too often!"

Angel's eyes sparkled. I was waiting for him to ask why but he remained silent. Whether it was a deliberate action for my benefit or not, I wasn't sure, but his hand stuffed into his pants and pulled his prick upright, tucking the stiffened head beneath the elastic waistband. "Got a problem?" I smiled.

"What about you?" Angel questioned.

"Have I got a problem?"

"No. What about bending over in front of you?"

Another casual remark caused me to gulp hard. But this time it wasn't accompanied by a wide grin but by parted moist lips begging to be kissed, and by seductive, smouldering eyes which sensually searched my own.

The door pushed open. Buster's solid physique filled the empty space. I saw his eyes sparkle bright at the sight of Angel in his underpants, even though I knew he had seen that sight, and more, many times. This time, however, Angel's nakedness was in the confines of Buster's workplace, without the possibility of excited stares being noticed. Except by me, that was!

"What you doing half naked, lad!" Buster barked. It was a playful reprimand really and I caught his wink before Angel bolted upright, searching his young mind for an excuse.

"Leave the boy alone, Buster. It's bloody hot in here and he's been working as hard as a Honk Kong prosy since you've been away."

Angel smiled, albeit a nervous smile as I came to his defence but still muttered, "Sorry, Buster."

"Hong Kong slut, eh! Doing what, I wonder!" teased Buster, slapping my shoulder then Angel's arse as he walked by and switched on the kettle. "Cuppa, Smudge?"

"Sure."

"Angel, darling. Want one as well? You must be exhausted by now, being here all alone with the biggest whore on the ship."

Angel giggled and said, "Thanks." Remembering my advice to give as good as he got, said, "I thought you were the biggest whore on board!"

Angel didn't even see Buster's move from kettle to his body, and in a flash his pants were down by his ankles, the only white part of his suntanned body standing out like a pair large snowballs as he bent to retrieve them. Swiftly he pulled them over his hips, his face as bright as the torpedo head.

In that hasty act of re-dressing, I glimpsed his soft cock as his pants waistband caught it and pushed tantalisingly into an erect stance. Buster also noticed and ripped the underwear back to Angel's ankles and with a bear-hug grip, spun him around. "Look, Smudge. She's all excited!"

This time even Angel's buttocks flushed! But that wasn't through his embarrassment. Buster had slapped his palm across the cheeks, fingerprints on one, palm print on the other.

"Shit, Buster. That fucking hurt!"

Buster resumed his coffee making. "What you doin here, Smudge? Cradle snatching!" I watched his eyes roll upward and his tongue flop out then ride over his lips, almost touching his nose, when he said that.

The reason I had come to his workplace was only to ask him a favour but I could sense that something much more interesting was in the offing. Angel didn't seem at all put out by Buster's attack on his bare bum and I could sense Buster was hoping his sexual frolic could be taken one step further. "Come to do the safety checks," I winked.

Immediately, Buster knew that that was a lie. He knew what job I did on board. "Right, the safety checks," he repeated, following my lead and waiting for the next clue to my plan.

"Yeah, the torpedo harness hasn't been checked for a month."

Angel remained engrossed with his cleaning, obviously unaware of the plan brewing.

"Problem, Smudge. The testing weights are down aft and the Bosun's locked them away by now."

I loved the way sailors were quick at taking up a line, conjuring up all manner of tales to defend a lie or gain advantage over some innocent soul. "I'm sure we can find some way to do it," I suggested. "Can't we, Angel?"

Angel hadn't yet realised that this devious plan was focussed around him and my reason for bringing him into the conversation was also part of it. "Do what?" he asked.

"Got to test the strength of the torpedo harness," explained Buster, getting into the jist of my plan, "but the weights to test it are locked up. Wonder what else we could use?"

Angel had no idea he was being baited. No idea that his body would hold the answer to all our problems. "Could use something heavy like those spare chains," he suggested.

"Nah! Not heavy enough and they'll probably slip off," I discouraged.

"Yeah, we need something pretty weighty, about eight stone," Buster enlightened.

Angel wasn't a thick boy, just ignorant of the ploys older sailors could use to meet their needs. "I'm eight and a half stone," he helpfully announced.

"Are you really?" I said, pretending to disbelieve him.

"Honest, Hooky!"

"You reckon Angel's eight stone, Buster?"

"Nah!"

"I am! Honest."

Buster and I moved over to the youth and took an end of his body each. Me bending and gripping his muscled thighs - my face close enough to kiss his cock. Buster gripping around his chest and beneath his sweaty armpits.

"What you reckon, Smudge?" asked Buster as we hoisted the boy off the deck.

"Eight and a half stone," I confirmed, slipping my hand beneath

Angel's briefs and caressing his buttock cheeks as I lowered him.

Angel, still the innocent, simply stated, "Told you so!"

Angel had been snared - hook, line and sinker! I moved to the door and pulled four of the damage control handles firmly down. It would take any unexpected visitors a while to open it.

"Right," said Buster, "we'll use Angel as the weights."

Angel smiled, pleased that he had been chosen. "What do you want me to do?"

"Climb on the torpedo," Buster ordered.

Angel pushed his palms down on the torpedo and raised his white-briefed buttocks onto the cold weapon. "Like this?"

My eyes bounced over the boy's bulge when his thighs closed and pushed it upwards. Buster's too flashed a crafty cruise over the boy's bulging cock, then at me. Turning, he opened a draw and pulled an item from within, secreting it behind his back.

Our minds were in sync. I knew exactly what to say. "That's fine, Angel, but to test it correctly, I need your weight to be dispersed. I think you'd better lay along the length."

"Oh, right!" Angel swung his leg over the solid weapon, straddling the beast. Gently he lowered his naked chest onto the cold surface. Reaching out, he grasped the harness chains closest to the head. His legs fell either side of the thick cylinder, parting his arse cheeks slightly, forcing his buttocks to arch upward. "This do?"

"That's perfect!" muttered Buster, his throat tightening in anticipation of his next move. Moving to the torpedoes head, he whipped a rope from behind his back and in a flash lassoed Angle's wrists and lashed them to the chains.

Angel wriggled frantically, his buttocks flexing and legs lashing out as he tried to dismount the torpedo. "Shit, Buster. What you doin? Smudge, tell him to stop!"

Buster pulled Angel to the head of the torpedo, bringing the cute face into his crotch. Meanwhile I positioned myself at Angel's side and slid his briefs down. I couldn't get them over his dangling thighs, so I tore the cotton and ripped them off.

Angel continued to wriggle furiously. "Smudge! Buster! Please stop. Please!"

Buster pulled his massive prick from his pants and pushed it toward Angel's panting and pleading lips. On the boy's second cry of complaint,

Buster shoved his thickening, throbbing cock halfway down the pleading palate. Angel gagged as it met his tonsils, wriggling even more forcefully. But it was to no avail, Buster was ramming home, parting the begging mouth wider apart with each forward thrust.

During his fight for freedom, I glimpsed Angel's cock and balls when they rolled from beneath his tummy, falling between his tightening thighs and down one side of the cold torpedo.

Although his mumbling mouth complained as it was filled with thick flesh, I could see his young shaft stiffened as he rode the torpedo.

Plunging my palm below his bum-crack, I pulled his prick free, lying it backward-facing down the weapon's steel shaft. Still Angel wriggled and mumbled complaint but as soon as I dropped my mouth over the head, first sliding my tongue over the cold steel, then around the growing bud, Angel began to relax and writhe at the sensation.

Running my tongue up the length of his cock, Angel's buttocks flexed, closing his inviting crack tightly. After I'd sucked one ball and then the other into my hot mouth, I saw the cheeks relax and his virgin hole spring into view. All-the-while, Buster continued to work inside the boy's mouth, pushing deep then withdrawing to the tip.

Buster's face was red and sweaty, delighting at being devoured; his eyes bright with the sheer bliss at the pleasure of seeing his shaft sink into the boy's pretty face. I managed to catch his attention. Immediately, he knew what I wanted and nodded to a draw. Inside, I found the lubrication.

Returning to a now solid sex and a more relaxed Angel, I continued to savour and slurp - balls then cock, cock then balls.

No longer was Angel fighting to be free. Indeed, there were whimpers of pleasure emitting from his mouth as I sucked on him and he sucked on Buster.

Another really deep and glorious gorge on Angel's cock and I felt the head expand, my tongue encircling the ridge of the bud. A dribble of cum surged from the head and I quickly swallowed it before pulling away. Angel groaned in complaint.

My greased fingers weren't expected by him and Angel yelped when I sunk them knuckle deep. On seeing what I was doing, Buster gripped harder on the boy's blond locks and began a frantic invasion of the moist mouth.

As I worked my fingers ever deeper, I could feel the boy's buttocks tightening around them. Angel was now submissive and willing. For several minutes I thrust one, two, then three fingers deep into him.

Gripping the harness bar, I pulled myself onto the weapon and sat behind the boy. Angel's cock was solid to the point of bursting, pre-cum dribbling down the side of the torpedo. Greasing my own sex, I pushed with one firm thrust. "Yes!" cried the boy as I impaled him on my prick. Angel had me to the hilt!

Robustly I rode the boy, banging hard into his buttocks, his soft sphincter sucking me deep. The harness began to swing with the ferocity of my fucking. Angel gasped and moaned in delight as I drove hard into his bum and Buster into his mouth.

A cry of "shit!" from Buster saw Angel cough and splutter as spunk siphoned in streams into his dribbling mouth.

Angel stretched his neck forward as Buster withdrew, eager to get every last morsel of cum, begging for Buster to ram it back down his throat. "Fuck my face, Buster. Fuck my arse, Smudge. Fuck me hard!" he cried.

Buster, willing to bring the boy off, shoved his sex back into the begging mouth. Seeing how gratefully Angel gorged on that, I dropped my naked chest onto his smooth back and began biting his neck and banging my bone hard and fast; my balls massaging the boy's dribbling cock.

Angel arched his arse upward, working toward my cock, rubbing his own over the torpedoes cold surface. With a delighted squeal from both of us, Angel shot his cum backward down the steel shaft and I sent mine sailing in streams into his hot hole as it tightened around my exploding dick.

A voice over the intercom startled us. "Leading Seaman, Wood. Engineering Officer. Are you there with Junior Seaman Heaven?"

Buster moved to the intercom. "Yes, sir!"

"What are you doing?"

"Some torpedo practice, sir!"

"Very good, Wood. Keep it up!"

"We will, sir!" Buster replied, taking up my position and me his.

VIRGIN SAILORS

ONE

My name is Ken. I've been a sailor for two years. No one knows I'm gay. Well that's a lie, really. Those sailors and civilians I've had sex with obviously do but generally it's not something I confess or make obvious - far too risky. Truth be known, my sexual confessions are usually the opposite.

It was two years ago today I offered up my soul, my life, my everything to a life at sea. But I wasn't alone when I embarked on that adventure. With me were Danny, Dave and Mike. Within a few hours those lads would be with me again. For the first time in a year our pretty faces will greet each other's once more - a plan made the day we were drafted to our respective ships. Hopefully, that will come about. But the navy had an uncanny way of destroying plans made by mere mortals like ourselves.

Before I take you to meet the lads, let me tell you a little bit about ourselves and our first year in training.

We are now all eighteen, only months separating us as we approach that ancient age of nineteen. But according to our farewell do a year ago, we are also virgins - drunkenly confessed at the end of that crazy night. But during training, we did all boast to having sex with girls. None of us believed the other. However, I never confessed to my acts of schoolboy sex with other boys.

You see, when you live in a small mess deck with thirty frisky lads, ranging from the ultra macho to the frighteningly timid, as we did, you needed to watch your every word and action if you didn't want to bring undue attention upon yourself.   That said, I would have to admit, I was constantly champing at the bit, desperate to broadcast that fact and that I adored guys, adored a good few of those naked lads who constantly bustled around me.

Deep inside, my tummy was forever knotted in pain and excitement as my eyes feasted on cocks and cute bums as we tiredly leapt from our bunks each morning. Many of those cocks still proud and oozing come from an early handshake.

Of those delightful bodies which daily tormented me, Danny's was the one that attracted me the most. His short, strong frame was simply stunning!

I recall that first day he stood in front of me as we queued to collect our uniforms. In his tight white jeans, there could be no mistaking he had a lot to offer a cock-hungry lad like myself. He looked edible and adorable!

Whilst we chatted and I swam in his every intimate detail, I didn't think he could look anymore delicious. But when he later slipped into that sailor suit, and those bell-bottoms hugged his cute arse and perfectly parted his pert cheeks, I almost fainted! Never had I seen such a beautiful bum!

I had no doubt in my mind that had his girlfriend been there - I prayed to God he didn't have one! - she would have surely pissed herself with excitement. I already had. But it wasn't pee which was oozing from my cock!

From that moment, Danny, I decided, would become my friend. My very close friend!

I'm not sure how Mike and Dave came into my 'special' friend category, it just happened. Perhaps it was because we bunked in a line, me sandwiched between Mike and Danny, Danny sandwiched between me and Dave. Or maybe, unbeknown to ourselves, we had similar sexual interests. Whatever it was, we were born to be pals.

Within a month the four of us were as one. Always together, we helped one another with our kit, played cards on our bunks at night, walked around the camp whenever we had time off, swapped gossip and jokes, swatted for our exams, and much much more. To be honest, we had become such close pals, they should have bunked us together in one huge bed! That said, there was nothing sexual going on between us. At least, I have no knowledge that there was.

So close were we, not a day went by when one of us wasn't wrapped around the other, having a friendly wrestle. And not a week went by when one or all of us paid the price for that - extra chores, kit-musters, doubling around the parade-ground and the like. We took it all in our stride.

There were only a couple of occasions, I recall, when things got a little serious. Like the time when Mike and myself became slightly aroused during a fun wrestle. The Petty Officer was sharp to spot the development within baggy pyjamas during that close embrace, and quickly intervened. Amazingly, too close a friendship with your mess mates was not encouraged. Indeed, quite often frowned upon. The resulting threat, to separate our little group, brought an instant easing down of our close-contact fun. I wasn't too upset about that, I still got close enough to the lads to be deemed as having sex during rugby, judo and other contact sports.

Funny thing was, I had no idea if any of the lads were deliberately trying to arouse or seduce the other. There was never any suggestion from any of them that they liked guys the way I did. Quite simply, we were just good pals.

But yes, the motives for my close encounters were pretty clear to myself, though constantly suppressed. There was no doubt in my mind I wanted all three of the lads more than they would ever know, especially Danny. Sadly, my only release for my sexual frustration came regularly after Pipe Down.

It was funny, and I have no idea why they did it, but we all bunked head to tail - one boy's head beside another boy's feet. Perhaps its purpose was to keep us from whispering to one another after lights out, the bunks being so close. But what the officers didn't realise, they had actually done me a favour. Thus positioned, I could lovingly glance across at Danny and Mike's pretty faces and observe their calm, cute expressions as they softly breathed, cuddling up to the fantasy lovers of their dreams whilst I gently tossed myself. But better yet, because of this position, I was a good deal closer to their bulging bedding than I would have been had we all faced the same way. And yes, often their bedtime bulges would be bigger than before, and be silently bouncing in sympathy with mine.

I've no idea why we gelled so easily. Perhaps it was Danny's presence, for it was he who was always the centre of attraction, or if not, made himself so - the one with the most skills. But even with his boldness, relative butchness and confidence, he still had an air of secretiveness about him.

I don't know how he managed it, but he almost always avoided punishment - not that he didn't deserve it! It seemed that everyone loved him. And of those that did, I reckon I was at the top of that list. Who did Danny love? I don't mean to be cruel to a friend here, but I think even he would be the first to admit that it was himself.

Mike, however, was the complete opposite. Reserved when not in our company. Always seeking help - mostly from Dave. Piss poor at sport, as was I. And, more often than not, sporting flushed, embarrassed cheeks.

Of the four of us, he got the brunt of the grief. Pity really, because he was such a lovely guy. With his gentle nature, he was easy prey for Gunnery Instructors, Physical Training Instructors and the like. Constantly, we shored his flagging ego. Built human supports around him. Even cheated for him during tests to give him better results and help ward off the endless bombardment of abuse. Sadly, there was little we could do for him in the gym and on the sports field. He paid dearly for that!

Dave was your suspicious type. Hated authority and often believed there was some ulterior motive in every order or request. He came close to getting a severe punishment the day he dared to question authority. He got a week of kit-musters and heavy duty for that outburst. We spent that depressing period polishing his boots and pressing his kit to get him through.

Although not overly bright, he always put his everything into the task at hand. If he had a fault, it was that he seldom admitted to not being able to do something. I remember, we watched him almost drown one afternoon in his attempts to prove he could swim, not willing to admit to us he couldn't. But despite his strong beliefs, Dave was a great lad. The type of guy who would die for you without even wanting to know the reason why.

Finally there's myself. I guess I'm a bit of all three of the lads. Okay at most things but not brilliant at any. Shy, but bold when I need to be. And, like the rest, always up for a laugh. The only other thing I knew about myself, which I suspect the others didn't, was that I was gay.

So gel we did. But with our inseparable friendship came a regular buffeting from three beefy trainees - also frighteningly bonded, I might add - who hated us. Who thought they were God's gift to masculinity. They nicknamed us the Four Must Be Queers. None of us were too bothered about that but we did keep our distance. Truth was, if you weren't getting the piss taken out of you, then you didn't fit in - anywhere!

We had many adventures, escapades, frightening moments and other nonsense in our lives during our year of training, but not once did we row or fight. We were inseparable friends, we did everything together.

I recall, we even started smoking at the same time. I guess it was a case of falling in line with the other lads, most of whom already smoked. We went through thirty in an hour. I was as sick as a pig afterwards. From that day on we were all hooked, and most of our cash went on fags.

None of us drank at that time, we couldn't. Us trainees were never allowed beyond the perimeter fence to find a pub. There was a bar for regular sailors on camp, but not for low-life like ourselves. We certainly made up for that the day we got our final results. The day we were rewarded with our first shore leave.

Ten pin bowling was another fun activity our money went on. We had a four-lane bowling-alley on the camp. Well, we had to spend our slavery pay somewhere, not that we had a lot of it.

I recall there was a beautiful wood-carved pin to be won by any lad who could reach the maximum score - a ploy to make us spend more cash. None of us ever won it. None of us ever managed to score over one hundred. As usual, we were far too busy larking about.

No, nothing was ever too serious in our lives at that time. That's a lie, really. Almost everything was serious when it came to studies, drill, divisions, kit inspections and all the other military crap.
"Discipline maketh a good sailor!" we were told. And how often we were reminded of that.

Because of our playfulness , punishments became a regular event for us, often unjustified, often cruel. But I guess the most severe, depending on the way you viewed it, was to be booted out. That awful revelation came about when two lads were found having sex in the heads.

Have I mentioned the heads before? That grown-up-potty-land without partitions, where you took your dump in full view of everyone. I can tell you that that certainly brought a flush to Mike's shy face the first time we sat opposite one another, desperate not to strain and make any rear-end noises. I don't ever recall seeing Mike enter them again when others were partaking.

As I was saying, getting discharged was the ultimate punishment for major sins. Two things occurred to me when news broke of those unfortunate lads. Firstly, I wasn't the only guy in the navy who liked having sex with other guys, so I was pleased I wasn't alone. But the other, more serious revelation that it was the end of your career if you did, was more worrying! It was quite obvious, then, that getting my much wanted sex with sailors was going to be a very risky business indeed.

Sex for me, therefore - apart from with myself - never materialised during my training. Well it kind of did, but I'll speak about that later. However, the lads still fed my mind with enjoyable, disgusting thoughts on a regular basis. Thoughts conjured up as we played rugby, did gym, showered, or other water sports. One water sport - sailing cutters and whalers - never got me horny, though. I was too shit scared! Constantly worried whether we'd tip the bloody boat over as we larked about. Like Dave, I wasn't that good a swimmer!

Actually, I think there did come a day when that nearly came about, the day we seemed to have more water inside the cutter than out. Danny suggested that we pull the plug from the bottom and let some out. Dave nearly did it! Well, he wasn't the brightest of boys.

The assault course, too, was a bloody nightmare and did little to enhance my sexual libido. I wanted to tell that pig of a Gunnery Officer that I didn't join the navy to freeze my balls off climbing netting, wade through waist-deep ice-cold water, crawl through tunnels and over twenty foot wooden structures; damaging my favourite parts and getting them plastered in muck. I joined the navy to shag some sailors!

Somehow, Danny seemed to enjoy it all and still looked delectable and delicious, even when covered from head to toe in muck. I guess the thought of me washing all that grime from his scrumptious body afterwards - God, if only he'd have let me do it! - helped create that delightful vision.

"In every job to be done, there is an element of fun," so Mary Poppins said. If us lads could have had a motto, then that would most surely have been ours.

No, there was no joy in mending kit, ironing and washing the bloody stuff....

Hang on, I just remembered, there was a lot of fun in washing kit! Yes, how could I forget our dhobi sessions. Those lovely days when we went to the dhobi house to wash our clothes. Thirty bollock-naked boys covered from head to toe in bubbles; larking around in a pool-sized tub as we cleaned it. Hell, that was fun! For me at least and I believe I slid my naked skin over Danny's soapy body more times than was acceptable. More times than I dare admit.

But no, there was no fun in learning how to march and do rifle drill in the freezing wind, snow and ice. No fun, either, in running the assault course when your fingers wouldn't work and you were shit scared. Even less fun in scrubbing showers with a toothbrush or painting coal white - can you believe it, we actually did those things! But as I said, even with all that crap and punishment going on, the four of us always managed to find fun somewhere.

Many things happened to us during our year of training, both good and bad. No, I didn't get my much wanted sex throughout that year, nor did any of the lads as far as I'm aware. No, none of us got such brilliant final results that we would become Admirals somewhere down the line. No, nothing particularly spectacular resulted from our year's training apart from one thing. The most important thing! I made three wonderful friends that year. Three lifelong, special friends!

TWO

The bar was busy when I strolled in. Well-bevvied sailors sang, swore, laughed and joked. Women were few and what there was of them were all servicewomen - WRENS mostly.

I pushed my way between a burly stoker and his skin. Skin, I should explain, is a navy term for pretty young sailor. And there were plenty of those, I can tell you! The stoker slung his arm over his skin's shoulder, keeping him close, so I moved around the lad and offered up a smile. Not a knowing smile, though. Just because an old salt had a skin in tow, didn't necessarily mean they were shagging each other. The stoker acknowledged with a beer-induced smile and pulled his skin even closer.

The beer I ordered arrived, warm and slopping over the lip of the glass, and was accompanied by a suggestive smile from the gay barman. But this wasn't a gay bar. Far from it. It would have been most unlikely, even for the most confident of gay sailors, to venture into such a place. No, gay barman in a sailor-town were quite the norm. I guess it was easy pickings for them; taking their choice of drunken horny sailors - straight or gay - at the end of a shift.

I smiled back at him as I bent and slurped a mouthful of beer, before taking my glass to a vacant seat. Somehow, with his return smile, I think he knew I was gay. It mattered little, mine would be one of the many faces he would clock during his shift as he searched for his nightly shag.

The stoker's palm now rested on his skin's bell-bottomed clad bum. And as I moved to a bay-window seat, I thought I glimpsed a kiss glance across the young lad's cheek. But maybe I was wrong and it was just my angle. Anyway, they seemed close enough to make love. For some reason I hoped they would - already had.

I scanned the occupants of the bar for any of the lads, none appeared to have got here yet. Anyway, I was a bit early as usual - discipline once more controlling my life. Being late was a punishable crime.

I began to wonder about the lads and how much they might have changed, physically and in personality. I doubted Danny would have lost his cheeky confidence, hopefully he wouldn't have lost his attractiveness, his sexiness. I'm pretty sure he wouldn't have gotten any taller, he'd done all his growing long before we'd left training. Long before he even started, I suspect. And for sure, another part of his anatomy couldn't have grown any bigger! I'll introduce you to that later.

Could Dave have become any brighter or Mike less shy over this past year? I doubted Dave would have reached professor standards, but I hoped Mike would have found more confidence in himself.

I suppose there were a lot of unanswered questions to toy with as I supped my beer and waited. Like, had any or all of the lads got hitched, now with a dozen sproggs in tow a piece? Or had any of them finally realised that they loved guys? Loved me, even! Those friendly kisses and hugs we gave one-another on our final night had certainly left a yearning deep inside of me for each and everyone of them. Each hug and kiss forever tattooed on my heart, especially Danny's overly long embrace. I laughed when those thoughts surfaced, my disgusting mind working overtime again.

I wondered, also, what ships or shore bases they might now be on. Indeed, all three may well be far afield - Hong Kong, Singapore or some other Far East station - and may not make this night. I checked my watch, it was still early, although it felt like I'd been here ages. I hated waiting!

For some odd reason, I began to toy again with each of the lad's sexuality. Was there any, even the slightest indication, that one of them might be gay? I guess, deep inside, I wanted to cement our friendship even further. Not to have to be lying about myself all the time. Living a double life. A case of 'love me love my dog'. For sure, there had been plenty of times when any or all of us might have been naughty with another. Often two of us would pair off and disappear for a couple of hours. Dave and Mike paired off together the most. Like I was closer to Danny, Mike and Dave were closer to each other. Maybe, just maybe, they were having a secret relationship throughout our training. I really hoped so.

I brought my attention back to the bar and checked for the lads again. It was rowdy and hot as hell as sailors sank beer and slugs of short chasers. The WRENS remained locked in their own corner, only the occasional approach of drunken sailors, which were quickly rebuffed, disturbing them.

WRENS are funny buggers!

Stoker and Skin were close enough to be lovers now, the skin completely legless and draped over his sea-dad's shoulder. They sloped off not long after. To where, I do not know. To bed together, I hoped. But there were plenty of other chunky or cute guys to observe. Like married couples they were scattered around the bar in pairs or foursomes. Some sat silently, others engrossed in sailor-talk or singing along with the jukebox or more bawdy songs. Others playing cards, fruit-machines, or just concentrating on drinking.

I scanned the bar yet again, increasingly more impatient, checking if any of the lads had arrived whilst my thoughts were elsewhere, then drifted into another daydream. And as I stared through the window and watched a frigate heading seaward, my thoughts wandered away to the week before I joined the navy.

The corn was golden and high, ears bobbing in the the breeze. My eyes were focused toward the woods as I sat in the yellow sea. So far only birds and squirrels had entered or exited. I was waiting for a friend. I had had sexual adventures with friends before: There had been the Thomas twins, Ben, and a lad who I couldn't remember the name of, who had been camped with a scout group in Farmer Wilmot's meadow. What all these lads had had in common, they had all been brief toss buddies. The twins - a regular hole-in-the-pocket wank on the school bus home. Ben - another toss up against the largest oak in the woods. And the scouting lad - a crafty toss in his tent.

Today was to be different!

Having matured into a fine youth, I was in no doubt what I wanted sexually. Today, for the very first time, I decided I would progress from wanking to something more satisfying. To assist me with this venture, a Canadian lad who was here for a vacation with his uncle was to meet me. We'd already met a few days back, up in the tree house. There we'd had the usual toss. This time, however, I had more exciting plans. Of course Jake didn't know this and more than likely would be anticipating another satisfying hand-job.

Also in my mind were other missing experiences - kissing and fucking for example. Sadly, fucking would still be a long way off. I doubted I would be able to persuade Jake to go that far. Indeed, that special activity would require a more experienced guy to teach me. Happily, I expected that to be remedied in the not to distant future. I was soon to become a sailor.

"Why a sailor?" Jake had asked up in the tree house. "To see the world?"

"To see the sailors!" I had excitedly replied, anticipating meeting an endless flood of men and youths all in need of that most desirable pleasure - sex!

And as I waited for him in the ocean of corn, staring skyward and watching swifts and swallows bob and weave in the blue sky above, I began to admire my own body, wondering if any sailor would fancy it. Working on the farm since a boy had developed me into muscle. Thighs, calves, biceps, abdomen and chest, all developed. But not overly so.

Occupied with these thoughts of future sailor lovers and the oncoming meeting with Jake, my cock had begun to grow and cramp my shorts. Gently I caressed it through the white material. Not enough guys had seen it as yet but I hoped that when they had they would love it's seven inch length and thick girth. Topped with a moustache-like tuft of fair hair, I was more than satisfied with what I'd be gifted with. And rolling the foreskin daily over the thick bud had given me ample pleasure since the day I realised that peeing wasn't necessarily its primary function.

Jake's dick was of a similar size. As yet I couldn't comment on his cock hair, having not seen it. I was sure I wouldn't be disappointed and guessed that his tuft would be jet black, matching the crop growing upon his head. My own pubics did just that, although slightly darker than the blond locks which fell sexily over my blue eyes. Perhaps it wasn't important but I also hoped Jake's body would be as smooth as silk, like my own. But being dark haired, I suspected that might not be the case. I'd already spotted a hint of a moustache on the upper lip of his extremely kissable lips.

I spread the stems around myself - a bed for boys to learn about boys - and continued to wait.

A shout from the woods brought my head above the corn...

Shouts from the far corner of the bar brought my attention back to my surroundings. Occasionally beer-drowned brains caused their owners to get somewhat macho over something as stupid as who's ship is the best. Even who owns what sailor-boy skin. Camp Barman was between them in seconds.

I didn't believe he was a brave bugger, though he definitely was, fearlessly placing his slim frame between the beefy marine and half-a-ton of drunken seaman. Rather, I had a sneaky suspicion it was more an act of wanting his youthful arms around that muscled marine, for his was the body he embraced in a frail bear hug.

With the assistance of shipmates and another brick-wall-of-a-marine, the fight was stopped. And then an act of comradeship which did and didn't surprise me. Marine gave Barman a lengthy kiss on the lips. Bellows of laughter and jeers filled the air on their mouths parting. Barman blushed as the two opponents threw forgiving arms over each other's shoulders and walked to the bar. Marine slapped Barman's bum and kissed him again. Barman beamed a happy smile and moved behind the bar to serve them.

I took a gulp of beer and grinned at him, suspecting he'd found his shag for the night. Barman smiled back. Almost immediately the group of WRENS up and left, mumbling something about "animals". An enormous cheer went up as they ambled out, accompanied by mooing from bevvied marines and matelots.

WRENS are definitely peculiar people!

I walked to the bar and ordered a rum, interrupting Camp Barman, who was now engrossed in what I suspected to be bed-talk with his man. I gave him a smile and a knowing wink when I paid for it. Barman's face lit up and he gave me a wide grin. Yes, he'd definitely found his shag for the night. If not, I had a distinct feeling I might be somewhere on his dance card.

I re-took my seat and sat in the blazing evening sun as it shone through the south-facing window and headed toward the horizon. The frigate was now well in the distance. Sailing to where, I do not know - a fishing patrol, a pretend war, some exotic island - who knows? For sure, the crew would be busy battening down hatches, preparing food, sending signals, testing weapons. Testing those weapons? Definitely!

I brought my attention back into the bar. Cheerful sailors were coming and going in various states of soberness. Only a quick visit from a Military Police Shore Patrol, checking for trouble, dampened our spirits. Barman continued to flit from customer to customer then return to the company of his chosen man. But still no sign of any of the boys.

I glimpsed a boy-sailor, sixteen if he was a day, sat beside the jukebox. He looked lost and lonely. I guessed he was based at a training establishment and as yet hadn't been snared by a caring sea-dad. I had no doubt that would be remedied the day he set foot on board a ship. He was beauty itself!

I managed to squeeze a smile from his lips - lips that most likely had only kissed a mother's face - when I caught his eye. With his short black hair, cherub cheeks and ruddy complexion, he reminded me of Jake.

Jake was in the shadow of a holly bush, scanning over the corn. Dressed in tight blue shorts and checked shirt unbuttoned down to the navel, he looked adorable.

"Jake!" I hollered, waving my arm above the chest-high corn.

"Ken!" he returned, his expression changing from one of possible disappointment to one of sheer joy on seeing me.

Grinning from ear to ear, he rushed from the shadow into the sunshine, his hair shimmering in shafts of silvery black. Excitedly I watched his upper torso bob above and below the corn as he bounded toward me, his shirt flapping behind him, parting to reveal his sunburned chest.

Already my cock was rigid!

Before he reached me, I ducked below the tall stems and shot away to my right. Jake's body cut a zig zag swathe as he searched for me. My excitement increased further when his black-haired legs stood before my flushed excited face. Panther-like I grasped both ankles, pushed my head between his thighs and below his buttocks, and pushed him over.

Jake fell face down. "Heck!" he yelled.

In seconds I was straddled across his lower back, half sat on his firm buttocks, hands pressed upon his stout shoulders. Jake was a good deal stronger than me, and with a bucking-bronco bound, sent me clear over his head. Instantly our positions were reversed but this time it was my front which took his full weight, the cheeks of his bum pushing firmly onto my stiff cock, his palms pressing heavily on each of my nipples.

It was me who was going to make the first move, I thought. Trick him into some serious snogging. So I was more than surprised when his naked chest met mine and his lips, full and fresh-smelling - orange juice, I think - smothered my own. I cannot describe how fantastic that felt, another boy's mouth over my own for the very first time. But the sensation which followed, when he darted his tongue down my throat, was just unbelievable! In fact, so glorious was it, I felt a jet of pre-come jettison from my cock and soak into my pants. So ecstatic was I, I didn't want him to pull his mouth away. I wanted us to swap tongues until I died from the pleasure.

Jake sat upright, wriggling his buttocks into my crotch. "You like that?" he grinned.

I didn't reply. I simply gripped his proud dick with my left hand, lassoed the back of his neck with the other and pulled our mouths back together. So tightly was my mouth on his, we could hardly breathe. In fact, I believe it was our own breath passing between us which was keeping us alive during that fierce embrace.

Whilst we continued to work on tongues and nibble on lips and ears, Jake had managed to wrestle his body from his shirt. Meanwhile, I had managed to wrestle his prick from his pants. And how good that felt, my palm barely big enough to wrap around it's girth as it stiffened and broadened.

I was delighted to discover that Jake's chest was smooth and silky, only a hint of black hair between his pecs. But under his armpits was a forest. Musty and moist, they smelt sensational. I sent my tongue deep into the hollows and lapped greedily on his fresh sweat. Jake giggled. However, his attempt to lick my less-hairy hollows were quickly rebuffed - being highly ticklish, it drove me crazy. But I did allow him to bury his nose into the sweat and hair, but even that was sensitive.

Lovingly we searched each other's bodies, both exploring for the first time places we had each longed to explore. Nipple buds were good fun. I hadn't noticed before how firm and protrusive they could become and I hungrily nipped and sucked on Jake's until they were red raw and twice the size of peppercorns. Jake loved that. Again it was too sensitive for me but I allowed him to suck mine gently enough not to make it unbearable.

We rolled apart for a breather.

I lay my arm across Jake's naked chest, and as I gazed puppy-dog-like into his big brown eyes, I believe I had never seen a boy so happy. My own happiness? I was in heaven!.

"Jake. You're beautiful. I wish we could stay together forever!" I sighed.

Jake remained silent and began to kiss along my chest, swirl his tongue around my navel, and unbutton my shorts. My cock was upright when Jake removed my shorts, hidden beneath my white briefs and pointing toward my navel; the bulging head clamped beneath the elastic waistband. Speedily he pulled my pants over my thighs. My cock sprang free. My eyes glazed, feasting on his long, thick dick when he did likewise. In an uncontrollable desire my mouth headed straight for it...

A group of sailors entering the bar had brought me from my enjoyable thoughts. My cock was uncomfortable in my bell-bottoms and I pulled it toward the waistband to make it less visible. So excited was I, I desperately needed a wank. But first I would allow it to subside before I dashed into the heads for that much needed release.

It was now approaching eight in the evening and the sun was setting. I thought I heard it hiss as it hit the sea. Old sailors said it did. The jukebox had been flung up a notch. Bowie screamed over the heads of rowdy sailors. Without a cue from any conductor, up went our voices in a crescendo of unharmonious noise.

"...saaaaailors fighting in the dance hall.

Oh man, look at those cave men go!"

Barman had now finished his shift, but not before ringing the Happy Hour bell - not that we weren't pretty happy already. Jolly sailors were all around me. Boys and men of all ages, shapes and sizes bonded together as one. A hive of males happy to be playing together. Dare I say it, but I have always found it wonderful how loving and caring men and youths can be to one another when women are absent. Nothing to bring out the macho shit in them.

Barman was sat close to his marine. Not too close, though. It wouldn't be safe for the marine to broadcast his sexual preferences too openly. Of course, sex amongst ourselves went on all the time but a blind eye was always best. What you didn't know or see couldn't harm you - or anyone else!

My Jake look-a-like appeared more comfortable now. A lad his own age had joined him. He was just as pretty. Just as virginal. Just as vulnerable to any horny sea-dad who might happen upon them. Jake look-a-like caught me feasting on his looks a second time and threw a smile as wide as a trawler net over me. I wasn't prone to embarrassment but I knew my face was hotter than my throbbing dick which was still in need of some urgent attention. Even more so now that the lad had rekindled those sexual thoughts of Jake in the cornfield.

I desperately needed another drink to calm myself.

A straight-looking barman had replaced Camp Barman, and after squeezing myself between a bounty of shapely buttocks, I reached the bar and ordered a single shot of rum from him. With a swift gulp, I sent it down my drying throat then moved into the heads.

Jake look-a-like sent another trawler net smile over me as I entered, but sadly didn't follow.

I threw the bolt on the cubicle door. Thankfully, all were empty, although a young sailor did have his head in a sink and was returning eight pints of beer from whence it probably came.

Removing my uniform, I hung it on the hook - come stains are somewhat obvious on blue serge. Jake look-a-like sprang into my mind as I teased my cock into an erection and conjured up visions of unwrapping his Christmas-present-of-a-body and plunging my prick into whatever hole he was willing to offer.

Gently I began to caress my cock, then more vigorously as those cornfield memories with Jake manifested in my mind.

A mass of freshly showered black hair met my nose as I buried my mouth to the base of Jake's cock. Without even thinking I might choke, which I did, I took every centimetre of him, so desperate was I.

"What you doing!" cried Jake in desperate gasps, sitting up and pulling my head away.

With a hard shove on his chest, I pushed him back down and plunged my mouth back to the base of his cock.

"We shouldn't be doing this. It's wrong!" he whimpered but immediately resigned himself to the pleasure of having his cock sucked upon for the very first time.

I caressed his abdomen affectionately, the ripple of muscles contracting as I brought my attention back to the bud of his cock. The texture was superb. Like a silken rosebud, it slid over and under my lapping tongue. With each lap I felt the ridge become more and more defined.

"Jesus, Ken. Oh, Jesus!" sighed Jake. "I'll come if you don't stop!"

I didn't want him to come so soon and eased off, but continued toying with the slit, teasing my tongue deep into its moist depths. As soon as the head began to loose it swelling, I returned to deep thrusts - tip to base, tip to base - bringing it solid once more.

"Christ, I'm coming!" yelped Jake. But before he did, I pulled smartly away. A small globule of white juice bubbled from the head. Hungrily, I lapped it off. It was my first taste of come. It was wonderful!

Although I desperately wanted my mouth filled to its capacity with his youthful juice, I slid my nakedness over his and we returned to kissing.

"Like being sucked?" I whispered, as I nibbled an earlobe.

Jake grinned then laughed kind of nervously. "Shit! I've never felt anything like that. I thought I was going to come seconds after you started." Then as an afterthought, asked, "You been sucked before?"

"Course!" I lied.

Jake searched my thoughts. "Yeah, right. We'll soon see." And with that he rolled me onto my back and his mouth was over my cock in a flash.

Desperately I gripped his head, entwining my fingers into his black hair, shoving his mouth further down my shaft. Instantly I knew what Jake meant by coming so soon because I felt a wealth of spunk burst from my balls and toward the bud.

Frantically I forced my prick into his pretty face. Jake pushed upward against my palms to escape my excited thrusts. I wouldn't let him pull away. I couldn't. Not now!

"I wanna spunk in your mouth, Jake. Please let me. Please!" I pleaded, wrapping my arm around the back of his head and pulling down even harder.

Jake's mouth met my pubics. I felt the head of my cock go past his tonsils and his throat tighten around the hilt. My balls lifted high as the bud of my cock expanded to bursting. "I'm coming! I'm coming!" I yelled.

It wasn't a punch exactly, more a firm push. But it had the desired effect and Jake, gasping for air, managed to break free. My come remained poised at the tip of my cock but thankfully didn't erupt.

"Shit, Ken! You trying to kill me? Choke me to bloody death!" he cursed, his face reddened from lack of breath.

My own face brightened with shame. "Sorry, Jake. Christ, it was so damn good I couldn't stop. I just couldn't!"

Jake released a forgiving laugh. "It is quite nice, isn't it?"

"Nice? It's bloody fantastic!"

"Had a blowjob before, eh?" he teased.

We resumed our kisses and cuddles whilst gently tossing each other, keeping our cocks firm. Not much was said during that loving embrace, just a few moans of pleasure as we each explored every inch of the other's body.

I loved the ladder of black hair which ran from Jake's navel to his bush of pubics - like some lay line indicating the direction I should take. Bum holes, too, we both found exciting. Tight and virginal, only one moist finger apiece managed to gain entry. Jake found it more pleasurable than I did. And when I tongued his hole, he writhed excitedly, begging me to lick deeper.

Instinct eventually brought us head to tail and found us slurping beneath balls, licking along cock shafts and, more frequently, cock heads. Two superb silkworms produced silver threads of pre-come from our excited dicks and was greedily lapped away.

Jake's breathing became rapid, his short gasps exciting me. My breathing took on a similar rhythmic excitement. Our heads began bobbing fiercely over our cocks and were soon joined by flexing buttocks thrusting frantically into delighted faces. Clenching Jake's, I pulled him powerfully into my mouth, thrusting his cock down my throat until I choked on its length and thickness. Jake responded likewise, cramming my dick deep into his.

Shooting a finger deep into my virgin bum and gripping one buttock cheek firmly with his other hand, Jake pulled me even deeper. The tightness yet softness of his throat was stunning and the sensation of young flesh rubbing together, belly on chest, sent my eyes rolling upward.

With each of Jake's swallowing actions, I could feel his throat muscles rippling down my cock shaft, culminating in an excruciatingly enjoyable pain as they ran over my cock head. Simultaneously, I felt his cock expanding to exploding on each of my desperate swallows.

Choreographed, it was. By some unknown sex God. By some lovemaking spirit who wanted to take two boys beyond mere pleasure. Take us to a place called Ecstasy.

We were dripping sweat and gasping now, spittle running from our mouths and over our chins. But neither of us was about to withdraw. We were swimming in a sea of sexual sublimity. Sailing to heaven. Joyously impaled. Soon, very soon, our mouths and throats would be swamped by a sea of virgin spunk!

We gripped each other's heads tightly as we were about to shoot, fearing they might be pulled away. Our buttocks flexed and thrust a final time. Both of us emitted delighted squeals as oceans of spunk, wave after wave of it, cascaded into youthful throats and was gratefully gulped away; each of us praying for the surge never to stop!

I heard the door squeak open and bang shut, then pee being sprayed into a urinal. My spunk hit my chest and the underside of my chin. A groan did escape my lips, but I fought the real gasp back to my belly for fear of being caught. Hastily I rolled some toilet tissue around my palm and rubbed myself clean.

The sailor didn't appear to be in a hurry to leave, so I pulled on my uniform and threw the bolt.

It was unmistakable, the cute bottom being offered to me as the owner bent and washed his hands.

"Danny!" I called, wrapping my arms around his slim waist and shoving my semi-stiff cock into his tight arse, pretending to fuck him.

Danny glanced into the mirror, then spun around when he recognised me. "Smudge, you're here!" he excited, using my nickname. "Mike and Dave here?"

"Nope. Probably got pissed or picked up a shag somewhere."

"Probably. Nice to see you. You look great!"

"And you, darling," I winked.

"Been strangling your nicker python?" he grinned, making a grab for my moist cock.

"Course," I chuckled. "What else was there for me to do?

Danny draped a friendly arm over my shoulder. "Come on, let's get a beer. Shit, it's good to see you."

"And you, you old scrubber!"

THREE

Jake look-a-like and his mate had vanished as we re-entered the bar. In many ways I was relieved for that. I doubted, even with Danny's gorgeous body beside me, I would have been able to keep my wanting eyes away from him. Especially as he'd just become part of my fantasy; albeit a small part.

Danny and I took our beer to the bay window seat still being reserved by my cap, and plonked ourselves down. Danny squeezed my hand. "Christ, it's really good to see you, Smudge.'

Yes, it was more than good to meet up with Danny again and absorb the beauty and elegance of his athletic body. But he wasn't the musclebound, weight-lifter type. No, Danny was your short, supple, muscular, gymnast type. A mere five foot five in his bare feet. But what he could do with that magnificent body was mind-blowing. What he could do with it in a bed, I had no idea.

Boxes, pummel horses, parallel bars and mat routines held no fear or problem for him. And the speed with which he did handsprings and somersaults over that mat was frightening. And whilst pulling my nine stone frame to the top of a rope took every ounce of my strength, Danny could hoist his torso to the top and back three times before I'd even gotten halfway.

It was no wonder then, that Danny was the envy of almost every sailor in our class. But my envy didn't come by way of his gymnastic skills. Mine came from the Physical Training Instructors who had the privilege of wrapping helping arms around his waist, or grip his slender, muscled thighs - almost to the point of touching the lump in his bulging shorts - as they taught him to perform those miracles. In fact, I was even jealous that, like me, they also had the privilege of seeing him naked when he showered. And what a sight that was!

Danny took two duty-free, 555 cigarettes from a pack, placed both in his mouth and lit them, then passed one to me. It was something he always did. Something I enjoyed. The closest I ever came to having his lips on mine. A kiss by proxy.

Both of of us inhaled deeply. But my deep breath was more an act of an increasing desire to engulf him in arms and smother him with kisses, such was my wanting for him which hadn't waned in a year's absence.

"Think they'll come?" he asked.

Engrossed in Danny's features - his greenish eyes; his fairly bushy eyebrows and extremely long eyelashes; his matching light-brown hair; his stubby nose and pinkish full lips; and his silken, almond-tanned face with petit ears perched on either side - I was a million miles away.

"Think Mike and Dave will come?" he repeated, gliding a finger, somewhat affectionately, over the back of my hand to gain my attention.

If I was to have answered honestly, I would have told him I didn't care. Told him I was more than happy with the two of us alone. For him to share all that had happened to him in the last year. For him to tell me that he hadn't got married, was still a virgin, and had understood what I meant in training about him being my 'special' friend. Tell me that he had saved himself for me, and me alone.

"Hope so. Be good to see them and get the gossip," I sighed.

"You got hitched yet, Smudge? Or got a bird on the go?"

I drew deeply on my cigarette. If only I had the guts to tell him I was gay. Tell him he could rip my nickers off me right there and then. "Nah. Likes me fun too much. You?"

Danny laughed loudly. "You're joking. Anyway, I'm too short. And the birds I've met only want to mother me."

"Ah, you poor little boy," I teased and leant over and ruffled his hair.

Danny flicked his locks from his eyes and gave a tut.

"So you never did become a PTI, then?" I asked, pointing to his Communicator's badge on his arm, which we both wore.

"Turned me down. Too short."

"Only part of you," I laughed.

"You're such a tart, Smudge," Danny giggled, having been reminded that I had firsthand knowledge of his ten inch cock - seven when hung loosely - which was even more enviable to his mates than his gymnastic skills.

I remembered the first time I saw it in its full glory. Reveille piped through the Tannoy at the usual unearthly hour. Out from the covers we both popped in our candy-stripped pyjamas. Out popped Danny's proud ten inches through the buttonless fly. Even a few of the stallions on my father's farm would have been in envy of it. I certainly was. Don't get me wrong. I didn't want to posses something of that size for myself; attached to my own body. No, I wanted it in my mouth. Up my bum. I wanted it to have and to hold. To worship!

Yes, that was the first time I glimpsed Danny's cock at its most splendid. Other occasions I had only seen it hanging loose in the showers, dripping come-like soap-bubbles from its bulbous head. Other times it was always hidden, tenting his bedding as he silently pumped it. All-the-while I would be pumping mine until I heard his tell-tale cough when he came, unleashing my own come seconds after.

"Surely the size of your cock counts for something?" I continued to tease.

Danny merely grinned, stood, adjusted his crotch - which had become slightly aroused - and headed toward the bar. "Fancy a rum chaser?" he offered.

I watched his shapely buttocks flexing as he manoeuvred between sailors all of whom were a good three inches taller than himself. But as far as I was concerned he would knock them for six. His arse was just wonderful. And the seam of his bell-bottoms which parted those firm, sexy cheeks was inviting beyond belief.

Once more my cock began climbing uncontrollably upward!

Whilst Danny waited to be served, I scanned around for Dave and Mike. Still no sign of them. No sign too of Barman and Marine. I had no doubt where they would be. In Barman's bed, for sure. And what a sight that would make - a delicate, cute lad with a massive marine stuffing him stupid.

I had a sneaky suspicion Barman would insist Marine keep his uniform on whilst he was being shagged, and Marine would have him handcuffed to the bed, humping his tasty little bum like it had never been humped before.

Two large rums banged down on the table, bringing me from my disgusting, enjoyable thoughts. My eyes immediately went to Danny's crotch, checking if it had increased in volume. Sadly, it was just its normal, massive self.

"The Buffer's a bastard!" saluted Danny.

"The Buffer's a bastard!" I repeated, gulping a good mouthful. I'm not sure where that toast came from, but it was one sailors often used. It was common knowledge that all Buffers were bastards, whether they were nice or not.

With the drinks Danny had consumed, now and before his arrival, his tongue had begun to loosen. "Still a virgin, Smudge? Slag like you, I doubt it!"

A question answer was the best avoiding tactic. "Me a slag? I bet that donkey dick of yours has been driven home more times than a Paddy's road drill!"

Danny smiled, a cunning smile. Perhaps even a knowing smile. "Chance would be a fine thing. Can't find anyone who can take it all!"

he boasted.

"Don't matter, does it? You can probably do yourself a blow-job whenever you want."

Danny's face reddened brighter than I've ever seen it flush.

"You dirty, lucky bugger. You do blow yourself, don't you?" I excited. "And you never told us!"

Danny jumped to his feet. "Shit, I'm bursting for a crap."

"Don't forget to wash your mouth out afterwards, you whore," I called after him.

Strange, but that was something I'd never actually thought about before. All that time together and he'd been blowing himself. No wonder I could never capture him. No wonder he always had a smile on his face. The lucky bugger. The bloody lucky bugger.

I suspected that when he returned he'd hit me with the same question. Course I wasn't a virgin. Not for a long long while. Trouble was, not once was there a bird-shag among those many encounters I could impress him with. I wondered if Danny knew this and he himself was in a similar position. Perhaps he was fishing. Testing the water. Waiting for me to reveal my gayness. Reveal that if he asked nicely, or if he just asked, there was a place for that lonely cock of his to languish in. Dare I tell him?

Jumping up, I set off for my own pee.

We passed each other as I headed toward the toilet. It was a tight squeeze between two beer-bellied sailors. I'm sure I felt Danny's cock deliberately brush against mine as I squeezed by. Or maybe it was just my imagination. But the quick peck on my cheek which he gave as our bodies rubbed together definitely wasn't.

I found the warm-seated cubicle he'd used and checked the floor, water, walls, everywhere for spent come. There wasn't any. I slashed two pints of the one I'd drunk, spraying it childishly around the bowl, zipped up and headed back to our seat.

A beefy guy was bent over Danny's shoulder and whispering into his ear when I returned. On seeing me approach, he up and walked away.

"Who's that?" was my strangely jealous question.

"Just an oppo."

I guessed Danny had many mates. I guessed, even more, that he had many lovers. Many male lovers. More and more I was convinced that he was as queer as I was. Problem was, how was I going to find out?.

"You still a virgin, then?" I threw his own question back at him.

"Told you. I'm too short and I can't find anyone who can take it."

I was determined to keep the conversation on sex. "So what's it like being able to blow yourself?" I asked, passing him one of the two cigarettes I'd lit.

Danny's face flushed again. "You're a filthy sod, Smudge. Is sex all you ever think about? I'm surprised you've still got a dick. You have got a dick, haven't you? Then again, you wouldn't need one. You probably take it up the bum!"

I sensed a slight annoyance at my sexual questioning but carried on. "So, do you swallow or spit it out?"

Danny glared at me but his eyes still had a knowing sparkle in them. "I swallow. Why waste all those vitamins."

Whether that was a truthful statement or a wind up, I had no idea. But the effect was to send my dick stiff beneath the table as the thought of Danny gorging on his own cock and gulping down a gallon of come swirled around my mind.

"So, what does it taste like?" I pressed.

Danny rose from his seat. I thought I'd pushed too hard and he was about to leave. Instead, he adjusted his bell-bottoms and sat back down. It was difficult to distinguish, being the size that it was, but I was pretty sure his cock was rising.

Danny roared a bubbly, drunken laugh. "It tastes a bit salty and sweet. You know, like sweet and sour sauce?" he winked.

I was stumped. That sounded like a truthful answer to me. Was he admitting that he did suck on his own dick? My excitement grew and my curiosity heightened. "Yea, that's what yours tastes like, but what about the other guys you've sucked?" I continued, pushing him to the brink.

Danny got the "Fuck" of "Fuck off" out but was stopped in mid-sentence by the same beefy guy who once more bent to his ear, whispered something, released an inquisitive smile at me, then disappeared.

"Who is he?" I challenged again, feeling even more jealous that he might be one of Danny's lovers.

"Told you. He's just an oppo," he said sharply.

My investigative attack into Danny's sexuality was unexpectedly brought to a halt by a rumpus at a table beside the bar. Stood on its beer-swimming surface was a well-built, well-hung, well-pissed sailor. His bell-bottoms and briefs were down to his ankles, the seat of his pants sitting in a sea of slops. Toilet paper had been rolled into a sausage shape and was being stuffed into his bum hole.

Up went the voices of those around him in song. The toilet tissue was lit and the sailors began a war-like dance around him. It was one of us sailors favourite routines - The Dance of the Flaming Arseholes.

At that critical moment, just before his hairy arse went up in smoke, out flew the dregs of beer, splashing over his bare backside and dowsing the ever encroaching flames.

With the spectacle over, the group staggered drunkenly from the bar, singing at the top of their voices, linked arm around waist in a kind of conga dance. Cheers went up around the pub as the brave sailor who had bared all and barbecued his bum left the bar.

"Did that on board. Farted halfway through and nearly blew me balls off!" Danny laughed.

"Lucky it wasn't your cock. Been enough cooked sausage to feed the ship," I sniggered, continuing with my sexual onslaught.

Danny wasn't taking the bait anymore. "Remember our boxing match the first week of training?" he reminded, flexing his hidden biceps like a weight-lifter.

How could I forget. It was just a pity that the fight didn't take place until after we'd became friends, then perhaps he wouldn't have hit me so bloody hard.

"Remember! You broke my bloody nose, you sod!"

Danny broke into a fit of giggles. "You should have seen your face. Talk about tomato head!"

I could laugh about it now, but not then. I never was a fighting machine. I didn't join the navy for that. I joined for the shagging. But the navy loved to do that kind of thing. Get boys to bang the crap out of each other just to prove how macho they were.

I recall there were no rules in that fight. No weighing of bodies to make sure it was fair. No questions to discover if one opponent had the skills of a World Champion or an uncoordinated set of arms and legs, as I did. Yes, I was bigger and stronger than Danny. But he was faster.

Like some demon insect he flitted all around me. Then with a hammer-of-a-blow, which totally surprised me, he spread my nose over my face. I found myself sat on my arse, stars spinning in my head, blood oozing from my broken nose, Danny hovering over me eager to land the killer blow. Wisely, I stayed put.

Had it been a kiss and cuddle competition I'm sure I'd have won, because once my body had wrapped around his, even a Sumo wrestler wouldn't have got it off - it was the first time I'd seen Danny in his tight shorts!.

"You weren't so hot at judo, though," I declared in my defence.

"Right. But I did get you in that head-lock which you never got out of."

How naive of him. Surely Danny must have realised that when my head became jammed between his strong bare thighs, my mouth pressed into that massive bulge, my nose inhaling that musty crotch smell, no way was I going to fight him off. And that embrace provided me with nights of wanking fantasies the likes of which he could never imagine.

"Dave was pretty good at judo, though. Almost got his black belt," I reminded him.

"Poor old Mike wasn't. Almost got a broken neck!" Danny laughed.

"What about that lad, Winkle the Wanker? I've never known a guy toss off as much as he did. Remember, he broke his bloody arm during rugby. I was nearly sick when I heard it snap. All that bone and blood."

"Sure stopped him wanking!" Danny giggled, unsympathetically.

"So what ship did you end up on?" I asked, quickly changing the subject even though I'd raised it, the thought of broken bodies almost bringing my beer up.

"Ranger. Crap ship. Crap captain and officers as well. But the guys are good fun. Bounces like a bastard even when we're tied alongside. You?"

I lifted my cap from the spare seat and showed Danny my cap tally. "Tornado. Been down Portland on a work-up for four months. Christ, you don't want to go there! Talk about guys being pissed with power. Everyone thinks they're a bloody Admiral, even the Midshipman! Anyway, we're back in Pompey for a break. I think we're off to the Far East for nine months at the end of the year."

"Great! You'll lose your cherry there!" delighted Danny, bringing us back to my favourite subject.

"And what makes you think I haven't already?"

"Cos you're too fucking ugly for British birds. Even WRENS if they weren't all lesbians. But I reckon some foreign chick will let you shag her!"

"Hey, you white trash. What's all this racist crap! And you'd better take a paper bag on your first shag. Big cock or not!"

"Joke, Smudge! You know I'm not a racist. And I think you're lovely."

I blew Danny a kiss. "Think so!"

Danny pointed his muddle finger skyward. "Fuck off you bandit! And where the hell is Mike and Dave?"

"Don't you like my company anymore?" I asked. "And there's me saving my virginity for you all this time."

"You a virgin! You might not have stuffed a bird yet, but I bet your arse got shagged stupid the first day you stepped on board Tornado. Probably put your legs over your head before some butch stoker even had a chance to get your draws off!"

"I bet you got shagged before you even reached Ranger," I retaliated. "Oh, I forgot. You don't need to, do you? Then again, perhaps your dick's so big you can shove it up your own arse! Anyway, you jealous or something?"

"I wonder about you sometimes, Smudge. I bet you do like a bit of bum fun, don't you?"

"Who doesn't!" I truthfully answered, but winked and blew him a kiss, placing my hands on my hips to make a joke of it.

Why did I do that? It was the perfect moment to come out. I guess it was just the way it had to be. Put up the shields just in case a cruise missile came flying from his mouth. I was only too aware how a gay confession could be a bit of an animal to wrestle with, especially if the person on the receiving end wasn't ready for it.

I decided to bring the conversation back to sport, one of Danny's favourite pastimes. "What about Petty Officer Mann. Remember him?"

Danny shuffled uncomfortably in his seat, slurped a huge gulp of beer and drew heavily on his 555. "Course."

I sensed I'd touched on something meaningful, some powerful memory from our training which Danny might not have wanted to recall. I watched his face contort slightly when his thoughts flashed back to training, but there was still a smile as he waited for my inevitable question.

"Remember? That afternoon when we finished gym and he kept you back. You were gone for ages. What happened? You never did tell."

Danny's expression continued to swing from a serious smile to one holding some sensitive information which he didn't wish to reveal. "I remember," was all he returned with.

I continued to search his eyes and watch his mouth suck nervously on his cigarette, waiting for him to spill the beans, but he just laughed.

Petty Officer Mann, the senior Physical Training Instructor in training. How could either of us forget him?

And Mann was just that. A man. A massive, muscled black man! But a man with the gentlest, smoothest face I had ever seen. His tremendous, solid body had not a hair on it. That was, apart from beneath his arms. In those constantly sweaty, fresh-smelling hollows, was the only hair of his I was ever privileged to see - a tight knit of jet black curls. I guess the hair on his head would have been the same had it not been shaved in a typical marine crop. But his cock hair? Well, I couldn't comment. None of us boys ever saw it. But he saw ours. Our pubic hair. Our bums and bollocks and dicks. Our virgin bodies. Yes, he saw every inch of our nakedness when we showered before his watchful, and dare I think it, lustful gaze. And what a gaze he had. Eyes so incredibly large, and of the darkest of browns I had ever seen. In fact, it was as if they had no iris. Just two black marbles surrounded by a brilliant white.

At five foot eleven, he was a powerhouse. I have no doubt his prick was also a powerhouse, for it was packed like two pounds of salami into shorts which were so tight, they looked as if they'd split in two during each of his regular Karate routines.

I cannot say I fancied him, I was far to scared. I believe we all were - except for Danny. But it would have been impossible for a sexually frustrated, young trainee like myself not to be in awe of his beauty.

As I said, he was incredibly handsome - model handsome. Biceps as big as my thighs were pumped up on each of his arms and two mountain pecs, sporting rich brown nipple studs, protruded from his chest. Like ridges on a cliff face, his stomach muscles were so defined and strong I think I could have climbed them and they would have easily taken my weight.

Then there was his buttocks. Black guys have the most wonderful buttocks. His were no exception. Beautifully rounded and strong, they were built for burying a cock into. Sadly, his were as tight as a vice, protecting a prize many a guy would have dreamt of winning.

And to complete that vision of male excellence, two tree-trunk thighs enabled him to hold that impressive torso high above me - which he often did - as I regularly begged him for mercy for some cardinal sin I had committed on the sacred gym equipment he constantly tortured me with.

Yes, that was Petty Officer Mann, the PTI who's fate we left Danny with late that afternoon.

Deep in silent thought, Danny was remembering that day, recalling that he wasn't overly concerned as he hung from the wall-bars and watched the lads file out. It was a regular punishment for him, for his cockiness.

Knowing that he was brilliant at sport, he got away with almost everything. That afternoon, however, was the first time he'd been kept back.

The curtains were drawn and the doors locked by Mann as he circumnavigated the gym. Eventually only shafts of sunshine shining through the open skylights high in the ceiling above; several shafts slicing Danny's suspended shorts-clad body across his naked chest and bare legs.

Mann disappeared into his office. Moments later he returned, catching Danny craftily resting his feet on a lower bar in order to take some of the weight. "Feet!" he bellowed, although his voice did have a softness in its authority.

Danny dropped them below the bar, his biceps tightening as they re-took his weight.

Mann re-entered his office but quickly returned. Casually he strolled over to the youthful body suspended tantalisingly before him. Climbing up the wall-bars, he fastened Danny's wrist with a soft skipping rope, winding the length several times around an arm, taking it across Danny's chest, then doing the same to the other.

Danny's breathing increased and his heart pumped hard and fast.

This was different. This hadn't happened in previous punishments. This was totally unexpected. This was frightening!

Mann climbed down and grinned up at his young trainee's bound body. It wasn't an evil grin. Even so, it filled Danny with a good deal of apprehension. Beads of sweat trickled from his armpits and down the sides of his chest. For the first time his confidant cheekiness had deserted him and he couldn't think of anything to say, not even a joke.

"You're a cheeky little sod, aren't you?" grinned Mann with an unnerving seriousness.

"Suppose so, Sir!" Everyone more important than an ant was called Sir by us trainees.

"Guess we've got to teach you a lesson, then."

Danny gulped hard. "Suppose so, Sir!"

Mann stepped forward and slapped his palms together.

Danny flinched!

The two firm hands travelling up each of Danny's thighs were not expected, and his stomach muscles tightened. The entry beneath the legs of his shorts were definitely not expected, and he quickly raised his feet onto the bar in order to pull away; breathing rapidly as the searching palms pushed higher and eventually engulfed his cock and balls.

"What you doing!" spluttered from Danny's drying mouth.

"Silence!" was the stern reply he was rewarded with from the cunning face staring back at him.

He hadn't wanted it to happen, hadn't believed it could. But as the PTI's powerful hands caressed beneath his cotton shorts, Danny's cock gained in girth and length, and eventually protruded from the right leg of his short as it was teased and tugged downward.

Speedily, the PTI unfastened Danny's shorts, and with a swift tug they came over his thighs and calves, falling to the polished floor. Danny's cock sprang upward and outward like a flagpole on the side of a building!

"Oh, boy. What a beauty! I guessed you'd have a really big dick," Mann sang in praise of the appetising sex.

Danny couldn't help himself, and smiled proudly as he watched his cock thicken and throb with an undisciplined excitement. Lustfully, the PTI rolled the loose foreskin over the bulging head and began to tease the swelling shaft with licks and laps, then more hungrily mouth along the shaft.

Danny gasped! Never had anyone, apart from himself, touched his cock before. Never had anyone's mouth, apart from his own, sucked on it before. And never could he have imagined the incredible difference of sucking his own cock than that of having someone else suck it. And he was stunned into a blissful submissive silence!

Mesmerised, Danny watched as his cock was manipulated by Mann's mouth. Magnificently it manoeuvred over the head, then to halfway down the shaft, then with a single thrust right to the base. Danny squealed with delight, he couldn't help himself! Almost immediately spunk siphoned in spasms into Mann's luscious mouth as it was brought back to the head, the final jet squirting over the his lips as the cock's contents were pumped into his eager mouth.

"Naughty boy!" scolded Mann. "Naughty, naughty boy!"

Danny apologised. He had no idea why.

"I think I'll have to spank you for doing that to me. Don't you think so?"

"Yes, Sir!" whimpered Danny. Again, for the life of him, he didn't know why he said it. Also, he hadn't the faintest idea why he was being turned on so by this master/slave situation. In fact, although he'd just shot a week's come, his cock was rigid and ready to fire another round into that ravenous hot tunnel.

"So you think I should spank you, do you? Spank your virgin arse!" Mann growled.

"I think so," Danny whispered.

"What! You only THINK so!"

Danny remained silent.

"Well. Should I!" screamed Mann.

"Yes, SIR!" shouted Danny.

Mann bent and unfastened his laces. Danny looked helplessly down at him, his heart racing as he watched the plimsoll slip from the stocking foot. Had he agreed to something the consequences of which he had not contemplated? Pain being his uppermost in his mind!

Flashing a row of pearl white teeth, the threatening face of Mann smiled before him, his wide grin menacing. Danny winced as the plimsoll was slapped heavily against the pink palm of the PTI's immense hand. He could change his mind, couldn't he? Say, no!

Teasingly, Mann ran the canvass plimsoll over Danny's stiffening cock. Again it sprang rigid and upward. Again he was filled with a mixture of apprehension and longing. Then, out of his young mouth came a babble of unexpected words. "Spank me, Sir. Please spank me. Spank me good and hard!"

Mann released another cunning grin and slapped the pump smartly against his palm. Thwack! it echoed around the empty gym. Again Danny flinched!

Anticipating the next slap would land somewhere on his vulnerable body, Danny screwed his eyes tightly shut. But the next sound he heard wasn't slipper on soft skin but the plimsoll falling to the wooden floor. Cautiously he opened his eyes. The brown-eyed, grinning face was still below his, staring upward; holding some unknown secret, some unknown intention in its expression.

Danny glanced down at the empty hand which moments ago held the implement of punishment, now unfastening a pair of shorts. His excited gaze remained rivetted upon the zip as it was parted. His excitement increased. Was he to be the first, perhaps the only trainee, to discover the contents of Petty Officer Mann's pants?

Danny gasped loudly when the shorts dropped. Suddenly there it was! Huge and throbbing and magnificent, a waterfall of pre-come oozing from an eye as wide as a letter-box. Black and thick and long, Mann's cock began to grow and grow and grow. Would it ever stop growing? wondered Danny. More importantly, when it had stopped growing, what was Mann going to do with it!

FOUR

"Your round," Danny indicated, clinking a gold ring against an empty glass.

I hadn't noticed that ring before. He definitely hadn't worn one in training. Where did it come from? Rings were definitely not your normal, everyday gifts. Rings only came from special people. Did Danny have a boyfriend? Someone who cherished him and bought him presents. Again a strange jealousy came over me.

"Nice ring," I commented, but really wanting to ask who gave it to him.

Danny twisted the gold band thoughtfully. "Beer!" he demanded.

I guessed that that was the end of that interrogation. No matter, I could easily come back to it later when more booze had filled his belly and brain, and loosened his tongue even more. Come back, also, to Mann, who Danny had obviously given a good deal of silent thought to over the past few minutes, but had yet to comment upon.

"How about a short chaser?" I suggested, thinking a stronger beverage would get him talking.

"Beer's fine. Night's still a virgin."

"So, are you," I winked.

I made my way to the bar. Perhaps I was being unfair, pushing him like I was. But I wasn't trying to upset him, I just wanted to know what he was into sexually. More importantly, if I fitted into that plan.

Of course, I could move things along by blowing my own cover. Tell him of some of my own sexual encounters. Tell him about a dockyard worker who gave me a blow-job fifty foot up the mast - not quite your Mile High Club, but a damn good place to have sex. Or I could tell him about the seaman who shackled me to the anchor cable down in the cable locker and shagged me senseless. Christ, was that cable cold!

More sensibly, I could invent a hettie shag story and observe his reaction. See if he was turned on by it. See if he'd come up with one of his own. Or see if he'd just turn around and say outright that he preferred guys. Preferred me!

If I were really kind, I could just leave the matter alone.

"You queer, Danny?" was one of the questions which jumped into my head as I juggled two pints through an ocean of sailors and walked back to our table.

I sat down opposite Danny. I noticed he was still thoughtfully twisting his ring around his finger. I also noticed that it was on his marriage finger; not that that meant anything. Guys wore rings on any finger, whatever one suited their fancy.

I raised my glass. "To absent fiends."

"If they ever get here," Danny sulked.

"Well it was a long shot," I reasoned. "Any of us could be anywhere!"

"Suppose so," Danny agreed, and twisted the gold band thoughtfully again.

"Game of pool?" I suggested in an attempt to raise his spirits.

"Pool's for girls," he rejected.

"Not swimming pools," I laughed. "Remember, Dave?"

Danny spluttered a mouthful of beer over the table as he burst out laughing. "Christ, he went down like a stone!"

"Yeah! I was wondering which one of us was going to have to give him the kiss of life."

Danny raised his eyebrows in an accusing kind of way. "Mann would've done it!"

We sat for fifteen minutes supping our beer and shorts in virtual silence. More happy voices suddenly filled the air as sailors started on a round of regular sea-shanties.

"This old hat of mine, has seen some stormy weather..." the gruff and sometimes high-pitched voices went up around us.   Neither of us joined in and carried on with our flagging conversation. Why that should be, I wasn't sure. There must have been so much to tell one another. So much that had happened to ourselves in that year of separation. I guess, for my part, most of those interesting events had been sexual ones with other sailors. I would have dearly loved to impart a few to Danny.

"So what's it like in your Wireless Office?" Danny asked, bringing our conversation onto work, a subject I'd have rather he left on the ship. "Ours is pretty small and the equipment's vintage."

"You wouldn't believe it. After all that training to become a Sparks, they put me on the bloody flag-deck. I'm a Bunting Tosser now."

"You're a tosser alright, but it's not bunting that's for sure!" giggled Danny, bringing himself back into the spirit of things.

"The vicar's daughter, she was there.

Up to her usual tricks.

Sliding down the banisters

And landing on her tits...."

This time we both joined in, bellowing,

"Balls to your partner.

Arse against the wall.

If you've never been shagged on a Saturday night
Then you've never been shagged at all!"

It was my favourite singing routine and it took a degree of skill to make up comical rhymes. Often they would be so funny, the chorus went unheard, or even unsung.

"Wasn't Ranger in that exercise in the Irish Sea? You know, Shake Up?" I asked after our unharmonious rendition had ceased, trying to get Danny talking again.

"Shit, yes!" Danny exclaimed. "Cancelled it because of that force twelve. Fuck was I seasick!"

"Yeah, you lot were okay cos your skipper took you back in. Our bloody tosser - Actually he's a good skipper, really - sailed us right through and out the other side. Lost a cutter, we did. Rolled over forty-five degrees on one big bastard. I nearly went over the fucking side! Christ was that some storm!"

Danny shivered. "We lost a guy over the side. Searched for him for two days. He was a CPO. They reckoned he jumped cos he stole the mess funds. Serves him right the greedy bastard! I wish the whole bloody bunch would jump overboard. Officers, that is. I hate that fucking ship!"

"Cheer up, you miserable bastard. Mike and Dave will be here soon. I'm sure they don't want to meet a couple of pissed off pals."

"Pissed pals more like by the time they get here," Danny complained. "My round, isn't it?"

"Thought you'd never ask. I've been dry for five minutes. And don't you get fresh with any of those lovely marines whilst I'm having a piss. Remember, I've been saving myself for you!" I winked.

Danny stuck two fingers in the air and walked to the bar.

I heard whispers in the heads, coming from inside a cubicle. Cautiously, after I'd peed, I bent and looked under the door. Four bare legs, one pair incredibly hairy, the other pair smooth and young, greeted my eyes. My cock jarred excitedly!

Christ that was risky, I thought. Especially in a pub full of servicemen. I guess the poor buggers must have been desperate. It was possible one of them was a civilian, one pair of pants not being a uniform. That was something I liked about gay civilians, they were more brave when it came to having sex whenever they got the urge. At the end of the day what had they got to lose? They might get the piss taken out of them if caught. At worst, they might get a bashing if they happened upon the wrong sort of servicemen. Hastily, I exited and left them to it. Mind you, I wouldn't have minded being in there with them. If only to discover who they were.

Danny jumped up as I sat down. "Better make room for this."

"Shit," I whispered as he walked away, "I hope he doesn't catch them!"

He was out sooner than I expected, almost before he'd time to get in. "Couple of bandits in there," he announced, with some disgust.

"What the eye don't see..." I defended.

"Thought you'd say that, Smudge." was his only comment as he slurped a huge mouthful of beer, slopping some over his white front and staining it.

"Fuck! Now look what you've made me do!" he grunted.

"Something must have got you all excited," I teased.

Danny shook his head like he was calling me a pratt or something worse, stood and moved over to the fruit machine. I couldn't understand his mood swings. He never used to be so touchy in training.

No conversation passed between us after he'd plonked his beer on top of the machine, and I was left to my own company. Thus stranded, the brief encounter in the heads brought sex back into my thoughts and I wandered off into memories of my first sailor shag.

There were loads of guys on my ship who I fancied. Not all were Greek gods but many were, or bordering on it. The choice of men and youths was infinite. Stacked three deep in the showers in the mornings and evenings, they waited to cleanse their grimy bodies. Balls, arses, stiff and semi-stiff pricks openly on display. Bodies of every kind up for grabs.

Big guys with little dicks. Little guys with big dicks. Guys with normal-sized dicks. Guys with twisted dicks, veiny dicks, thick and thin dicks. Every kind of cock fantasy you'd ever wished for there for the taking. Problem was, which boys did and which boys didn't play?

Thus frustrated, there I was, stumped. A sex-starved, goggle-eyed, sexual neophyte with no idea of how to let my preferences be known without totally fucking up and being labelled a fairy for the rest of the cruise. But I needn't have fretted because I was soon to discover that like-minded, more experienced souls had a natural instinct for recognising young guys like me who were champing at the bit to suck on a dick, or have one rammed up their bum. And within a week of being on board cocks of all shapes and sizes were being thrust at me from every quarter.

Quite suddenly, I was spoilt for choice!

And so it was Paul's web I unwittingly wandered into early one morning as he welcomed me with open arms. And legs! Yes, Paul, my first playmate - who's prick was small, who's personality was big, and who's sexual prowess was paramount.

Gay - he wasn't. Married - he was. A sex machine - without question! If Paul thought something could be fucked, then he'd fuck it. And did he fuck me? On a daily basis we found some nook or cranny on board where we'd secret ourselves and he'd shag the arse off me.

Always equipped with condoms and lube, he banged me up against bulkheads, in the showers, in the heads, in small locker spaces barely big enough for both of us to fit. Regularly, his short, thick cock fired up my backside more times than the guns on the bow. But it was our first screw which was the most memorable.

It was the middle watch. Paul had been given the task of cleaning the showers. I'd been up on the flag deck in the pissing rain and wind, sending signals by Aldis lamp to ships bouncing about in the force eight gale. Frozen to the bone and sodden through, I ambled down aft for a hot shower to thaw me out before I bunked down.

An "OUT OF ORDER" notice greeted me on the shower door when I reached it - all notices were obeyed without question if you didn't want to be strung up by your bollocks. I thumped the door in disgust and began to head forward.

It was a pleasantly soft voice which called after me. "S'ok, kid. You can come in if you're quick."

I spun around. There stood Paul naked to the waist, bare footed and covered in bubbles up to his knees.

My first thought; his voice didn't suit his attractive, weather-beaten face.

My second thought; that cock of his - beautifully outlined through a pair of snug-fitting, wet, Hong Kong, silken shorts - looked a superb and a easy morsel to swallow.

My third thought; had he noticed my cock tenting my towel on receiving my second thought?

"Come on, kid. Quick, before someone sees you!"

I'm not sure if it was my imagination but the gap he provided when he opened the door to allow me to pass seemed pretty narrow. And his hand which hung crotch height and brushed against my cock as I entered, most surely could have been placed elsewhere.

"Thanks," I said, retrieving my towel from the deck, convinced that during our close encounter he'd magically unfastened it from my body.

"Use the end shower but don't pull the curtain, I've just cleaned them," he offered in a kind of order.

Having observed so much nakedness since the day I'd joined the navy, being seen nude no longer embarrassed me. But a little voice inside my head was telling me that this guy was actually banking on a good all-round view of my bollocks and dick. To be honest, having had no sex since Jake in the cornfield, I was actually pleased to be exhibiting myself.

Casually, I soaped my chest, arms and legs. Thoughtfully, he continued to mop the floor. I felt somewhat guilty that I was interrupting his chores, so I decided I'd better get on with it and quickly started on my cock. Gently, I lathered its thick length, but as usual with the cleansing of my private parts, the damn thing had a mind of its own and began to rise. Embarrassingly, it was almost up to half mast.

I glanced somewhat self-consciously over to my mopping friend. He appeared to be engrossed in his work. But then, just before I brought my attention back to the task at hand, I glimpsed his mirrored eyes focussed lustfully on my ever-increasing dick. Turning half in my direction, he left me in no doubt what I was supposed to see. Upright, clearly visible, solid and thick, his dick was pushing desperately against his soaked satin shorts.

"Nice to have a good shower after coming off," he smiled, then grinned craftily as he turned full frontal and observed my gaze drop from his cheerful face directly onto his broad cock.

It was the way he said "coming off" which made me desperately want him to drop his kit and flash his stiffened dick which was teasing me to the point of coming, but I decided to play it cool. "Sure is."

"You're a good looking kid, you know. I'm Paul,'he smiled, his words so soft and gentle, they seduced me like some sexual olive branch as he sexily sighed them.

"Ken," I smiled shyly, then turned away and began to soap my buttocks, drawing my palm invitingly into the hairless crevice. In my excitement, my cock bolted upright against my tummy, pointing invitingly toward my navel, not another drop of blood able to gain entry.

There was no doubt in my mind that I wanted him. No doubt, either, that I wanted him to be the first sailor to fuck me. Wanted this rugged-looking lad to take away my rear-end virginity.

His palm was unexpected as it stroked down my soapy spine, stopping at the crease of my buttocks. My cock twitched excitedly!

"Never guess what I've found?" he whispered seductively and confidently into my ear. "A rubber!"

Surprised by that information, I spun around to face him. Our cocks collided. I couldn't believe my eyes, he was bollock naked. His well-built body glistening. His dick proud and ready to perform! With the passion of a famished child I pulled him into the spray, wrapped my arms around his silken skin, frantically kissed his mouth, fell to my knees and began sucking his circumcised sex. The width filled my mouth but the length didn't. But I didn't mind, so grateful was I to be gorging on a cock.

Paul rubbed my recently-shaven head. "That's nice, kid. Been waiting a long time for that, have you?"

Mumbled moans of pleasure were all I responded with as I continued to swallow his appetising prick, stroke his large, loosely-hanging balls and rub his taught abdomen.

His tattooed forearm rubbed against my cheek. "Want me to fuck you?" he asked, lifting my chin and gently raising my face upward. I hadn't wanted to appear nervous, I wanted him to fuck me more than he could imagine, but somehow my body-language spoke differently.

"Your first fuck, eh?" he deduced, correctly. His expression compassionate but an obvious excitement hidden beneath.

"Mmmm," I nodded, my mouth still filled with cock.

Paul pulled me gently upward, lifting me by my armpits, bringing my smooth blushing face close to his stubbled one.

"A virgin, eh?" he delighted but not in a lecherous way. "S'ok, kid, I won't hurt you. But if you don't want fucking, you just carry on blowing me."

"I do!" I blurted. "But you'll stop if it hurts, won't you?"

Paul planted his succulent mouth onto mine and sucked my tongue into his whilst lovingly caressing my buttocks with both hands. "We'll take it nice and slow," he comforted, kissing my nose, forehead and eyes.

I gripped both our cocks and began rubbing them together. Although I was positive Paul wanted to get down to fucking, he allowed me to return to my knees and continue to mouth him.

"Ready?" he asked, just as I thought he was about to shoot his load.

The truthful answer to his question would have been that I wasn't - I was pretty damn scared - but deep inside I couldn't wait for him to be inside of me, fucking me, loving me.

I stood, kissed him once, released a smile, turned and offered him my virgin buttocks. Tenderly he caressed my arse, torturing me with his touch. Then, soaping both palms, he slid one between my buttock cheeks and the other over my cock. The sensation was electric and I could have easily come the moment he began pumping my prick with one set of fingers and probing my backside with the other.

Biting into the nape of my neck, maybe to distract me from the oncoming pain, he plunged two fingers deep into my tight hole. I held a yelp of pain behind my teeth as they went knuckle deep!

"Is that okay?" he tenderly whispered, nibbling affectionately on my earlobe. Words had deserted me and all I could do was sigh.

Soon his fingers were slipping easily from finger-tip to second knuckle, soaping my hole, lubricating it for a painless entry. I whimpered as they worked faster and deeper whilst he continued to pump my cock and kiss my mouth. "Fuck me, Paul," I pleaded.

Paul needed no encouragement. He'd been breathing excitedly for some time. With a movement so swift I hardly noticed, his fingers slipped out and were replaced by the throbbing head of his cock, spreading my hole wide apart. A cry of pain rushed from my mouth!

Paul stopped his penetration. "You Okay!"

"Don't stop!" I begged. "Go all the way!" It seemed the easiest choice - get the pain over in one thrust.

Paul obliged and buried the remainder of his sex, pubic deep, into my arse. My next muffled cry was the last complaint he heard.

Warm spray cascaded over both our heads, running down our excited bodies between my back and his chest. I could feel his pelvis and wet cock-hair slapping against my relaxing buttocks as he thrust and withdrew. My squeals of delight echoed around the cubicle, far too loudly. Paul placed his palm over my panting mouth to muffle them.

"Like that, kid? Like me fucking you?"

"God, yes!" I gushed, biting and sucking frantically on his thick fingers.

Taking the soap, Paul lathered his palms, rubbing them over my cropped head then over my pecs, tweaking my nipple-studs hard. Another delighted screech escaped my mouth as he simultaneously bit into the nape of my neck.

"You ready to come?" he breathlessly asked as his muscled buttocks flexed and drove his cock deep into my virgin hole.

To be honest, again I could have come seconds after his thick dick had stretched me wide apart, but I wanted him to continue fucking me until the spray dissolved our bodies.

"Not yet!" I gushed as he sank his cock to the base.

Paul quickened his pace, furiously biting my shoulders and pumping my soapy dick.

"Yes, Paul!" I squealed. "Fuck me hard!"

My chest slammed against the Formica bulkhead as Paul drove fast and deep. "I'm coming, kid," he thrilled, pumping my cock vigorously, my foreskin slipping rapidly over the sensitive bud. My legs trembling so badly they almost gave way, such was the sensation zipping from my head to my toes.

"Shit, kid," he called out as he rammed his cock full in and sent a bounty of come into the condom.

"Jesus, Paul!" I cried, as my own jet spurted in a single stream against the Formica bulkhead and was washed away by the hot spray.

"Boy, that was some fuck," delighted Paul, hugging his chest into my back.

"Wasn't it just!" was all my panting breath was capable of.

Paul turned me around, bent and licked my dick, then kissed me. "Tell you something, kid. You're gonna have a lot of fun on this ship."

"Reckon so?" I laughed.

"Take my word for it!" he grinned, slapping my arse.

FIVE

My cock was stiff again. Would it ever go down!

Danny remained beside the fruit-machine, feeding coins into it's greedy mouth. His cute arse still begging me to be bouncing upon it, begging me to be licking it, just begging me. Being in his presence was driving me crazy! That said, something was wrong. Something was bugging the little bugger. If only I knew what.

I continued to torment myself with his cute arse as he played the machine, bringing it into every conceivable scenario I could muster. I called over and asked him if he was winning, but he barely acknowledged me. I guessed my worst fears had come true. Over the past year he'd changed. Become more aggressive, more intolerant. In training I could have camped it up until the cows came home. Not anymore, it would seem.

My mind worked overtime thinking about the lad who had interrupted our conversation, and that ring. Danny's sparkling, gold ring. What did it all mean? What the hell was going on!

Continually, he had asked where Dave and Mike were. Had he finally realised I was gay, and hated it? Maybe hated me! He certainly appeared to have little sympathy for the lads having it away in the heads. I couldn't think of a time when we were in training when that would have bothered him. Not even when the boys got caught did he bat an eyelid. I don't believe he even comment upon it. Danny had definitely changed.

I decided, I would make no more advances toward him. No more innuendoes. My heart sank!

Again I asked if he was winning. Again he continued to feed the hungry mouth and ignore me. Locked in thought or hypnotised by the flashing lights. Occasionally a clatter of coins clinking into the empty tray did bring life into his miserable body. Already I could see the remainder of the evening turning into a nightmare. Mike and Dave not turning up and leaving the two of us with our separate thoughts. Me thinking I'd love to be in bed with Danny. Danny wishing I'd piss off and play the faggot with someone else.

I prayed he'd would win the jackpot!

Bollocks, I suddenly decided. If he was going to stay on his own and play the misery guts, then I sure as hell wasn't going to sit there like some gooseberry on a date. I was going to search out a shag!

The pool table was vacant for a change, only a skin slamming the white into various pockets. I trotted over and asked if he wanted to play with me. I'm not sure whether he got my gist, but he dissolved me with a red hot smile when he agreed.

He was pretty crap at pool, but he wasn't crap looking. About seventeen, I reckoned. Already, I'd undressed him. God, did he look gorgeous naked! His curly locks were fair rather than blond. And his body was incredibly thin. I'd already thought I would need to feed him before I fucked him. Put some more meat on him just in case I broke him in two.

Lustfully, I dwelt on his buttocks as he bent before me. I could see they were begging me to bang my dick between them. They were certainly more interesting than the game.

I played as badly as I could, so as to make his abominable play look better. It didn't help.

"How about leaving this bar and coming down the sea front for a fucking good shag or blow-job?" was what I desperately wanted to ask him. Instead, I threw a sexual joke and told him that had the pockets got some hair around them, then he'd probably get his balls home more often. I know it was a pathetic old chestnut. But I guessed, being so young, he might not have heard it before. Anyway, he did laugh, wounding me with his broad smile.

By now I'd almost forgotten I was here with Danny, so absorbed in beauty was I. Already I was planning the best location to lure the lad into if I was given the green light. Danny didn't appear to be concerned at my absence and continued to feed his hungry friend. I wondered if he'd glanced across at me when I wasn't looking. Thinking I was some perverted, sailor slut corrupting an innocent skin. I guess if he had, then he was right. Sex for me was a difficult thing to resist if on offer.

Remarkably, I managed to conjure a black ball game, purposefully missing several easy shots which were jeered at by drunken sea dads, who had now placed their names on the waiting list. I don't have to tell you why?

I had also managed to manipulate the lad's name from his mostly tight lips. Succulent sucking lips, I might add! Zak was what he'd returned with, stabbing it into my groin like some sexual dagger.

Just to save face, I slammed the black deep into the pocket, winning the game.

I decided it was time to make my move and was just about to slay Zak with a request for him to join our table, when up pops this tart - from below the floorboards, I think - and flashes her enormous tits in his angelic face. Zak beamed delightfully, wounding me again as he thanks me for the game and is dragged away. My heart sank and my cock stopped twitching.

"She's going to eat you alive, kid. Suck you in and blow you out in bubbles!" was my whispered, jealous comment as her huge arse and body moved through the doorway, pushing his boyish one before her.

"I wish I was a girl on the game!" was my final insult to myself.

I turned to play the next guy chalked on the board but changed my mind and moved my sexually frustrated body back beside Danny's, ready to torture myself yet again. Almost reluctantly I plonked myself down, staring feebly and wantingly into his arse.

The night was going rapidly down the toilet.

I decided, I would have to come clean and clear the air. Tell Danny I was gay. Not for his sake. For my own. I was torturing myself!

Danny glanced over his shoulder checking if I was okay, smiled, then went back to playing the machine. As he reached for his pint, he caught sight of one of the many photographs decorating the wall. One was of a group of boy-sailors dressed in white shorts and shirts, sat beneath the wall-bars of the very same gym we had trained in. In an instant Danny was back in the gym, tied to the wall-bars!

Mann brought his large hand around the girth of his cock and pulled the foreskin down, revealing the bulbous purple head. Several times he ran it back and forth over the bud, working the pre-come around. Danny's eyes danced excitedly over the thick sex as he witnessed it swell and seep yet more silvery semen from the eye. Still he couldn't believe he was being stimulated so by the sight of Mann's cock; his own throbbing in sympathy.

Mann grinned and slapped his cock above his navel. "Ready for this, boy?"

Danny licked his lips subconsciously, his cock twitching in anticipation. "Yes, Sir!" he barked.

Mann began to ascend the frame, stopping as their cocks met, then began gyrating his hips and rubbing his massive sex into Danny's. Glancing between the formidable thighs, one on either side of his, Danny had thought his own cock was huge. Not anymore! Only now, close too, could his feasting eyes appreciate just how big the cock really was!

Mann grinned wickedly when he caught Danny's lustful gaze. "Like my big dick, boy?" .

"Yes, Sir!" enthused Danny, still surprising himself but knowing it was the truth.

Mann climbed ever upward but stopped again, his hardened biceps either side of Danny's head taking his weight. He began to massage his heavy black dick powerfully into Danny's naked chest. Danny breathed in the heady scent of Mann's crotch and lowered his head, impatient and desperate for the strong sex to reach his mouth as it was brought higher. The massive dick trailed strands of pre-come over his chest and on underside of his chin as it was brought ever higher.

"Fuck my face," Danny pleaded.

"Fuck my face, Sir!" corrected Mann with a slap across his trainee's cheek.

"Sir! Please!" begged Danny, stretching his neck and lowering his head in a desperate attempt to reach the gigantic sex.

Mann was teasing for sure, temptingly bringing his dick close to Danny's mouth then pulling away. Then, just when Danny's lips had managed to part over the dribbling bud and began to savour and suck, Mann pulled away and climbed back down, bringing their faces together again.

The force with which the PTI's tongue was driven down his throat almost caused Danny to gag - the long, soft flesh almost as large as a young lad's cock. Rapidly it ran over Danny's teeth and wrapped around his tongue, then darted several times toward his tonsils. Passionately Danny sucked on the succulent member, slipping his own small tongue into Mann's mouth whenever possible. Mann reciprocated, savouring Danny's with so much force he almost sucked it from his head.

Gasping and dribbling spittle, once more Danny begged for the huge cock. Again, slowly and deliberately, Mann climbed the frame and brought it close to Danny's pleading mouth. But still he didn't ram it home.

Whimpering now like a wanting child, his own cock solid and bursting pre-come, Danny almost screamed for Mann's sex! This time Mann obliged but only half of the thick cock was all he gave, still continuing to tease and tempt Danny.

"You want my dick that badly, boy" he tormented.

Danny didn't speak, his tongue lavishing all that it could reach, lapping away silver pre-come, reaching out for the defined ridge below the bud and darting deeply into the moist eye, desperate for the whole length.

"Naughty boy like you, you don't deserve it!" scolded Mann, pulling away again.

Danny opened his mouth to scream another plea. Mann thrust forward and plunged his prick halfway into the begging mouth. Danny's lips parted wide as they accepted its girth. Almost immediately, he sank his teeth into the rigid flesh. No way was Mann going to take it from him this time!

Mann yelped and his body jarred as the teeth sank into his cock. "Want it that bad do you, boy?" he laughed.

Danny stared childlike up at him but didn't speak, but continued to gently grip the shaft and lap upon it greedily. Excited to the point of hysteria, his dick jettisoned a spurt of spunk. Splat! it sounded as it struck the gym floor.

"So long as you're sure," Mann grinned, then bent and twisted Danny's nipple.

Danny's mouth gaped open in a sudden yelp of pain! Instantly the gigantic cock was thrust forward. Down it shot in one swift movement past his tonsils and deep into his hot throat.

"It's all yours, boy!" Mann roared wickedly.

Danny gulped hard and couldn't breath as the pubic bush met his upper lip and nose. He could feel the muscles of his throat contracting in spasms over the bulbous head as he swallowed. His eyes began to water.

Although he was gagging with such a quantity of cock to consume, Danny began to move his head back and forth, bringing the bulging bud to his tonsils then plunging his lips back to the cock hair.

Mann grunted and groaned with the pleasure, excited by his trainee's face thrusting down the length of his cock. "Boy, you're a born cock-sucker," he praised.

Danny continued to gorge gluttonously on the huge black shaft, desperate for Mann's spunk to jettison and swirl into his mouth. Frantically he fought his arms against the rope, eager to free them and engulf the flexing buttock-mounds which were forcing the fattened cock further and further into his throat. Again Danny couldn't help himself and a huge dollop of come spat from his cock and hit the gym floor.

Without any warning or sound from Mann, and just as Danny had withdrawn back to the cock-head, the mammoth prick exploded! Danny gulped hard as a monumental amount of come erupted from the colossal cock and into his mouth. Simultaneously, his own dick burst forth, showering the floor in a series of sensational spurts. In an almighty manly gasp, the withheld breath rushed from Mann's mouth. And with a final determined thrust, he sent his heavy cock far into the depths of Danny's throat, discharging the remaining spunk. Once again Danny gulped hard, his own cock continuing to spew a river of come as he gratefully savoured the last of the delicious juices, eager to swallow every morsel.

Mann grinned wickedly, slapping his sticky dick against Danny's face and wiping the head against the lips. "That's round one," he tormented.

Danny licked away the last droplets of come from around his lips, glancing curiously up at him, a new wave of apprehension and excitement sweeping throughout his vulnerable body.

Sweat streaming in rivers form his body, Mann climbed down from the frame, unwinding the rope from wrists and arms as he descended. The red marks from being restrained were clearly visible. Gripping Danny around the back of the neck, he led him into an adjoining room where vaulting boxes and other gym paraphernalia were stored.

"Up on the box," he ordered.

Without questioning the command, Danny sprang onto the equipment and sat facing him, a wary expression on his face.

"Lying face down!" commanded the PTI.

Danny threw his body across the length of the brown leather top. Swiftly the PTI grabbed his ankles, dragging him backward until his cock swung level with an open handgrip, his arse bent invitingly over the edge.

"Don't move!" Mann commanded and walked into his office.

Danny remained silent and still, studying the implements the PTI tortured his boys with - pummel horse and the like.

Moments later Mann returned. In one hand he held condoms and lube, in the other a solitary plimsoll. "You're a damn good sucker of cocks," he praised, "but let's see if you fuck as good!"

Danny gulped hard and his buttock cheeks clenched tightly together. A wave of apprehension sweeping over him. Yes, to suck on that large prick had filled him with an excitement he'd never known before. And to have come in Mann's mouth and him in his was a thrill the likes of which he'd love to experience again at the soonest opportunity. But the imminent act looming over him was not one he'd been anticipating, or one he was likely to enjoy. The PTI's prick was dangerously large. There could only be one outcome. PAIN!

Mann squeezed the virgin cheeks. Danny pulled them tightly together! "Guess we've got to get your cute little arse to relax," he grinned.

Danny swivelled his head toward the tormenting face, catching sight of a plimsoll in flight. Screwing his face into a grimace, he awaited contact. Thwack! the rubber sole smacked against his right cheek. Thwack! it struck upon his left. Thwack! yet again as it struck both.

"Shit!" screamed Danny as yet more blows struck, bringing both buttock cheeks into a crimson flush.

"Relaxed now!" Mann thundered.

"Yes," Danny almost cried, tears beginning to sparkle his eyes.

"Yes, WHAT!" shouted Mann, sending yet another blow perilously close to Danny's exposed balls.

"Yes, Sir!" yelled Danny at the top of his voice.

"Good boy," Mann rewarded. Danny thinking what a strange thing for him to say.

Relieved that the punishment had ceased, Danny reached back and stroked his reddened cheeks. They felt hot under his soft palm. If getting fucked was less painful than that, perhaps it wouldn't be so bad after all, he considered.

It was such a pleasant surprise. Totally unexpected. Wonderfully enjoyable. Instead of a thick cock plundering his passage, Mann's tongue - that same delicious tongue which moments ago was in Danny's mouth - now foraged deep into his hole, darting delightfully into its musty darkness.

Danny's cock bolted upright!

For a few minutes Mann sucked on the young, hairless balls, tenderly rubbing his palms around the fiery buttocks. Steadily the soft balls rose and fell inside his mouth. Danny daringly reached backward and gripped the shaven head, pulling the working face deeper. It was the first time he'd touched Mann and he was a little apprehensive. Mann, however, didn't appear to mind and continued rimming the youthful backside.

The lubrication came next. It felt cold as it replaced the hot tongue. That in turn was followed by a thick finger which probed his hole, causing Danny to wince. A second and then a third finger joined the first but the painful feeling quickly subsided and he soon found himself arching eagerly backward on each of Mann's explorations.

With the polished dexterity of a surgeon, Mann worked deeper into the virgin hole, deftly pushing and probing. His fingers touched a sensitive spot just inside the sphincter. Danny's brain exploded and his cock jarred upward. His whole body erupting in spasms of electrified pleasure.

Writhing excitedly, Danny wriggled backward onto the working digits. Again his cock was dribbling profusely, the silver strands streaming down the side of the wooden box. This was not what he'd expected. This was fantastic! This was sensational!

It was the removal of the fingers which caused Danny to moan in disapproval, so enjoyable were they. But that was soon replaced by ecstatic, joyful cries when Mann pushed a springboard up against the box, planted his bare feet at the head and drove his cock deliberately deep into the virgin arse.

Danny's insides exploded in fire, the brilliant sensation sending his eyes rolling upward and his head spinning. "Fuck me, Sir. Fuck me good and hard!" he encouraged.

That was no problem for this PTI. He could do a hundred press-up's in minutes. Press-up's into a young guy's arse? He could do those until he dropped!

"You like getting fucked, eh?" asked Mann. "Guess we'd better make your first time something to remember."

Groans of delight and approval emitted from Danny as Mann changed gear and sent his dick pounding rapidly from head to hilt, his large balls slapping against his trainee's legs. Urgently Danny reached for his own cock, desperate to pump it at the same time. Mann got there first and with several explosive movements brought it to the brink. Danny shoved his arse smartly backward, ensuring he had every millimetre of the thick black cock constantly pummelling his backside.

Their breathing took on an air of desperation as each became increasingly possessed with the pleasure of fucking. Come in both cocks was already climbing upward. Danny's poised at the tip and ready to erupt at any moment. Mann continued to pump his trainee's prick, ready for his own climax.

The box began to rattle, such was the ferocity of their fucking. Both gripped tightly to steady themselves, Danny on the side of the box, Mann on Danny's hips.

"Yes! Oh, yes!" Danny squealed in encouragement as the massive cock hammered home.

It was to be the PTI's penultimate thrusts which were the most sensational, pulling his cock completely out from Danny and plunging it fiercely back into the quivering hole. But on his final penetration, instead of tossing his trainee, he grabbed the youthful cock and pushed it through the hand-grip on the box. Danny went delirious with excitement. There could be no mistaking where his cock had disappeared. It had vanished inside a hot mouth!

Unbeknown to him, hidden in the box was a youth. Another sexual prisoner of Mann's. Another trainee. Lustfully the glorious mouth lavished on his cock, sucking it furiously. Mann, knowing who was hidden there, cried out, "Shoot, boy! Fill that pretty face with spunk!"

A whimper of excited anticipation escaped from inside the wooden prison, the owner's mouth working faster and deeper in response to Mann's command. Without another word of encouragement needed, Danny thrust backward onto Mann's massive cock and forward into the sucking mouth. "I'm coming. Sir, I'm coming!" he squealed.

Down went the prisoner's mouth to the base of Danny's dick. Up went Mann's cock to the hilt in Danny's hole. Out shot stream after stream of thick come into the prisoner's ravenous mouth. Out shot another into Danny's greasy arse and was captured by the rubber. Out from the box emitted the final howl of pleasure as the captive swallowed an ocean of spunk, delivering his own onto the gym floor.

<u>SIX</u>

Danny was so engrossed in losing money, I lost myself with thoughts of Mike as we waited for him to show. I wondered how he had got on since we went our separate ways, and if that angelic face of his still blushed red on every awkward or sensitive situation. I was often amazed that it did. Being of mixed race, you wouldn't think he would show a blush, but he did.

I have to say, that if any of the lads were gay, then Mike was the most likely candidate. Seldom, when any of us were inventing hettie shag stories, or doing the 'look at the tits on her' kind of thing when a dirty mag materialised in the mess, did Mike comment.

I cannot say that I fancied him more than I did Danny, but he was only a short head away on that finishing line. I guess it was Danny's height and athletic body which gave him that small lead. But Mike's glorious, caramel-coloured skin certainly sent delightful shivers down my spine on more occasions than I would care to admit.

The same height as Dave, around five ten, he was also slim and hairless over chest, arms and legs. But with his mixed race, he had those fantastic tight black curls under arms and poised prettily over his long thin prick. And that prick wasn't bad either, though nowhere near as big and thick as Danny's. Even so, I would have gladly slurped along its length and brought yet another flush upon his cheeks, but this time one of joy and satisfaction.

Of course, the other wonderful, more important part of his anatomy which excited me was his fantastic bum. It was even more delightful than Danny's. Being of mixed race, it was like most other black bums, perfectly rounded. I also hoped it was a virgin bum.

I recall, there was a time I got really close to it, for longer than I ever could when we larked about or played rugby. It was the only time we were allowed beyond the perimeter fencing. It was during our final week of training. For the first time ever we were told that we could have Saturday and Sunday off. And if we wanted to, we could go beyond the boundary fence. Go hiking.

We were sat in the mess deck, the four of us, glumly glancing across at one another. Mike and Dave were playing cards - snap, I think. About the limit of their intelligence. Danny, beautiful Danny, was reading a raunchy book, occasionally stroking his dick, albeit subconsciously. I'm laid on my bunk, mind wandering over this and that. THAT being mostly of what it would be like to suck on Danny's huge cock!

"Come on you lot, let's do something. Danny, let's walk around the camp. Anything!" I suggested.

Grumbles greeted my enthusiasm, along with 'No money' groans.

I could see it was going to take some sure-fire plan to get the lads off their backsides. "Christ, we gonna sit in this bloody mess deck all weekend?" I attacked. "We can still do stuff without no money."

"What?" was the duet reply from Mike and Dave.

"I'm reading," the whisper from Danny.

I jumped from my bunk and tossed a rolled up tissue over to Danny. "Here, you might need this. I'm not staying in this dump with you miserable buggers any longer."

"Where you going, Smudge?" Danny asked, pulling the tissue flat and inspecting it as if wondering whether I'd used it to wipe my cock last night.

"Going for a hike!"

A twinkle of enthusiasm sparkled in Danny's eyes, another in my groin as thoughts of him bedded down in a tent with me and huddling close to my body sprang to mind.

"Well?" I urged.

Danny slung his book inside of his locker and jumped up. "I'm game, Smudge," he said.

I was suddenly filled with excitement and my voice almost trembled when I telephoned the Stores Petty Officer to reserve our gear, imagining Danny and myself in the countryside together - larking, walking, singing and hopefully shagging!

I could dream, couldn't I?

We kitted ourselves out in our Number 8's - our working clothes - blue shirt, darker blue trousers, studded black boots, green gaiters and comforters. Although it was sunny, as with all things in the navy there was a dress code. For hiking our comforters - blue scarfs - would replace our caps and would be folded in two and turned inside out to form a woolly hat. Thus dressed, we would look presentable for any public or officers who happened upon us.

"Remember," we were constantly told, "you are still in the navy wherever you are."

How could we ever forget!

"Hang on. We're coming!" was not the duet of voices I wished to hear, and I'm sure Danny's jaw didn't drop as low as mine, or that he had been thinking, as I was, that coming was what we had in mind. But together. Alone!

"Sure," I said, trying desperately not to sound disappointed - did I mean angry? After all, we were all mates and we would have fun together. But fun of the sexual, frolicking kind? I doubted it. Then again, that was only my randy thoughts and most likely not any of the lads.

Mike and Dave were soon kitted up - sailors can dress in seconds - and the four of us were heading across the barracks.

An over-enthusiastic stores Petty Officer, excited by our adventurous spirit, or by us, went over the rules, our supplies and a whole host of other nonsense before letting us go. He was far too camp for my liking. We had a good giggle about that once out of his clutches.

Once free of the camp, we climbed the first hill toward the main road, planning to hitch a lift to our starting point. I had managed to cool my anger and disappointment that Mike and Dave were tagging along, my new found excitement brought about by Danny's bottom bouncing buoyantly before me.

There was something erotic about Danny. The way he dressed. The way he walked. And, of course, his looks. Most sailors, definitely me, resembled a sack of spuds in our working clothes, but not Danny. His trousers and shirt fitted him perfectly, hugging tightly against his fit body, his buttock cheeks clamped so tightly together he could have placed a cigarette paper between them and held it there without effort. I often wondered whether he had a lustful admirer in the stores - maybe the same Petty Officer who had sent us on our way - who crafted his kit, made to measure, purposefully to torment and tease us. To torture sex-hungry boys like me!

"Geddy-up, Danny," I encouraged, giving myself and excuse to slap his biteable bum.

"Tart!" smiled Danny, "I reckon you're a bandit, Smudge," he stated - correctly.

"Course," I laughed, and grabbed a handful of buttock.

Mike and Dave were bowling along up ahead, almost marching. It's funny but we always seemed to march. Habit, I guess.

"What's the rush!" shouted Danny. They didn't even look back and continued stride for stride, almost hand in hand.

"Let's beat them," I suggested, nudging Danny and edging him on. A boy-like excitement surfacing within me.

We slung a silent left then galloped away up a side street, boots clomping on the concrete, back-packs slapping our shoulders, giggling like a couple of schoolgirls. A good three hundred yards and we slung a right, cutting them off at the brow of the hill. Puffing slightly, we plonked our bums on a grass verge, lit fags and waited.

Mike and Dave reached us but marched by, not even noticing we were there.

"Going somewhere, sailor?" Danny called out, jumping to his feet and putting his hands on his hips. "Want to take me along?"

The boys swung about. "Where the fuck did you two come from?" they said in stereo. I was positive they must have been twins in a previous life.

"You two been shagging, or something? We've been here ages!" I teased.

"You bet," they answered together.

We reached the main road, at least a road with traffic, and raised our thumbs at passing cars and lorries. Hopefully, our lift wouldn't come by way of an officer or higher rank from our barracks. They could be pretty cunning, ready to trap spirited sailors and report them for antics innocently confessed.

Ten minutes passed and still no lift.

"Better roll up your trouser leg, Smudge. It'll take a tart like you to get us a lift!" sarked Danny.

"Just bend over and wiggle your arse. We'll probably get three lorries parked up there in no time," I retaliated.

"A double-decker bus and all the passengers," Dave threw in, he being slightly better at playful banter than Mike, who was clearly straining his brow, desperately trying to think of a suitable slanderous statement.

Our lift came by the way of a farm-hand type - brown locks, blue eyes, legs like logs and hairy arms displayed beneath rolled-up sleeves. Mike and Dave pushed Danny and myself aside as they climbed into his cab, relegating us to the open back.

During our four mile journey, I noticed the hunk wrestling with attempted conversations, and caught his eyes several times in the rear view mirror searching mine.

Danny unfurled the Ordnance Survey map and laid it on his lap, calling me close to examine our intended route. It was a must for him - taking charge. I suspected he would zip through the ranks. Always reading. Always top of the class. Sadly, always unavailable.

I slid my finger over his to the spot he was indicating. He didn't seem to mind or notice that it was an intimate gesture. And even when the brakes of the truck were suddenly slammed on to avoid some wild animal, and I wrapped my body around his claiming that he'd saved me from certain death, did he flinch. How much of a tart did he want me to be before he gave in, before he gave me some encouragement?

I allowed my body to remain close to his, absorbing his body heat, absorbing whatever my imagination could draw from it.

The driver ditched us at the disused railway station we were aiming for, receiving a four way thanks and a packet of fags for his trouble. He looked pretty pissed off, though. And I felt his wink at me indicated that he'd rather have had Danny or myself sat up front. Sat on his lap!

"Nice bloke," I nodded to Danny.

"Bandit," was Danny's one word reply. I wasn't sure whether he meant me!

Mike flinched at that remark and I could see his mouth opening for a reply in the driver's defence, but he said nothing. Dave grunted, unconcerned.

There was no way around the railway station onto the track. Dave solved that problem by kicking the door open. Mike did have a go but we all moved back, unsure where that long leg of his, which couldn't kick a football, would land. Whether he'd break it and we'd be heading back in an ambulance.

We did a quick scan of the map and had an argument of how to read it and work the compass. Well, none of us were particularly good at this stuff. Let's face it, when you are at sea there's only sea!

Although we'd set off late, ten miles was the day's agreed hike. Our target was to be a row of pylons marching over the countryside. And beyond those, about a mile on, a farm. Plan was to bed down overnight, legally or illegally, in the farmer's barn.

Danny, self-appointed navigator, gathered us around and pinpointed our position on the map.

"Are your sure?" were the doubting words which slipped from Mike's mouth.

Kind of confident that Danny did know what he was doing, we began to our trek over the railway sleepers and toward our destination.

"When was your first time, Smudge?" asked Dave. Sex was never far from his thoughts.

So it was going to be one of those bonding, let's get intimate about our sex lives kind of marches. But did he mean with a boy or girl? I wondered.

"When I was twelve," I boastfully lied.

"Twelve!" from all three.

"Yep!"

The boys stopped and stared at me. "Keep walking!" I urged, not wanting interrogative faces staring at me.

"How old was she, then? Ten?" quizzed Danny.

"Sixteen," I continued to lie. "My cousin."

"Your cousin!" all three again, and with even more excitement from Dave.

"Yeah. When my uncle and aunt was out one day, she dragged me up to their bedroom and we did it. I thought she was putting it up her bum," I laughed.

"Bet you'd have liked that better!" giggled Danny.

"Christ, your cousin! Twelve!" Dave amazed.

I noticed his cock begin to bulge!

"You couldn't have come and your dick would have been too small," deduced Mike.

"Still the same size!" Danny threw in.

"Been peeking you pervert?" I parried.

"So what was it like?" Dave more eager to get to the nitty gritty, his cock now solid down his right thigh.

"It was incredible. Tickled like fuck towards the end and I had to ask her to stop. But she wouldn't and kept going until she shivered all over and her big tits wobbled like crazy."

"Fuck!" shouted Dave. I thought his cock was about to burst from his pants, and I'm sure I could see a wet patch developing.

"Was it just the once?" Froth was forming around Dave's mouth as he asked for more information.

"Nope. Did it every Saturday. 'Til I was thirteen. 'Til I could come."

"You can come!" laughed Danny.

"Okay, donkey dick. When was your first time?" I asked.

Danny's face flushed bright. He wasn't expecting his turn to come so soon, if at all.

"Well?" I pushed.

Danny pulled the map from his rucksack. "Better check our bearings."

"Well?" repeated Mike and Dave.

Danny's face was now brighter than the red underpants he was illegally wearing!

His first, he reluctantly revealed, was in the back seat of his Dad's car. It was brilliant. He came loads. He sucked on her tits all the way through. She loved it and wanted it again and again. They did it five times.

We knew it was a load of crap but refrained from laughing. I'm sure I'd read the book myself. Maybe the very one he'd been reading before we left. I suspected Danny was a virgin!

Because we loved him dearly, we didn't say a word. In fact Dave was enjoying it so much, he scrambled behind a bush for an extremely long pee.

We continued to trudge the track whilst Mike broke into his losing his virginity story.

"Do you hear that?" asked Dave, relieving Mike from his obvious embarrassment.

"What?" I asked.

"It sounds like a... TRAIN!" yelled Danny.

A couple of ear-splitting blasts on a horn saw our party divided in two - Dave and Mike rolling down one bank, Danny and myself down the other.

A locomotive sailed by, pulling a snake of goods wagons.

Dave's head appeared over the bank. "Disused railway line, eh!" he pointed accusingly at Danny, pulling a variety of foliage from his hair and rubbing his nettle burnt hands.

"Whoops," giggled Danny.

Our giggles quickly changed to all out laughter when Mike's bedraggled body bounded into view. By the sweet aroma wafting over the rise, he had landed in cow pats!

"Shit your pants, Mike?" I roared with laughter.

Danny grabbed me around the waist and fell into a heap of giggles, rolling us back down the bank. Mike discarded his rucksack and headed straight for him. Dave rugby-tackled Mike, bringing him down before he reached us. A brief argument broke out but Mike quickly saw the funny side of things after we'd cleaned him off.

A knew buoyancy was in our legs and hearts as we continued the trek. I guess it was our new found freedom away from authority figures. Even the sight of seriously black clouds looming over the horizon couldn't dampen our spirit.

"The cabin boy he was there
 Looking all forlorn.
 The captain, he soon cheered him up
 When he let him blow his horn," sung Dave.
"Balls to your partner.
 Arse against the wall.
 If you never been shagged on a Saturday night,

Then you've never be shagged at all," we sang the chorus together.

"Christ it's cold," shivered Danny, delving into his rucksack, retrieving his sea-jersey and pulling it over his head. Each of us did likewise. And that was no understatement, the wind had picked up somewhat. Stupidly, because it was sunny when we'd set off, none of us had thought to bring foul-weather clothing. We were now beginning to wonder if that was wise because with each mile we trudged, ever closer came the darkened sky.

"The local whore she was there..." sang Danny.

"And she'd been smoking grass.
 Pulling carrots from the fridge
 And shoving them up her arse!"

"Balls to you partner..." we went into the chorus again.

Danny suddenly had a worried look on his face as he scanned the horizon, and did another check of the map. I draped myself over his body and wrapped my arms around his waist.

"Better find some shelter soon," he said as the sky opened and rain the size of golf balls splattered on the track. "I reckon we're still a couple of miles from the farm."

The four us us began to leg it as the rain came thicker and faster.

"Little Danny, he was there....." I sang as we ran.

"His cock was really throbbing.
 Bending a boy over the vicar's lap
 He gave him a jolly good knobbing."

Danny took a swipe at me and I ducked. "That's not funny!" he sulked.

"But you wish it were true!" I teased, flicking his comforter from his head.

There was no chorus this time, we were more concerned about finding shelter, namely a wood close by the pylons up ahead. It was relatively warm in amongst the trees but Mike became more and more concerned as the rain turned to snow and began to settle. He was right to be worried. Not surprisingly, Danny had got us lost.

After a further few mile's trudge through the wood we still hadn't found Danny's farm refuge. But it was as we came out the other side of the wood and discussed whether to remain in its relative shelter or move on in search of the farm that Dave spotted what he thought was accommodation. Cautiously we crept close to a battered old caravan hidden in the darkness. Mike lit his lighter but it had no illuminating effect.

"Anyone home!" shouted Dave as we crept toward it. There was no reply so we rushed it.

The door was ajar. Dave jerked it open and peeked in. "Empty!" he joyously announced.

There was an instant scramble to get inside but Dave beefed himself up and barged in first, claiming one of the two seating areas which were about bunk size. Danny got the other.

We lit fags whilst we got our ground-sheets out and wrapped them around our freezing bodies.

"Might as well crash 'til morning," suggested Dave.

We all went along with that idea, and after foraging out some grub, we settled down for the night.

At first I was pretty pissed off that Mike and myself had been relegated to the stale, piss-smelling floor riddled with bugs and other creepy crawlies. But after I'd persuaded him to snuggle close to me, pulling our ground-sheets over both our bodies, explaining that we'd be warmer that way, I was more than happy. I was even more surprised that he agreed.

It was impossible for me to sleep, being so close to him, but the others were already emitting slumbering sounds. Even Mike, who sounded as if he was into some erotic dream, was unaffected by my closeness. For a sleepless hour I lay beside him, pressed tightly into his slender body, eyes wide open, breathing in his body scent.

Sexual desire is such a powerful energy, so difficult to control. And as I wrestled with mine, like it was some crazy monster, my hands mentally travelled around Mike's slender waist and between his powerful young thighs, tightly grasping his delightful brown cock. Having fed my mind with such erotic thoughts, my cock bolted upright beneath my trousers. I began breathing excitedly. I couldn't help myself. After all, I was where I'd so longed to be, snuggled into the warmth of one of the lads.

Mike rolled onto his side, his buttocks nestling into my crotch. He was slumbering like a baby, breathing shallow and contentedly. My arousal hit fever pitch!

Yes, I had seen every inch of his naked body, even his long, thick cock when hard. Yes, I had touched him playfully over most parts of it many many times. But I'd never slept with him!

Daringly, I placed my arm around his waist. He whimpered slightly as I gently squeezed closer. Already I had formulated an excuse should he wake.

"I was so damn cold," I would tell him.

Ever lower went my hand. I couldn't help myself. My palm found his cock. It was stiff. Incredibly stiff! I slipped my other arm beneath his waist, replacing my right hand with my left. My breathing raced away as my palm gently brushed against his swollen sex.

I daren't even think of the consequences should he wake!

I wanted to stop. Knew I was in terrible danger. But couldn't! I rested my lips on his neck and breathed in the heady smell of sweat from our walking. Desperately, I wanted to prize open his fly and bury my hand inside, and stroke on that throbbing cock and toss it off until it erupted in creamy come.

The vein in my left temple was pounding fiercely. I glanced quickly at Danny and Dave lying not a foot above us. Both were sound asleep. I kissed Mike's neck gently, pressing my hand more firmly against his cock. Still he did not stir.

My cock was painful, crammed tightly in my pants. I could feel the wetness of pre-come against my tummy.

Unable to contain my urges any longer, I decided I would go for it. Myself, that is!

I popped my fly open and prized my prick free. It felt so good as it escaped its prison and rose to its full potential. Demon like, I licked on Mike's neck and gently squeezed his cock, occasionally rubbing as I became more and more possessed. My head exploded when I felt his bum arch backward. Thoughts of fucking him swamped my mind. I grabbed my cock tightly and began pumping. All to soon, I was pulling my cock toward myself and rolling onto my back, fearing the deluge would land on his backside.

A sudden groan emitted from Mike's mouth as he rolled onto his right side toward me. I managed to free my arm and roll away as he wrapped himself around me, his hand only inches from my dick and lying in my fresh cum. My heart and mind galloped, excited and afraid, but Mike didn't wake.

I couldn't believe my luck, I'd had sex with Mike - if I could call it that. And I'd gotten away with it!

Ringing bells brought me from my thoughts and avalanche of attention over to the fruit-machine.

"Jackpot!" Danny jubilantly announced, turning in my direction as he bent before a large cup which was catching coin after coin as they clattered down.

SEVEN

Dave glanced at his Rolex watch as he sat in a taxi heading toward the bar where he was to meet the lads. Planning his life had always been a touch and go affair; yet again he was late. It had been only days ago that he'd suspected it unlikely he'd make the meeting, the ship having been sent on a hectic exercise in the Irish Sea. It was only an hour ago that he had the same suspicion, him being otherwise occupied.

He ran through an encyclopedia of excuses he held in his head. Kept back for a couple of hours by the Officer of the Day for not being dressed smartly enough was his chosen one.

Dave flicked open his wallet and scanned the wad of notes, then pulled out a fiver ready to pay the driver. A cheerful smile filled his face. I'm worth every penny, he mused, tucking the wallet safely into his bell-bottoms, an increasing excitement rising inside his belly at the thought of meeting the boys.

As the taxi raced through the town, jumping two red lights and almost sending a drunken sailor sailing over it's bonnet, he wondered what stories he could impress the lads with when he arrived. For sure, they would have plenty of their own. A few similar to his, no doubt. Life on any ship was pretty much the same, and even the runs ashore took on a similar theme - getting pissed, causing havoc, stealing trophies, getting shags; imaginary or otherwise. Anyway, there was usually some event during the course of a month which was different from the run of the mill, and if there wasn't you simply made one up. Truth was, as long as the adventure was exciting or got a decent laugh, then it didn't matter whether it was true or not. In fact, the more unbelievable the better.

Sex was always a favourite theme. Apart from stories of drunken escapades, it was the number one topic. Whether that sex gossip was straight or gay, made no difference. Of the two, it was usually the queer stories which were the most eagerly received. Not gay confessions about oneself, though.

Dave remembered a tale his mate, Taff, had told one drunken session. Taff and this junior stoker had been travelling home on leave. They were on a night train heading toward Edinburgh. In the carriage with them was a muscular soldier. After sinking a good quantity of booze between them, they decided to crash.

It was about dawn when Taff was rudely awakened by a Ticket Inspector raising the blinds, filling the carriage with unwelcome daylight and demanding tickets. Sleepily, he began foraging in his creased bell-bottoms. At the same time he also realised that the soldier was no longer with them, just a single large mound covered by the stoker's sleeping bag on the opposite seat.

Noticing his young friend hadn't stirred, Taff gave him a gentle kick. Willing to assist with the waking of the slumbering friend, the far-too-jolly Ticket Inspector whisked the sleeping bag back.

Taff had said he'd always remember the expression on the Inspector's shocked face when they were both greeted by the soldier's flexing white bum as he stuffed his cock into the young stoker arse; the Inspector hastily announcing that he'd come back later.

Yes, those were the kind of sordid tales sailors loved. Dave reckoned he could use that one if conversation got slack. But there were a host of others he could use. One in particular which he knew would definitely appeal to the lads came from another guy on his ship, who had also been a trainee from the same barracks as them. He had told Dave that he happened to pass by the gym one evening and noticed the curtains had been drawn. Glimpsing through a crack, he was totally shocked to discover PTI Mann giving a trainee a blow-job, the lad having been tied to the wall-bars.

Dave laughed loudly as he imagined imparting that knowledge, positive the revelation that Mann relished sucking trainees' cocks would astound them. Whether they thought it true and believed him, didn't matter. It was a gem!

"All right back there, Jack?" the obviously gay taxi driver called as Dave continued to giggle girlishly in the back.

"Fine! Just remembered something funny."

"You sailor-boys certainly are a queer lot," the driver grinned into his rearview mirror and laughed along with him.

Wasn't that the truth, thought Dave. If only the top brass knew just what a queer lot sailors really were, and what they really got up to.

Take his own life. If the lads would be shocked by Mann's little secret, they'd be totally overwhelmed by his! And that secretive lifestyle started soon after leaving training, not long after joining his first ship. But it wasn't planned. Indeed, Dave would have been the first to deny that he had any inclination to wander down the path he eventually did.

It all began one hot, sunny afternoon. He'd been wandering through a park, casually strolling between flower-beds and around shrubs and bushes, when he spotted a guy following from behind. Stopping to light a cigarette, Dave noticed the guy had also stopped. He thought little of it and soon moved off. Glancing back, as he turned toward the path leading to the exit, there was the guy again, no closer but no nearer, just keeping the same distance between them.

Dave plonked himself on a park bench and from the corner of his eye had a closer scrutiny of the guy as he approached. His first thought that he might be a mugger was soon dispelled, simply by the fact that they weren't the only occupants of the floral surroundings; calculating it most unlikely that he'd be attacked in broad daylight. His second thought, that perhaps he was from the same ship and was about to identify himself, was also dismissed when the young man continued walking by. But his third thought, when the chap beamed a broad smile and rubbed his crotch on passing, left Dave in no doubt what was going on. The guy was a queer. Not only that, he was coming onto him!

Dave was stunned. He'd never met a queer before, let alone been propositioned by one - albeit in his own imagination - and continued to draw thoughtfully on his cigarette. All the while, he continued watching the guy walk away, noting that the glances back in his direction were far more frequent the greater his distance became.

Surprisingly, Dave's cock had grown in his pants. Clearly embarrassed, he shoved it to one side, unable to believe what was happening. Yes, he was still a virgin. Would jump at a chance for his first fuck. But with a guy? No way!

With a final, lengthy stare, the young man exited the park. Dave breathed a sigh of relief and moved over to a drinking fountain and splashed his face, cooling himself and reducing the reddening of his cheeks.

What was that all about? he wondered. Not the guy flirting with him but his resulting arousal. Christ, he'd seen enough stiff cocks and naked lads since becoming a sailor, but not once could he remember getting a stiffy because of it.

He'd even had sailors slapping his arse and giving crafty grabs at his dick, even sneaky kisses, but even that had never brought his cock up. To be honest, the only time he did get hard was when the sailor bunking next to him used to give himself a good old rub before crashing, but even that had never bothered him, suspecting that to be secretly tossing at the same time was a normal reaction.

Feeling self-conscious, Dave decided to leave the park, but instead of taking the same exit, made tracks for the opposite one, ensuring they wouldn't meet.

It was a beep on a car's horn, as he trailed his fingers along the metal railings, which caused Dave to swivel his head in the direction of the parked vehicles. His heart kicked heavily against his ribcage and his face glowed brightly. There was the same chap, cozily sat in the leather upholstery of a red Porsche.

"Want a lift, kid?" he confidently asked.

Dave was totally dumbstruck and unbelievably nervous. "No!" was all he could utter, which came out more aggressively than he'd intended. He offered up a conciliatory smile. The last thing he wanted was some ugly scene on his hands.

"It's no trouble, kid. Where you going?" he persisted.

It was just as he turned to walk away that the similar feeling of arousal and curiosity once more engulfed Dave. "Where you going?" he asked, more out of curiosity and with as much disinterest as he could muster.

"Wherever you want," came the same confident reply, this time accompanied by a wink.

It was a superb machine. One that Dave would have loved to be able to afford but doubted would ever come about on a sailor's pay. A tingle of excitement and suspense rushed between his thighs and throughout his body as it roared away. Dave smiled shyly at the handsome guy, unable to believe he'd actually jumped in beside this total stranger.

"Take you for a spin, if you like. If you're not in a hurry to get back to your ship."

It was too good an opportunity to miss, zipping along in a sports car, and all thoughts of where this meeting might lead completely dissolved from Dave's mind. "Sure," he agreed.

"I'll take you over the Downs. I can really give you something up there!"

Dave grinned innocently, rubbing his knees excitedly like a child and nodding agreement, totally missing the point. Liam, who had now introduced himself, gave a helping hand and intimately stroked his own palm over Dave's knee and toward his young crotch. Dave, completely engrossed with the power of the Porsche, hardly noticed.

And so, it was over the hills and valleys of the Downs that Dave was taken at phenomenal speeds. But it was on the highest peak that the Porsche was brought to a halt within the confines and secrecy of a small Copse. It was also at that precise moment, when the engine had ceased purring, reality swept back into Dave's life, realising that a price was about to be paid for his roller-coaster ride.

"Better get me back now?" he timidly requested, dropping his palms nervously between the safety of his thighs and over his cock.

"S'ok, kid. Relax. Don't worry, I'll get you back on time," Liam smiled without a hint of a threat in his voice. "Look. We both know what I want," he continued, covering the back of Dave's hand with his palm. "A horny young sailor like you, must like your sex. A blowjob's all I want."

"Sweet shit, he wants me to give him a blowjob!" Dave thought. "Christ, I haven't even had one myself before, and now this guy's wanting one from me for a poxy ride in his car!"

Trouble was, Dave knew they were miles from his ship and it looked increasingly likely he would have to oblige if he was to get back. He gulped hard but dare not pull his hand away from his cock and leave Liam's perched perilously close.

Liam's hand slid beneath Dave's and began caressing.

"I'm not sure, mate. I'm not into this kind of stuff," Dave informed, desperate not to sound as nervous as he was.

"Money, is it?" Liam suddenly surprised him. "S'ok, kid. You sailors always want cash." And with that he flipped open the walnut dash, pulled out a twenty and tucked it beneath Dave's crotch, giving it fondle.

Dave gulped hard as the hand gently squeezed. His face glowing brightly, embarrassed that his dick had become excited. He still managed a smile.

Fuck it! he suddenly decided. Twenty bloody quid's twenty bloody quid! And with that, a softly spoken, "Okay," slipped from his drying lips, which was quickly followed by a more serious, "But you don't come in my mouth!"

Liam laughed loudly. "Come in your mouth! It's me who's sucking you, kid! Course, if you....."

Dave interjected quickly, eager to demonstrate that he was in control of the situation. "I meant, do you want me to come in your mouth," he shyly smiled.

Liam laughed again and bent over and kissed his sailor's cheek. "Thought that's what you meant," he beamed, but without making Dave feel like a novice. "Course I want you to come in my mouth. I hope you've got a good whack."

"I got twenty quids worth!" Dave proudly declared, relaxing with every passing second, now with a painfully stiff cock bulging his bell-bottoms at the thought of getting his first blowjob, but inwardly praying he wouldn't embarrass himself by shooting his whack in seconds.

"Haven't had sex in a week, not even a toss," Dave tormented.

"Great!" delighted Liam and swiftly set the imprisoned sex free and in a flash had Dave's virgin cock pressed deep into his palate, rolling his tongue around the protruding ridge of the head.

With a gasp, Dave fell backward against the leather seat, his whole body quivering. The sensation was unreal, unbelievable, unbearable. And his fear that he would come instantly almost materialised on the first deep thrust of Liam's mouth as it sank down his spittle-covered shaft. Quickly Dave clenched his buttocks, desperate to hold back the bounty of come climbing through his cock.

Liam felt the young thighs tighten as they valiantly attempted to control their spasms of delight as the spunk rose in the virgin cock. Prizing his sailor's muscled legs apart, he sank his head down to the base of Dave's cock, working the final inch in rapid movements, eager to bring him off.

Liam wasn't bothered if his sailor-boy was in uncontrollable agony with the pleasure of having his cock gorged upon, knowing only to well he had a virgin in his mouth. He only wanted his mouth filled to overflowing, filled with what he hoped would be an abundance of virgin come.

With a sensational gasp and a painful tightening of his tummy muscles, Dave let loose his juice. "Jesus!" he yelped as Liam returned to the top and tongued rapidly around the head of his pulsating cock, gulping down the promised wealth of come.

Deliberately, Liam continued to work lovingly up and down the dripping shaft, draining every last ounce of the sweet liquid, lavishing the thick head until it began to soften in his mouth. "Worth every penny," he finally announced, licking a dribble of spunk from around his lips. "Christ, kid. You could make a fortune in this town!"

It was from that day's delightful adventure that Dave discovered the key to his fortune and became a rent-boy sailor. Selling and sowing his seeds for all who would pay him handsomely. And the surprising thing he discovered about himself, he loved every minute of it.

But what he enjoyed the most about his clients, apart from their money, was they all liked different stuff and had their own fantasies. Every punter became a new adventure.

Some liked bondage. Others a bit of splashing and spraying fun. And a good few a touch of the old slap and slap stuff. Dressing-up was also a regular requirement - schoolboy, maid, his sailor's uniform, you name it. Naturally, most wanted nothing more than fucking or sucking fun. But whatever their fancy Dave didn't care and could handle almost any requirement; having a whole repertoire of raunchy games he could play. All he did care about was they paid him ridiculous amounts of cash for his services. Lucky for him, that was always the case.

And that was precisely why he was now late and dashing across town in a crazily driven cab. He'd just been servicing a client. And like all of his punters, this one had money to burn. Simon, his new punter, liked his boys bound up in a leather harness, and that was costly. Two hundred pounds to be precise.

"Cabin Boy, Jack," the gay cab driver called, pulling up beside the pub and bringing Dave from his thoughts.

"I bet you'd love one!" mused Dave, paying the camp driver and jumping out.

<u>EIGHT</u>

Danny and myself bending over a pile of pound coins was the first sight which greeted Dave when he entered the bar and spotted us at the table beside the fruit machine. Reaching us he grabbed a handful of coins, which had been stacked into a ten pound pile, and quickly turned away.

"What's your game, mate!" Danny hollered into the back of the tall sailor, grasping his shoulder and swinging him about, myself taking a forearm.

"Dave!" we both delighted when we were greeted by his Cheshire cat grin.

"Well, fuck Smudge's arse," cried Danny, embracing Dave in a tight bear-hug, his head coming just below Dave's chin. "I was just about to knock your bloody head off!"

"Take a man, not a midget," Dave laughed, lifting Danny clean from the floor.

"I ain't that small."

"Yeah, I remember," Dave winked at me.

Danny gave me a poke in the chest, his old self re-kindled, possibly because of his recent win. "Shit, your as bad as this one. You guys with little dicks are all the same."

"Who's got a little dick? Christ, mine's really itchy today," I laughed, bending and scratching just above my knee.

Just to outdo me, Dave scratched his ankle. "Mine too!"

All three of us threw arms about each other, "The Buffer's a bastard," we declared in unison, laughing and slapping our palms together.

"Jesus, I've been here five minutes and you miserable buggers haven't even bought me a pint, you cheap sods. And where's Mike?" asked Dave, dropping the stack of coins back onto the table.

Danny scooped the coins into his cap. "Mike's not here yet. What do you want, Dave? Lager? I'll get them when I cash this lot up. Fifty bloody quid, it is!"

"S'ok. This one's on me," Dave insisted, flipping open his bulging wallet to reveal a wad of crisp twenties.

Both our eyes opened wide at the sight of so much money. "I reckon it is!" I declared. "Your granny died?"

"Probably sold his arse," Danny giggled.

"Probably sold yours when you weren't looking," I suggested.

"Sold my granny!" Dave corrected. "But I reckon we'd get a few bob for this if we tried hard enough." Making a grab for Danny's big dick.

"Bandits!" Danny parried, snatching a twenty from Dave. "Lagers with rum chasers. Right?"

"I'll do the rums," I offered as Dave's eyebrows raised.

"Bollocks. I said my round and my round it is. You greedy sods!"

Dave and I sat down and began to chat. Before we'd got into any meaningful conversation, Danny returned with three pints of lager in one hand and three tots of rum jammed between the fingers of the other. "Quick!" he screamed. "Before I drop the fucking lot!"

"Shouldn't be so fucking clever," laughed Dave, holding onto my arm as I reached to assist, dying for Danny to send them crashing to the deck and bring undue attention and jeers from drunken sailors upon himself.

"Should've balanced them on your dick," I broke down in a fit of drunken giggles.

The tots went away first, in single gulps.

"To dead grannies," toasted Danny.

"To Danny's dick," toasted Dave.

"To your arse," I followed.

"To the Buffer. The miserable bastard!" we all finished, starting on the pints.

Chat soon bubbled between us. Danny's spirits had once more soared and I was more than pleased for that. My intended revelation that I was gay was soon shelved.

Danny moved us into training memories. "Remember when we had to climb the mast? Smudge thought we'd got away with it because of all that snow, then shit his pants when the bloody stuff melted."

I shivered to the bone. "Don't remind me."

Danny prodded me. "Christ, you were whiter than the bloody snow by the time you'd gotten halfway."

"And that's as far as he got!" Dave reminded. "Didn't some six year old kid help you down?" he laughed.

I shivered again. "Yeah, I've never been so fucking shit scared in my life. And he wasn't six. He was about fourteen. Some Commander's son. My legs were shaking for the rest of the day."

"You went to the top and over the Devil's Elbow, didn't you Danny?" Dave asked.

The Devil's Elbow was at about fifty foot. It was where the rigging jutted out. If you climbed it, your feet would be dangling in mid air. It was a real pant filler. Luckily there was a way through for cowards - for me. The Half Moon was the highest you could climb the netting. The highest point you could go without permission. From that point on it was a straight pole to the button at the very top, about ten foot of it.

"No problem," Danny proudly praised himself. "Never have been scared of heights."

"Only tall birds," I mocked.

"Yeah, he's probably had to climb enough ladders just to reach their tits!" Dave laughed. "I didn't go over the Elbow, though," he grimaced. "Too bloody scared. But I got to the Half Moon. That was bad enough."

"I'm not so bad now. I've been up the mast on-board quite a few times," I said.

"I could have been a Button Boy," Danny boasted.

"A belly-button boy without that ladder," Dave giggled.

"Remember those couple of days on that hike thing?" Danny asked, moving us into another training memory. "And that flea-infested caravan? Shit, I nearly froze me balls off that night!"

"Shouldn't have jumped on the bunk so smartly. Serves you bloody right," I said

"You tell him, Smudge. You and Mike had the right idea. Kept yourselves nice and warm all night, didn't you?" he winked with a soul searching smile.

My heart skipped a beat and I fought against my flushing cheeks. I was pretty sure he knew what I had done that night. "Yeah, slept like babies we did."

Dave swept another knowing smile over me and changed the subject. "And that blooming train! That sure as fuck got us off the railway line!" he chortled.

"Remember? Short arse here wanted us to jump on and cadge a lift," I said.

"Well it wasn't going that fast, and it would have saved us a bloody long walk," Danny defended himself, glancing at his watch. "Christ, soon be closing. Mike's not going to make it."

"If you recall, there was a branch line a couple of miles down the track," I continued with the train story, "and if we'd have jumped on then we'd have most likely ended up in Scotland." I glimpsed my own watch. "I think you're right, Danny. I reckon Mike must be at sea somewhere. Well, at least the three of us made it," I said with a smile for both.

"Pity," Dave saddened. "I like Mike. Poor bugger was always embarrassed about something."

"Could've cooked eggs on his face, half the time," Danny grinned.

"Sure took a lot of flak, especially from that big bugger Mann," said Dave, puffing out his chest. "You even had a run in with him. Didn't you, Danny?"

"We've already done that one," I told him, giving Danny a searching look. "Doesn't want to talk about it."

"Why?" Dave asked, raising his eyebrows as he was prone to do.

Danny lowered his gaze. "Nothing to tell."

It was a good moment for Dave to spin his story about Mann, although he'd probably have loved to have waited until Mike had arrived. He went into the details of the lad secured to the wall bars and the resulting blowjob. Making things more sordid when he thought it needed colouring. Danny fidgeted in his seat throughout and at one point looked as if he was going to move to the heads or fruit machine.

By the time Dave had finished, he had a roaring hot flush.

I glanced across at Danny when Dave had finished. I was sure he was in some kind of mental agony but then again it could have been the booze brightening him. "You're pulling our plonkers," I laughed.

"Truth," Dave insisted, crossing his heart.

"Wouldn't surprise me. Always thought there was something queer about that bastard," Danny gruffly accused.

"That's good coming from you, Danny. You were his favourite. His little Olga Corbett," Dave giggled.

"That's right," I supported. "Little Miss Handspring!"

"Little Miss Hand-job!" Dave exploded, again spluttering beer everywhere.

"Wasn't you was it, Danny? Tied to those wall bars," I winked.

"Bollocks!" was Danny's sharp reply.

I reckoned it was time to change the subject, Danny's annoyance fermenting. "I see you're on Defender," I said, pointing to Dave's cap. "You were in exercise Shake Up as well, weren't you? Who would have thought we'd all end up in Pompey, and on the same exercise?"

"Got dragged into Shake Up at the last moment. Carrier escort," Dave revealed. "Did you see that plane go down?"

"Shit. It came down quicker than Danny's draws. Got a recommend for that because I was the first bugger to spot it," I praised myself. "I wasn't even a lookout. I just happened to see the pilot eject when I was sending a signal to the carrier."

"Clever clogs!" Danny dampened.

"Just cos you're always stuck in a stuffy office," I retaliated.

"If some of us are brighter than others," he fought back. "Bloody flag tossers!"

"What's this!" Dave burst in. "You two fallen out or something? And anyway big dick, I'm a bunting as well. Some of us have to be big and strong enough to brave the waves."

"You tell him, Dave. You'd only need to piss on the little bugger and he'd be washed over the side!"

"Not if he tied his dick to something," Dave broke down, laughing so loudly his face almost burst.

"So what's the emergency frequencies?" Danny asked, getting all technical to prove he was brighter.

"Don't know, but I know a hot slut's emergency number," Dave continued to tease.

"Smudge gave you his phone number, then," Danny dived in, not wishing to be outdone in the piss-take battle.

"'Course. I put it in every telephone box in Pompey," I hit back.

Dave didn't bat an eyelid at that remark. Although, unbeknown to us, that was close to the truth for him. But his adverts hadn't been placed in phone boxes, they were discreetly coded and placed within gay magazines.

"So, Dave, is this mare any good or is she an ugly bitch with the pox?" Danny cruelly questioned.

"Well hark at Miss Pretty Pants. Your original crab-infested cock-sucker!" I said.

"At least I'm not a bum-bandit's scrambling net," Danny fought back, fearing he might be loosing the play.

"I don't wear string vests," I said. String vests were a regular joke amongst sailors, who believed them be an indication of gayness. "I don't even wear nix."

"You're so desperate for a shag, you wouldn't have time to get the buggers off!" both laughed, their jolly words colliding into one another's.

I just loved the way sailors could create this wicked, friendly banter. Some were just brilliant at it. All too often, especially with the young skins, an older sailor would feed a line for himself or another old salt to follow up on. Almost always the lad, and even more experienced sailors, fell into the trap. It was seldom serious stuff but allowed us to keep life on-board light-hearted, even during the most awful of times.

"Anyway, Mr. Wonderful. How come you're still a virgin? Danny's still a virgin, Dave. Can you believe that? Says his cock's too big!"

"Not too big for your slack arse!" Danny hit below the belt.

"Danny a virgin? I think not!" Dave answered in his defence, but quickly destroyed the ego he'd just inflated by adding, "Who's donkey dick do you think sired Desperate Dan. You know, that horse that won the St. Ledger?"

I almost fell from my seat in laughter. It was a brilliant shot over his bow. "Is that right, Danny? And there's you accusing Dave of shagging mares!"

"And who do you think sired Slack Arse Annie!" Danny fought against the tide.

"Truce!" called Dave, sensing it was getting too personal.

"Mary, Mary. Quite the fairy," Danny threw in my direction, in a final bitch.

"Have you two been like this all night. Christ, I'm surprised you haven't slit each other's throats by now," Dave bringing some sensibility back into things. "So is it true? Are you still a cherry boy, Danny?" he asked, slapping his own face in punishment for another irresistible attack.

"You sure Smudge didn't pay you all that dosh for shagging his arse!" Danny continued to fight.

"I don't know, Dave. These virgins are all the same. So sensitive!" I nailed him.

The booze was going away far too quickly but we didn't stop. "Your round, Danny?" I calculated. "Better get yourself a short," I wounded with a final height joke.

Danny slapped my head as he walked around me, causing me to spill the remaining dregs of my pint. I made him move smartly away by making a grab for his dick.

After he'd vanished into the sea of sailors, Dave asked me if I thought Danny really was a virgin. I could only tell him that that was what he had told me.

We chatted for awhile about the exercise in the Irish Sea then about some of the other places he'd visited. Unlike myself, he travelled to Malta and Gibraltar and around a good few ports in Europe. He'd also visited Amsterdam. There was a good opportunity to bring gay sex into our chat at that point, but for some unknown reason I suggested that he'd probably seen a lot of tit and pussy whilst over there.

"And the rest," was his somewhat revealing reply.

Unfortunately, my opportunity to follow up on that was halted when Danny staggered back, slopping beer from the over-filled glasses, positively more pissed than he had been an hour back. "Any sign of Mike?" he asked, placing the glasses heavily on the table and sending booze in all directions.

"You're pissed?" I accused.

"And you're not?" Danny slobbered.

"Here we go again," Dave sighed. "You two should become a couple, you're forever fighting."

"I'd love to marry him," I truthfully teased. "I'll be faithful to you, Danny. I promise," I tormented, fluttering my eyelashes at him.

"Reckon Smudge is a bandit?" Danny asked Dave, who was scraping slops from the table with a cardboard beer mat and onto the wooden floor. "Reckon he takes it up the bum, do you?"

Dave gave me a penetrating look. It went so deep I felt I'd unwittingly given him the answer. "You know what they say?" he softly smiled and winked at me. "One up the bum, no harm done."

I laughed at Dave's quote often used by sailors but it left me with a strange feeling that he was actually defending me, even approving of my actions if it happened to be true. If I was to tell any of the lads that I was gay, then Dave most surely should be the first.

"Sure. One up the bum, no harm done," Danny sarcastically repeated.

He said it far too loudly and the group closest to us laughed and roared, "One up the bum, no harm done, lads!"

Danny's face erupted red, and he jumped to his feet and legged it to the heads, aware that he'd brought unwanted attention upon himself.

"One up the bum, no harm done, darling!" the sailors taunted him.

"I reckon he must be a virgin," Dave said after Danny was out of earshot. "Seems a bit touchy about sex tonight."

"Been touchy since he got here. Guess he just don't like queers," I replied, searching Dave's expression carefully for any reaction but he only acknowledged with raised eyebrows. "You still a virgin, then?" I asked, inwardly hoping that he was, at least concerning straight sex.

Dave laughed softly then went into sordid tale of some lass he'd screwed this very afternoon whilst her husband had been watching them and tossing himself off. It was such a good tale, I thought he should have saved it until Danny had returned, if only to enlighten him on sexual matters. In actual fact the story was massive fib and the truth was he'd actually been servicing his latest punter, Simon.

It had been the first time Dave had been suspended in a leather harness - hanging there like some succulent piece of prime meat - hands handcuffed behind his back, his body naked apart from a skimpy, leather jock. Simon, too, had been dressed from head to toe in a black leather outfit and wearing a hood with small spy holes and an opening over the mouth.

There could be no doubt that Dave was apprehensive, he was a damn big bugger was Simon, and his heart pumped painfully in his chest with the fear and thrill of it all. But soon all fear was forgotten and replaced by enthusiasm and excitement as the fearsome, leather-clad figure began to tantalise and titillate as it circumnavigated his suspended torso. Gently cracking a ten-stranded, leather whip over buttocks, back and chest.

Behind Dave now, Simon kissed at the powerful young shoulders and biceps, then over the nape of his sailor's neck and behind his ears. Worshipping the suspended body, he worked his way to the tight, firm buttocks and began biting into them. Adoringly he rotated his boy-sailor and began a tongue search of Dave's navel, avoiding the beautiful bulge beneath the leather jock, saving it until last. Biting, but not too hard, Simon nibbled on the nipple buds, each firming slightly with the attention they had been given. Kissing now, ever more passionately, his tongue slid around the adorable, youthful chest. A moan of delight meandered from Dave's mouth.

Aware of the pleasure his purchase was submerged in, Simon continued his tantalising tour of the handsome figure. Tenderly, he teased and tweaked from tip to toe every centimetre of his covetous youth. Dave's dick began to fill his leather jock as the masked head mouthed and manipulated its contents. Simon's eyes sparkled with delight as he watched the cock's excitement unfolding before his wanting eyes.

His sailor sufficiently stimulated, Simon moved for the magnificent mound bursting from the leather pouch!

Popping open the press-studs on either side of the leather jock, Dave's proud prick pushed the shiny sheath clear. Simon moved upon the mouthwatering meat. Instantly, it vanished into the blackness of his mask. Dave moaned, frantically writhing and wriggling his hips into the working face, stunned by the pleasure of his restriction. All the while Simon continued to work furiously over the youthful, firm flesh, sucking around the balls, teasing and torturing Dave to the point of making him scream for more.

For a half hour the punishment continued - tweaking tits, biting nipple buds, tugging on cock, more lashes across the vulnerable body, and finally the return of the sensational mouth as Simon rewarded Dave with glorious sucks to his cock, gulping it deep then withdrawing when he felt the head swell and the spunk serge.

Finally, Dave's body was spun about and the massive condom-covered cock was driven home in one painfully enjoyable thrust. Fiercely, Simon's dick was plunged back and forth into the darkness of the hot, lubricated passage, the buttock cheeks gripping tightly around its gigantic girth. Desperately, Dave wanted to grip his own cock and crank it violently and bring himself off. But Simon was a master and kept him handcuffed whilst continuing to make him suffer the pleasure of being controlled.

In a final frenzy of sexual oblivion, Simon's cock was suddenly withdrawn and the sheath pulled away. Simultaneously, Dave was spun about. And whilst Simon frantically pumped on his own cock, his mouth moved back and forth over Dave's and began to gorge glutinously, gathering every millimetre into the depths of his eager throat.

With a desperate sigh from Simon and a gratified whimper from Dave, one whack of come shot over his sailor's muscled calves and another gulped into his ravenous mouth.

"Bloody hell! You kinky bugger," was all I could say after he'd finished his threesome tale.

I suspected it was the truth. I had no reason to believe otherwise. But during that extremely descriptive account, I had noticed a kind of sensuality about him that I hadn't seen before. I found it unnerving and yet compelling. The kind of sensuousness you are confronted with the first time you see a naked boy. Dave had definitely discovered a good deal of confidence during the past year, exhibiting a sexual awareness he'd never possessed before.

I began to imagine that girls simply dissolved at the feet of this handsome friend of mine whenever they were in his company. I suspected that he wasn't gay after all. I was truly disappointed.

Danny moved through the busy bar and sat back down. His hair and face were wet from the dampening he'd given them.

"One up the bum!" the sailors roared a final jibe.

This time he took no notice and his face remained its normal colour.

"Had this really good shag in my office a few weeks back," he excitedly informed.

Dave and I shot surprised glances at one another!

Danny spotted our disbelief and shuffled in his seat but continued with his story. "We had this Cake and Arse party going on - Cake and Arse was a term us ratings used for officer's parties - and this bird's wandering around the lower-deck, lost. Well, that's what she told me," Danny winked, implying that she was actually searching the ship for a shag. "Anyway, I was duty signalman and she starts chatting to me outside the Wireless Office. I asks her if she wants to see what a Wireless Office looks like inside. Birds love all that technical stuff," he claimed with a knowing wink.

"Bit risky," Dave broke in. Wireless offices were out of bounds to everyone who wasn't a communicator. As for taking a civilian inside one..... Well that would have cost Danny his job!

"Yeah, I know," Danny admitted, becoming more confident with every word he uttered. "But that's what made it so exciting! Anyway, no sooner than I've locked the door behind her, when she's on her knees and pulling out my stiff cock."

"Did she scream!" I laughed.

Danny ignored me and continued to get into his tale, an increasing excitement brewing. "I couldn't believe my luck!" he delighted. I wanted to say nor could I, but I kept mum and let him continue. "Shit, she opened her mouth so fucking wide I thought my balls were going to vanish. I'm watching her face as she's munching on my dick. It was so fucking fantastic, you'd have thought she hadn't had any food for a year!"

"Danny can blow himself, Dave. Did you know?" I broke in as I was reminded of that massive cock being gorged upon.

"Shit, Danny!" grinned Dave. "Can you really blow...."

"Will you shut the fuck up!" Danny snapped. "Do you want to hear this story or not?"

"Carry on, kid," came from the adjacent table.

Danny glimpsed the silent faces beside us, turned slightly in their direction, wiped some perspiration from his brow and continued. "Anyway, her mouth's swirling around my cock head then slamming down to the base of my prick and back again. My legs are shaking like fuck and my cock's covered in red lipstick. At one point it became so red, I thought she was actually eating the fucking thing," Danny laughed.

We all remained silent, rivetted by his every word. I even had a hard on.

"Then it happened!" Danny paused to swig some beer and draw gratefully on the cigarette I'd lit for him. "Just as I was about to shoot my whack, up she jumps!" he gasped, throwing his arms into the air.

"The fucking bitch!" a sailor cursed from the adjoining table.

Danny grinned and paused to take another swig of beer and an even longer drag on his cigarette, keeping his captive audience in suspense. "I thought that was the end of it," he continued, "but then she dives into her handbag and pulls out a rubber. Put it on with her mouth," he enthused. "Fuck, did that turn me on!"

All ears were locked on his every word, waiting for the juicy bit.

"Suddenly, she whips my bell-bottoms down," Danny demonstrates with exaggerated arm movements. "Shoves me backward onto the seat and jumps right onto my dick!"

You could've cut the silent air with a knife, so engrossed were we. In fact, I think the whole bar was listening!

Danny seemed unaware and began to play out the final scene. "Then she starts bouncing on my cock like she was riding a force twelve in a jam jar. My prick was throbbing so hard, I think my balls were under my chin!"

A couple of laughs emitted from behind me.

Danny continued, getting more excited by the minute. "All of a sudden she starts spinning the seat round and around, and bouncing harder and faster over my prick, ramming her pussy all the way down. It was like fucking on a merry-go-round. I had to bite my lip cos it was so fucking great!" he declared. "Suddenly, she screams so loudly, I had to put my hand over her fucking mouth to shut her up. Still shrieking and bouncing like fuck, she comes her lot and soaks my leg in her juices. My head exploded! No shit, I shot so much spunk I could feel it oozing out of my rubber. Was that some fuck, or what!" he finished.

I was just about to clap, for it surely deserved one, when he hit us with a punch line.

"You won't believe this, but when I takes her back to the quarterdeck, she turns out to be the bloody Captain's sixteen year old daughter!"

For a brief second their was stunned silence. Then, with an almighty cheer from the group of sailors beside us, "One up the bum, no harm done!" soared into the air.

Danny's face blushed brightly again!

"Brilliant!" Dave declared.

"Fucking brilliant!" I seconded.

"Truth!" Danny blushed, taking a gulp of beer into his mouth, then lighting a cigarette between trembling fingers and turning away from the mocking group.

Danny's moods were certainly swinging. One minute saying he was a virgin, next having a go at queers, next divulging a sleazy, straight sex story. I was truly baffled.

"So, you're not a cherry boy, then?" I asked.

"'Course not," Danny frowned. "Lost count of the amount of shags I've had. Just leading you on, Smudge. I know how much you like virgin lads," he taunted.

"Don't want to marry you anymore," I pretended to sulk.

"So, what's this about you giving yourself blow-jobs, Danny?" Dave asked. "Can you swallow the whole thing?"

"Swallows his own come," I disgustingly revealed.

"Do you!" Dave delighted, without revealing it. "You should wear a rubber, you know. Can't be too careful these days."

"Especially some of the places he's supposed to have stuffed his prick," I suggested, doing a very poor horse impression.

"I don't suck myself!" Danny bickered as we entered yet another battle of wits. "It's just Smudge's queer mind. Truth is, he'd love to suck it for me!"

"Don't get all shirty again. Christ, if I could suck my own cock, you'd never get me off it!" Dave laughed.

"Me too," I declared, licking my lips and laughing along with him.

Danny realised he was working himself up again. "Suppose most guys would love to be able to do it," he admitted.

"So, you do!" Dave dissolved him.

"I guess I have," Danny resigned himself to defeat.

"Told you," I said, delighting in his declaration.

"Lucky bugger," was Dave's easygoing answer.

"What's the plan, then? We going to wait until the end for Mike or move off to a club?" asked Danny.

"We're going to wait, you impatient bugger. He'd have waited for us. Right, Dave?"

"Ken's right. Mike might've got held up somewhere and it'd be a real bummer for him if he'd come a long way and we weren't here. Anyway, it's Saturday and I've got a weekend pass until Monday morning, so there's no hurry for me."

"I've got one too, so I'm fine with that," I agreed. "Staying at Sally A's."

Danny was outnumbered and gave in, although his pass only lasted until Sunday evening.

"And what's all this cuddly Ken crap?" Danny quickly jumped down Dave's throat. "He's a Smith and all Smiths are Smudge, Smiffy or Bum Bandits!" he corrected, with his usual dig at the end.

I had picked up on Dave calling me Ken, but didn't give it much thought. I couldn't remember the last time when any sailor had used my real name - nicknames being the norm on ships.

"Thought I'd give him a treat," Dave replied, slapping me heartily on the shoulder. "After all, he never uses a nickname for any of us."

"I ain't got a nickname and it still ain't right," Danny disagreed. "Smudge he's always been and Smudge he'll stay. Right, Smudge?"

"Don't really think about it anymore," I told him. "In fact, for one moment I wasn't sure who the hell Dave was talking about."

"See!" said Danny rather drunkenly and patting my shoulder. "He likes being a Smudge. Don't you, Smudge?" This time patting my head.

It was real pissy talk and I had to laugh at Danny. "Think I'm a bloody horse or something, do you? Why don't you give me a lump of sugar," I suggested, as Danny continued to pat me like some favourite animal of his.

"Careful, Smudge. You know what he does with horses after he's got friendly with them!" warned Dave.

"Tell you the truth, I'm so bloody horny after his disgusting story, I don't think I'd mind," was my beer-induced confession.

"Told you, Dave. Your darling Kenny's a bandit," Danny unable to resist attacking my sexuality again, and calling me Kenny to emphasise the point. "But I'll forgive him this time because he loved my shag story."

"If only it were true!" I wickedly went for him. "But I'd love to shag you,

you little runt!"

Our referee was quick to step in. "My round, right? Shall we stay on shorts? All this lager's bloating me."

"And makes you want to piss all the time," we both declared, jumping up for our umpteenth pee. Dave came also.

We had our rowdy piss like a bunch of silly schoolboys, but not before both Dave and I had drunkenly asked Danny to show us his big cock. Quite unbelievably, he did. But when I asked if I could see it in its full glory, he declined, doing another 'bandit' routine on me.

Dave's squeeze on my backside brought me instantly about as we walked behind Danny and left the heads. "It really is great to see you again, Smudge. Take no notice of Danny's queer nonsense. I'm sure he doesn't give a toss," he comforted without me seeking any. "What am I saying? You can take care of yourself."

I have to admit, his words did stun me and I wondered if he was opening a door for me and all I had to do was walk right in.

"Yeah, I know. Thanks anyway, Dave. And it sure is good to see you again. Shit, you look better than ever," I said, rubbing his silky black hair and disturbing the little quiff which fell sexily over his forehead. "Actually, there was something I wanted....."

"You two coming or what! Chatting like a couple of tarts. Dave, get those bloody rums in!" demanded Danny.

Dave gripped my arm affectionately. "What was you saying, Ken?"

"Tell you later. It's not important," I said, moving him in front of me and giving his bum a gentle pat.

NINE

It was nine in the evening. Mike was sat in a lumpy sofa, before a smoked-glass occasional table. Upon it sat a bottle of Navy Neaters rum and an over-filled glass with two chunks of ice melting on its surface. Mike knew where he should have been but wasn't in the mood to leave his flat.

Mike was pissed!

Somewhat glassily, he glanced around his spacious flat, taking in a couple of pictures sat upon his sideboard. One was of himself and the lads taken whilst they were in training, and the other was of himself and Naresh taken at a party.

An unwise selection of moody love songs, Barbara Streisand and the like, swamped his thoughts.

He took a hefty slug of rum, and although the glass wasn't empty, topped it up. His head fell against the back of the sofa. "Oh, shit!" he whispered to himself. "The guys are going to hate me if I don't turn up."

"All I need is the air that I breath,

And to love you..." slipped around the picture-covered walls and soaked into his brain. Mike did and didn't want to hear those sorrowful sounds, but continued to disappear into their depressing depths.

In the hall, the telephone rang. Mike let it ring.

For a few moments, he kind of waltzed around his lounge, a rum assisted smile slipping across his face. His dance took him into the bedroom where he spotted his gear laid out for the evening's meeting. Again he was tormented as to whether he should shower and put them on, and do the dutiful thing and go and meet the guys.

Sorrowfully, he flopped back onto the sofa and sank another slug of rum.

The phone ringing again and the answer machine clicking in, brought his thoughts away from the direction his chosen CD was constantly taking him. He knew it couldn't be any of the guys, none of them knew his number, let alone where he lived.

"Mike! Are you in? Pick up if you are, darling. It's your Mum."

Mike ignored the message from his mother, the third this evening, and continued to torment himself with the meeting which he desperately did and didn't want to attend.

He never had been prone to outbursts of any nature, but after he topped his glass up yet again, he slammed the bottle down. The expensive smoked-glass didn't shatter, but a forked crack shot outward to each corner.

"Shit!" he shouted as a few tears welled into his eyes and escaped onto the reflective surface.

Mike stared down at his sorrowful self. "I can't go on like this," he muttered into the unhelpful face staring back at him.

Again he raised he weary body and began smoochily gliding around his lounge, dragging a finger over highly polished furniture as if checking for dust.

Reaching for the photograph of himself and Naresh, he carefully picked it up, kissed it once, pulled open a draw and placed it inside. It was as if he were desperately trying to lay something to rest. Almost immediately, he plucked the it from its hiding place and replaced it.

Mike drew a deep breath into a chest which had been built up with gym work since he'd left training, and decided a decision had to be made. Circumnavigating the sofa once more, he took another hefty gulp of rum and began to discard his clothing.

The shower was hot and refreshing as it soaked his skin. Carefully, he lathered his fine torso - buttocks, cock, balls and back. Chest, arms and legs. Those actions used to be sensuous, stimulating, desired. Not anymore! Not since.....

Mike suppressed those thoughts before they had time to take hold again. He'd promised to meet the boys, and that's what he would do!

For a half an hour he massaged his soapy skin, several times dunking his throbbing head beneath the fine spray in an attempt to rejuvenate his not-so-sober self. Constantly he fought back visions of other loving hands doing it for him.

With a determined effort, he brought his thoughts onto the lads, wondering what they were now like, in looks and character, and whether they would have made the chosen destination for this night's meeting. He wondered, also, if any of them had had such a painful time as himself. His mind reluctant to succumb to thoughts of joy.

A soft, white towel, as large as himself, comforted him as he wrapped its radiatored warmth around his nakedness and towelled himself dry.

Bypassing the bedroom and his awaiting clothing, he plonked his nakedness back onto the sofa and started again on the rum. The ice bucket, mostly water, offered up a couple more chunks of ice. Their entry into the warm rum almost spilled the contents over the lip of the glass.

Mike supped another huge mouthful to bring it back to a sensible level.

Again his mind toyed with whether he should go to the pub or not, the sad music taking another swipe at him.

"Fuck this shit!" he cursed his own indecision, and ejected the sorrowful CD and replaced it with a more thumpy, dance number. The deep base began to do the trick as it vibrated around his flat and through his body.

Mike released an enormous laugh. His first today. Which may well have been more to do with the excessive amount of alcohol he'd drunk rather than his happiness.

"What am I like?" he asked himself. "It's not the end of the fucking world. Shit, the Cabin Boy's only ten minutes down the road!"

Quite suddenly, he was champing at the bit!

Yet another slug of rum fired the depths of his throat, and the glass refilled.

Mike found the bedroom, somewhat shakily, accompanied by his ruby-red friend swirling in an unsteady glass. With some effort he removed his dressing-gown and replaced it with his clothing. Several times his lips went to the increasingly empty glass. His stereo continued to feed thumping sounds into the flat. And a couple of times he did a drunken dance routine to help liven himself up.

His mirrored image looked unsympathetically back at himself as he checked his attire was in order - flies up and the like. He didn't really notice his reddened eyes brought about by sorrowful tears and too much booze.

Preparing to leave his flat he stopped at the pair of pictures sitting on his stereo. He kissed each of the boys, then, more affectionately, he kissed Naresh.

Placing that treasured picture carefully into a draw - another attempt to lay his past to rest - he shouted, "I'm coming, guys!" Draining the last of the rum from his glass and zapping his stereo into silence with the remote.

TEN

Danny, Dave and myself retook our seats beside the bay window, a double rum and ice apiece accompanying us. Outside the night was dark. The sea front was busy with an assortment of different characters enjoying their evening out. The dockyard looked like fairyland with its multitude of lights. But only sailors could know the truth of what life inside that starlit sailor-town was truly like.

Dave was still the most sober of the three of us and continued to keep the strange battle between Danny and myself under control. The clock above an array of navy plaques was at a quarter past ten. For the past hour, the bar had discharged some of its drinkers, but now, creeping toward closing time, it was as busy as ever.

Continuously, the sailors sang cheerful songs and sank their beers and spirits chasers. The pool table, too, had a handful of more professional players gathered around it. In one corner, a group of sailors were playing pontoon, the pot hidden in a sailor's cap. Gambling, although illegal, was a regular pastime. In fact, one group of hardened gamblers on my ship even had a roulette wheel.

It was something I seldom got involved in. Whist and Ludo - Uckers was what us sailors called Ludo - was about my limit. That said, Uckers was one game which was taken very seriously amongst ourselves. Like civvies would have their pool or darts tournaments, ships almost always held a similar championship for Uckers. The heated exchanges between opponents of various mess-decks could get very strong indeed. For sure, they would make the battle between Danny and myself seem like baby talk.

"Such a shame about Mike," Dave interrupted our thoughts as each of us stared towards the sea.

"Yeah. Could be anywhere," I sighed, feeling more tired by the minute from the amount of booze I'd consumed.

"Do you know what ship he got drafted to?" Dave asked. "Hunter, I think," Danny told him, swaying slightly in his seat as he drunkenly raised his rum to his lips.

Dave searched his memory for signals he'd recently read. "I'm sure I read something about her. Wasn't there some trouble on board when she was down in Devonport? She was brought back to Pompey afterwards."

I shrugged my shoulders. "Don't know, Dave. Can't say I've seen anything about her. If you're right, though, Mike must be in town. If there was trouble, she would have definitely come back because I'm sure she's a Pompey ship."

Danny conjured up a new awareness in his sozzled brain. "I think you're right, Dave. Yeah, I'm sure I read something about her. Shit, I can't put my finger on what it was all about, but I'm sure you're right."

"Well, if he is on her, but we don't really know if he is, I'm pretty damn sure he wouldn't miss tonight," Dave smiled, the expectation that he would eventually arrive cheering him.

I had no doubt that of the three of us, Dave was the one who would like to see Mike the most. For he was the one who usually went to his aid on those distressing days he constantly wrestled with whilst we were in training.

I didn't mean to dampen Dave's spirit but I told him that Mike may well be elsewhere.

"Reckon he would have phoned the pub if he was in Pompey and couldn't make it," Danny suggested. "I could phone Hunter!" he suddenly thought

"As pissed as you are, I think not!" Dave rejected.

"Yeah, they'll most likely send a shore patrol and we'll all end up in cells," I concluded.

That awful experience was something I could readily relate too. On my last birthday I'd gotten more than pissed, and the Military Police, who constantly toured the town, deemed me too drunk to return to ship when they came across my unstable body. I did their stupid walk along the white line routine and as a result spent the night in cells. A reprimand was all I received, but that night in the nick was punishment enough. Military Police can be pretty nasty buggers, even when they're trying to be nice!

"So what's Malta like?" I asked Dave.

"You been to Malta, Dave?" Danny asked, bringing his body upright from the slouching position it had slipped into. "What's it like down the Gut? I hear there's shags on every corner."

Dave was scanning the bar, I could see he was becoming more and more disappointed at the absence of Mike. "Malta's great. Everything's so cheap..."

"Even the birds," Danny broke in.

"Especially the birds," Mike informed. "The Gut's crawling with girls on the game. That's some street, the Gut. Runs for about a mile, small bars on either side and all down hill. Fine when your on your way down and getting pissed. Different story when you trying to stagger back up."

I screwed up my face. "I heard the water tastes like sewage?"

"Who wants to drink water?" Danny laughed, raising his rum.

"They reckon if you fall in Malta's harbour and swallow any of the stuff, you're as good as dead. Have to have every injection under the sun," Dave enlightened us.

Danny winced, he hated injections. Even fainted in training, and that was whilst the guy in front of him was having his jabs.

"Can't be as bad as India, they toss dead bodies in the Ganges," Danny said, rubbing his arm.

"Been to India have we?" I belittled his information.

"Read it somewhere."

"You can read!" I started on him. Well it had been awhile since I last slagged him. Danny didn't take the bait.

I noticed Dave do another sweep of the bar in search of Mike. "Malta's got this lift which takes you close to the start of the Gut. About two hundred foot high. I tell you, Smudge, you'd wet your nickers if you went on it. For every three foot it goes up, it suddenly drops two. Sure as heck made me glad to reach to top."

"Wouldn't have frightened short arse. He loves big things. Don't you, Danny?" I tried to bait him again.

"Did you get your leg over, then?" Danny ignored me, bringing things back onto sex, my favourite subject.

"Mind your own business," said Dave, tapping his nose. "Not all of us want to tell the whole bar about our sex lives."

"Didn't get a shag," Danny interrupted, looking in my direction for support.

"Oh, I must tell you about Sugar's bar in Gib. This gay bar we all went to for a laugh," grinned Dave as he began to recall an hilarious event.

I was all ears. Dave talking gay talk was more interesting to me than Danny's straight shag stories. Even Danny's eyes took on a sparkle.

"We'd gone with some old salts," Dave began. "With us we had this young, cherry boy skin."

"Who's calling who a cherry boy?" Danny intervened.

"Hark at big dick," Dave couldn't resist coming back at him, "Your original one shag wonder."

Danny opened his mouth to defend himself. I got in first, "Go on, Dave."

"Anyway. Sugar's is packed. God was it camp! I'm not sure how many sailors were in there. It was out of bounds, you know?"

"Naughty boys!" I scolded.

"Queer boys!" Danny got his tuppence worth in.

Dave gave an unconcerned tut at Danny's remark. "Well, it was pretty obvious who the gay guys were but mixed amongst them were some real dishy lasses."

Danny began to pay more attention. Dave laughed at him, knowing what was coming.

"This old salt, who must have been there loads of times and knew a good few of the punters, takes us over to this really beautiful bird and introduces us. Simone, she is. Well, what can I say," he laughs. "Knocker, our little cherry, is smitten. And after the cruel old salt had plied him with every conceivable concoction the bar had to offer, he ends up on a sofa with her, giving her every inch of his tongue."

Dave took a swig of rum and passed cigarettes around, sheer amusement written all over his face. "Come closing time, Knocker is well away, stroking her legs and feeling her tits, his excitement clearly visible," winked Dave. "With that, the old salt says we should leave them to it and for us to move onto somewhere else, a cunning grin filling his bubbly face. Once we're on our way to the next bar, leaving Knocker to his fate, he gives us the low down. Simone is a guy!"

"Fuck, no!" I cried, inwardly delighting in that vision. Danny, for some reason didn't comment.

"That's not all," Dave excited. "Knocker does a runner, doesn't come back to the ship! It's on the day that we're going to sail that he appears, shackled to two Military Police."

"The poor little bastard!" I sympathised.

"Bandit!" was Danny's unconcerned remark.

Dave broke into a fit of giggles, and took a gulp of rum. "But that's not the worst of it," he continued, tears of laughter streaming down his cheeks. "Behind them is Simone. She's in hysterics. Black mascara streaming down her pretty face. She's screaming at the top of her high-pitched voice, 'Please don't take my sailor away!'. You can't imagine the wicked taunts that that brought from the sailors on the upper-deck. The ship was in uproar. It was just unbelievable!"

Although that mental picture was most definitely hilarious, I couldn't help feeling sorry for the lad. "The poor kid. Did they kick him out?" I asked

"That's the amazing part," Dave laughed. "The skipper believed Knocker's story that he'd fallen in love with this GIRL and couldn't bring himself to leave her. All he got was two weeks stoppage of pay and leave."

"Good for him. But I bet he took some flak, the poor little bugger?" I said.

"Sure. But that passed in a few weeks. Tell the truth, I think he had a few new mates after that," Dave winked.

"And a sore arse!" Danny muttered.

Dave raised his eyebrows but neither of us went back at him.

"Your round, Smudge," Danny ordered, clinking that gold ring of his against his glass.

This time I couldn't let it go, I just had to ask. "Where did you get that ring?" I asked.

Dave leant over and grabbed Danny's hand. "That's a wedding ring!" he announced.

Danny wriggled awkwardly in his chair as he pulled his hand away, his face turning into wine. "Okay, I'll come clean. Look I wasn't holding anything back or telling lies or anything," he got all defensive. "I was waiting until we were all here to tell you. Now that Mike's not coming, I might as well do it. I'm married."

"You're what!" we both declared in disbelief.

"Married!" Danny reaffirmed. "A month back."

Dave being as polite as ever congratulated him. Me not being such a kindly old soul laid into him. "Fine one you are, Danny. Feeding me shit about being a virgin. Not telling me that you're married. Making up shag stories to impress..."

Dave stopped me before I lost it. "Just say you are happy for him, Smudge."

I guess I was becoming unreasonably annoyed because he was now beyond the grasp of my eager paws, and no longer was there any point in me trying to seduce him. "Who is she and what's she like?" I mellowed.

"Jane. She pretty good-looking. A year older than me."

"Taller!" I couldn't resist.

"Taller," he replied, but there appeared little enthusiasm in his reporting of the details of his new wife. "That guy who came over to me earlier? Well, he's my brother-in-law."

At least one mystery had now been solved. Even so, I couldn't help wondering if Danny knew his brother-in-law was gay, for I was pretty certain he was! "Rums?" I asked, not divulging my suspicions and not really wanting to hear anymore.

I gathered our empty glasses on conformation that that is what we all wanted, and was just about to head to the bar when I spotted a familiar face. "Mike! Isn't that Mike? Shit, he looks more pissed than we are!"

Danny and Dave glanced toward the door. "Fucking hell!" cried Dave as he watched Mike stagger around a table and nearly knock it over. "I'd better fetch him."

"And quick!" Danny agreed.

Whilst Dave went to retrieve Mike from an impending disaster, I went for rums for the four of us. On returning, it was a wonderful sight to be greeted with as Dave and Mike wrapped loving arms around one-another in a very long and affectionate hug. I could see it was quite an emotional moment for both.

When they parted I gave Mike my own very special embrace. Danny, however, didn't even bother to get up, and merely shook Mike's hand. Well, I guess he was married now and that might've dented his masculinity!

Greetings over, we sat down, Mike almost missing the chair completely. Even before he'd spoken a word, I could sense there was something wrong. The look on Dave's face as our eyes met confirmed my fears. Mike was in trouble!

Danny didn't seem to notice Mike's obvious distress and went straight for his jugular. "What you doing in civvies? We said we'd wear our uniforms!" he barked.

Mike left that question alone. "Sorry I'm late. All sorts of things held me up," he drunkenly apologised.

"You okay, Mike?" Dave asked with some concern.

"Sure. A little pissed, that's all."

"Aren't we all!" Danny grinned.

"That's a fact," I confirmed.

"So where's your uniform?" Danny couldn't leave it alone.

Mike snapped back, unusual for him. "I'd have come in a bloody dress if I wanted too! Anyway, who are you? The fashion police, or something!"

Danny grunted.

"Take no notice of Danny. He's changed a lot since he got hitched," I attacked.

"Hitched. That's a joke!" laughed Mike.

"What's so fucking funny about that?" Danny went for him again.

"Don't matter," Mike laughed at him again.

It wasn't the best of reunions, now that we were all here. In fact, it was heading in a decidedly uncomfortable direction. I put it down to the fact that we were all well gone.

Dave quickly attempted to bring the tone down. "You look great, Mike. Lovely tan," he teased. "Been abroad?"

"Actually, I have," Mike revealed. "In the Far East for the last couple of months."

"Makes Malta look pretty tame," Danny tormented Dave.

"If you're going to be a bitch for the rest of the night, why don't you piss off and shag your wife!" I unforgivably hit back at him.

"If you two don't pack it in, I'll bang your heads together," Dave angered.

There was no doubting he was capable of doing so but it was unusual for him to contemplate such a thing. I could sense that he wanted the two of us to lay off of one another and get Mike talking. To discover why he was in such a state. Problem was, with our ongoing battle it was difficult.

Dave wrapped his arm around Mike's shoulder. "You sure everything's alright? You seem a little, well..... upset."

"I'm fine. It's just been a pig of a month," Mike reassured him, brushing the back of his hand beneath his eyes. "Tired, that's all."

"How come you've been in the Far East, aren't you on Hunter?" Danny probed.

Mike shook his head.

I could see he was holding something back. I expect Danny could also. I decided to come to his aid. "So what's it like over there? I bet it's bloody great! Where did you go, Singapore or Hong Kong?"

Mike gave Danny a lethal look. One which I didn't think he was capable of. "Singapore. It was just brilliant. I tell you, that Tiger beer's wicked! Three pints and you're on another planet."

"Danny's on another planet after three sniffs of rum," I told him but wished I'd kept my mouth shut.

"Smudge's a bandit, Mike. I bet you didn't know that. Navy's full of 'em," Danny accused, almost incapable of speaking without slurring his words.

Dave remained silent, taking in the situation, observing carefully both Danny and Mike's reactions. Mostly Mike's.

"You can be such a pratt for such a small guy," Mike went for Danny, surprising both Dave and myself.

Danny jumped to his unsteady feet. Dave was up before him and shoved him back down. "I thought this was a reunion of friends?" he questioned, glaring frighteningly into Danny's eyes.

"Shit, sorry guys," Danny mumbled. "Guess I'm up to my shoulders with booze."

"Up to your shoulders with chips," I declared, knowing he was outnumbered three to one.

"And you, Smudge. Stop baiting the little bugger," Dave warned.

I could never remember when Dave had gone at me like that, or Danny to be honest. I glanced across at him and smiled an apology. Still he was engrossed in Mike, who had a vacant expression on his sorrowful face.

I held out my hand toward Danny. "Truce?"

"Truce," Danny agreed.

"Then give us a kiss!" I just had to add.

"Smudge!" Dave glared.

Mike laughed loudly and knocked his rum back in one. I quickly passed him mine. I decided I'd had enough. Mike picked it up and sent it away.

"Steady," a concerned Dave cautioned, holding onto Mike's arm.

Mike grinned at him. "Still got room for a few more. It's alright, I can get as pissed as I like now."

There was information in that statement for all of us, but somehow Danny and myself didn't grasp it. But Dave's inquisitive look suggested that maybe he had.

"You're such a lucky bugger, Mike. All I've done since I left training was a bloody work-up at Portland, and a load of gruelling exercise in the pissing rain and wind," I complained.

"Guess you're right," Mike agreed. "Really great to end up in the Far East with all that lovely sunshine," he said. I found his enthusiasm unconvincing.

"And those Singapore shags!" Danny added. "Get your leg over, did you?" his same question to Dave repeated.

A bolt of lightening turning the bay-window white, and the loud crash of thunder which instantly followed, brought surprised shock to each of us. The good old British weather doing its usual trick. Hailstones began clattering against the panes.

"Shit, look at that lot!" Dave alarmed. "And right on chucking out time."

"That's nothing," said Mike. "When it rains in Singapore, you almost drown standing up. Got these paper umbrellas what smell like rat's piss to keep you dry. I thought they were just trinkets that trippers took home, but you can hardly see the sky for them when a monsoon starts. Everyone's carrying one."

Danny appeared to have slipped into silent thought, his shag question having not been attended to.

"Bring anything exciting back, apart from an umbrella?" I asked Mike. "Mind you, that might be a handy thing soon."

"Like a nice little Singapore shag!" Danny woke up.

Mike rolled up his sleeve. "Got this Rolex watch. I know it's a fake but it looks like the real thing. And I bought a Nikon camera, but I don't think that's fake."

"Bet you paid a load of duty on them?" Dave cheered as Mike's spirit appeared to be rising.

"Didn't declare them," he smiled.

"Naughty boy. I've heard of guys who have got caught years after they've brought things back," I told him.

Mike lowered his gaze into the two empty glasses before him, his cheerfulness seeping away once more. "Don't think I need worry about that anymore. Danny, you going to get the round in before last orders?"

"Not for me," both Dave and I refused.

"Come on you miserable buggers. You'll be off soon. Have a tot with your old mate," Mike pleaded.

"Okay," Dave reluctantly agreed, but I knew he didn't want Mike to have anymore. "I'll pay for them, Danny," he offered. "Get what you want for yourself. Just a single rum for me, though."

"And me," I fell into line.

"Double!" Mike ordered.

Dave gave him a uneasy look. "Where you staying, Mike?" he asked, more to discover where we would need to take him. "Smudge is at Sally A's and I'm booked in at a B & B. We've got weekend passes. Don't know where Danny's at, but he's got to be back on Sunday."

"Oh, just up the road. Got a week's leave."

"Lucky bugger," I said.

A couple of sailors, with street girls in tow, bundled into the bar to escape the storm. One of them nearly sent Danny and our rums flying. Surprisingly, being in the mood he was, Danny didn't make anything of it. Cursing under his breath, he placed the drinks onto our table, gently this time. "I remember!" he excitedly announced, giving Mike the strangest of looks.

"What?" I asked.

Danny thought for a while as he pulled out cigarettes and offered them around. We each took one.

"What do you remember?" Dave repeated for me.

"Those signals. You sure you weren't on Hunter, Mike?" he asked.

Mike looked uncomfortable and sent half of his double away. "Told you!"

"I'm sure you were." Danny disbelieved him. "You showed me your draft the morning after our farewell party. I'm positive it said Hunter."

Mike shrugged another denial but looked very uneasy.

"Does it bloody matter?" Dave snapped. "And leave Mike alone!"

Unexpectedly, an unknown fire sparkled in Mike's eyes, the likes of which I'd never seen before. "It's alright, Dave. I can take care of myself."

"So, you going to tell us what you remember, Danny?" I prompted.

Danny grinned cunningly, staring right into Mike's eyes as he went for him again. "Hunter," he began, puffing heavily on his cigarette, "was brought back to Pompey because they caught a bunch of queers on her."

Mike's gaze remained rivetted to Danny's face, frighteningly so.

"Big deal!" I said.

Danny continued his assault, his insides fired with a kind of hatred I had never witnessed before. "I'm telling you. Mike's damn well lying. He was on Hunter. Okay!" he rounded on us. "I read the bloody signals and those which followed. What's your surname, Mike!" he demanded.

"Stop this shit now!" Dave flew at Danny, gripping his arm like a vice.

The unexpected hostility made me shiver. I'd never seen anything like this within our group before.

"It's okay, Dave. Let the little bugger say his piece," Mike insisted, a eerie calmness coming over him. "My surname's Barns, as you well know!"

"Yeah I know!" Danny cruelly delighted. "I also know you were part of that queer shit. Admit it!"

Neither Dave or myself could believe our ears, or the viscous way in which Danny was delighting in attacking Mike.

The fist which slammed upon the table, when Mike brought it crashing down, certainly brought me from my mesmerised state. Angrily, he bent toward Danny. For an instant I thought he was going to punch the little sod's lights out. Then, quite calmly, he softly said, "It was me in that box, Danny. Me!"

I didn't have the faintest idea what Mike was on about but Danny did. Oh yes, Danny sure did! And as we waited for his response, we watched him turn from an angry red into a ghostly white. Before our very eyes the blood drained from his shocked face!

Without warning he jumped to his feet and raced from the bar, knocking over ours and another table on his way .

"Thanks, Danny. Didn't want to drink the bloody rum anyway!" Mike hollered after him.

"What the fucking hell was that all about?" I asked, still stunned and shaking by the ferocity of it all.

Dave looked helplessly at Mike, waiting for an answer. Any answer.

"Doesn't matter," Mike sighed and fell back into his seat. "Look, guys,

I'm staying only ten minutes walk away. Pub's closing now. You want to come back for another drink or some coffee?"

"Sure," Dave comforted, rubbing Mike's shoulder and glancing over to me for my nod of agreement.

"What about Danny?" I asked.

"Fuck Danny!" was Dave's abrupt reply.

Mike squeezed a smile from his lips and reached for both our hands. "Cheers, lads. I really appreciate it. There's something I have to tell you," he tearfully announced.

The three of us stepped from the bar and were soon being buffeted and battered by the stormy weather as we headed in the direction Mike had indicated. Dave and myself on either side of him, holding him upright.

ELEVEN

Mike felt the heat of our warm bodies and found them comforting as we huddled together against the storm. He knew he was so drunk he could hardly walk. His thoughts were elsewhere - his attack on Danny and the resulting disappearing act. He wasn't too upset about that. Danny deserved it.

As we braved the elements, Mike's mind wandered away to the day Danny had been tied to the gym's wall-bars by Mann. On the pretence of sending him into the store to stow some gear, Mann had in fact ordered Mike to climb inside the vaulting box once our class had left. As always, Mike obeyed without question.

On this particular occasion - Mike had done this before - instead of jumping straight inside the box, he peered around the door, eager to discover who he would be sucking this time. In amazement and disbelief, he watched as Danny, one of his closest friends, was secured to the wall-bars by Mann. His excitement increased as he watched Mann seduce his prey. But then, quite unexpectedly, Danny appeared to be enjoying his imprisonment - if Mike could call it that - and he soon heard him begging for Mann's massive cock.

Mike wasn't bothered by his own excitement. He knew he liked guys. After all, that was why Mann often used him in his seductive sorties. That said, not once had Mann seduced him.

Becoming even more aroused, he watched Danny sucking the massive cock and beg for more each time it was withdrawn. So excited was Mike, he spent a good deal of that observation wanking himself, eagerly anticipating the moment when Mann would bring his prey to the box and fuck his arse. As always, that finale would culminate in the trainee's cock being pushed through the handgrip whereupon Mike would have his feast.

Having seen Danny's huge offering many times, he couldn't wait!

Now, as he trudged drunkenly toward his flat, supported by his loyal friends, Mike could not understand Danny's evil and cruel attack upon him. Especially when he was at his most vulnerable! There could be no doubt that Danny was totally turned on by his sex with Mann, and was most likely gay himself. Mike couldn't understand why was he now attacking gays himself?

His thoughts shifted to Hunter. Danny had been right all along. He had been on her. He remembered the day he joined the ship. A shy and vulnerable trainee. A trainee who like guys!

It was in his Mess, as he changed from his uniform into evening-wear, that he glimpsed the most beautiful guy he'd ever set eyes upon. Shyly huddled beside a locker was a sailor-boy skin of the most adorable kind, dressed only in a pair of tight blue briefs, his crotch hair visible in wisps on either side of them. Mike was swept off his feet!

Black-brown eyes caught Mike's focussed gaze, and a pair of thinnish lips parted over perfect white teeth and released a wounding smile. Mike smiled back at the shy-looking, Indian lad.

Whilst he continued to dress himself, he was constantly drawn toward the slim, smooth figure standing before his own, taking in all of that heavenly body he possibly could before each delicate part was covered by clothing - his micro-dot nipples, dark and flat; his undeveloped chest with a ripple of ribs showing through; his waist, so thin, you could possibly touch thumb to fingers if you held it in two hands; his tantalising bulge beneath the blue cotton briefs, not overly large but a delight yet to be revealed; and finally his hairless arms and legs with just a hint of muscle on each.

The youth was like some treasured ornament of the highest quality. One that you would dearly want to possess and cherish. But one you would always be in fear of breaking, so fragile and vulnerable did he appear.

It took some time to get to know Naresh - his name revealed some days later by a friend. Unlike Mike, he was a radar operator and having different jobs their paths didn't cross that often. On the evenings when they were both off watch, they would sit together and play cards or other board-games. It was during these enjoyable times that Mike discovered more and more about Naresh and began to fall in love.

Naresh was an abandoned child from an early age and he'd spent most of his young life being juggled from foster-home to foster-home. He saw the navy as a way out of that viscous cycle. Despite his unhappy childhood, he had the most pleasant nature and was always happy, although often painfully shy. But beneath those dissolving smiles he drove Mike crazy with, there lay a hidden sadness which ran deep. A constant desire to be loved. Constantly, Mike wished he could be the one to supply that much needed comfort but being shy himself was unsure how to go about it. Also, there had been no indication from Naresh that he had similar sexual feelings. Mike suspected his closeness was more to do with his desire for friendship.

Over that first month there had been little physical contact between them, only the occasional embrace during a friendly wrestle. Mike found that satisfying but knew he would dearly love to embrace Naresh. Gently kiss every inch of him as he peeled away the layers of his of uniform. It was a thought which constantly tormented him during his nightly relief.

Remarkably, not once did Mike discover the delicacy which lay hidden beneath Naresh's cotton briefs. But it was often temptingly close but always hidden. Sometimes fully erect or rising. It drove Mike crazy!

But then came this incredible weekend, the weekend when both were off watch at the same time.

Naresh had often told Mike that he would dearly love to be able to leave the ship for a break but didn't really have the cash to stay at the Sally 'A' or a B & B. With excited enthusiasm, Mike bravely offered

Naresh a weekend with himself. With equal enthusiasm, Naresh agreed.

Mike was fortunate enough to have a flat he could use, his parent's holiday home. Because his ship was based at Portsmouth, they had offered him full use of it. To treat like his own home. Somewhere to escape too. Mike had quickly jumped at the opportunity. It was a good place to relax on those nights away from the ship or on shorter weekend breaks when he didn't have enough time to travel to his folks.

Dressed smartly in civvies, Mike and Naresh soon found themselves, hold-alls in hand, marching over the gangway, the warm sunshine greeting their freedom. And with that unexpected freedom emerged a brighter, more confident Naresh.

A visit to a bar seldom used by sailors brought them closer to Mike's flat. Naresh wasn't really a drinker but accepted a pint of beer. The alcohol soon had him giggling.

A further ten minutes stroll, after they'd abandoned the bar, took them to a street with Regency style housing. After climbing three steps, they were standing at the doorway of the ground-floor flat. Excitement caused Mike to fumble with his keys as he opened the dark blue door. But the unexpected hug of thanks given to him by Naresh upon entry almost made his heart stop. Such was the overwhelming desire of Mike to be close to Naresh, he almost gripped his tiny waist and lay a passionate kiss upon his lips.

After Mike did the usual tour for new friends, and fixed drinks, the remainder of the afternoon was spent relaxing in the garden, where they continued to chat and sip rum and coke. Naresh became increasingly merrier as each hour passed.

Proudly, Mike witnessed him mellow, believing he had done the right thing, although he did have some concern that the reasons he'd brought him here were somewhat selfish and probably sexual. However, he had already decided that he would make no advances toward Naresh.

As they became more comfortable in each other's company, so the antics started, and they began chasing one another around the flat - bedroom, hallway, second bedroom, lounge and bedroom again. On their second entry into the master bedroom, they flopped onto the bed and began to wrap their bodies around each other and wrestle. Mike's heart pounded painfully in his chest and his cock became rigid as they excitedly rolled on top of one another. He wasn't sure if Naresh had spotted the stiffness in his pants but his cheeks flushed brightly believing he had. Although he would have gladly stayed locked between the lad's arms and legs, Mike pulled away.

The afternoon whizzed by as they relished in the joys of being alone together. And as the evening drew in they watched TV and listened to music; first sat apart then more closely on the same large sofa. A romantic film finished their wonderful day, bringing tears to both their eyes.

Approaching bedtime, Mike slipped into the guest's bedroom to check it was clean and tidy. It always was. Naresh stayed on the sofa, relaxing to the music, having selected a romantic song.

"All I need is the air that I breath,

And to love you..." painted the walls in a sound which would have been pink if coloured.

As Mike folded down the duvet and fluffed up the pillows on the spare bed, he too was moved by the emotive words, thinking how true they were; knowing that he had found the love of his life. Painfully saddened, he moved back into the lounge.

So badly he wanted to cuddle Naresh into his arms and sleep with him. He no longer thought about sex with him. He just wanted to hold him close and draw out the loneliness from his gentle soul and replace it with love.

Naresh asked him what he'd been doing. Mike told him he'd been preparing the spare room. His next question, when he asked why couldn't they sleep together almost bowled Mike over, and it took an unbelievable amount of control not to leap onto the sofa and engulf the lad he'd fallen in love with.

In an excited nervousness, Mike agreed.

They showered separately, although the thought of both of them beneath a fine spray was more appealing to Mike. And as he washed, he imagined both of them naked and soaped from head to toe in bubbles. An instant erection sprang between his legs but somehow he managed not to play with it.

Whilst Naresh took his shower, Mike turned out the top light and switched on the bedside lamp, its red bulb painting the bedroom in a warm, seductive glow. Slipping naked beneath the duvet, Mike always slept naked, he eagerly awaited his return.

Looking wet, cute and cuddly, Naresh moved back into the bedroom dressed in Mike's over-large dressing-gown. His delicate, nut-brown, hairless chest peeped through. His fine black hair flattened on his head.

He looked stunning and sexy and.....

Mike's cock bolted upright, he couldn't help himself!

Excitedly, he awaited the removal of the gown, anticipating viewing for the very first time what treasure had for so long lay hidden beneath Naresh's briefs. Immediately the gown parted and fell to the floor. Mike's eyes opened wide, sparkling with excitement, instantly focusing on the crotch. Just below a neatly tied navel indented on a flat brown tummy, the obligatory briefs - red this time - teasingly covered the small bulge. Mike smiled warmly, easing Naresh's obvious shyness.

Drawing back the duvet, careful not to reveal his own arousal, Mike offered Naresh the place beside himself. His excitement increased even further but he was also aware that just because a friend had asked to share his bed, didn't necessarily mean he wanted to share his body. With a shy smile Naresh jumped in and lay on his back.

For sometime that is how they both remained, Mike too afraid to make any contact with the delicate skin which tormented him so painfully.

They chatted as they lay closely together, skins barely touching, Naresh thanking Mike for bringing him over for the weekend, and saying how relaxed and happy he felt in his company. Mike reciprocating by saying it was the best weekend he'd spent in a long while.

After a lull in the conversation, Mike guessed it was time for them to sleep, and wished Naresh good night. Reaching over his hot body to switch out the light, a waft of arousing fresh sweat and deodorant meeting his nostrils, Naresh unexpectedly kissed his chest.

Mike's hand dropped away from the lamp and touched his soft cheek, his eyes searching Naresh's deeply. No words of encouragement were needed from the beautiful mouth parted sensuously before his own, and their lips met in a passionate kiss. It was for both the first time either had kissed another guy. And the way in which they did indicated that it had been something they had longed to do for some considerable time.

For a long while that is how they remained, mouths locked together, youthful tongues searching, their young hearts competing as they excitedly raced.

It was Mike who pulled free first, rolling onto his back, a strong passion driving him wild, eager to devour every inch of Naresh. Somehow he held back. Immediately, Naresh scrambled on top of him and brought their mouths back together. Mike threaded his fingers into the fine strands of wet hair, pulling their bodies even closer. Gently and affectionately he slipped his palms over the nape of Naresh's slender neck, then down over the shoulders. With each electrifying dart of Naresh's tongue, Mike's body was charged with even more passion.

Mike moved his palms ever downward and over the lower regions of the satin smooth back, around the slender waist, and finally onto both buttock cheeks. As he gently caressed them through the briefs, he felt Naresh's soft, young cock spring to life. Speedily his palms moved inside the cotton pants and over the bare buttocks.

Mike could restrain himself no longer, desperate for their cocks to touch. Carefully he slipped the briefs over Naresh's bottom, thighs and knees; all the while their lips locked in kisses. With some clever manoeuvring, he hooked the pants with his foot and pushed them over the ankles. Naresh kissed him ever more passionately as youthful flesh rubbed youthful flesh.

Their hips began to gyrate enthusiastically rubbing tummy against tummy, cock against cock. Sticky slivers of pre-come spilled from the eye of both cocks and was rubbed into tender skin as their bodies gently gyrated together.

Both had waited so long for this moment that soon the gentle touches became more powerful. More intense. Passionately, tongues searched palates, playfully entwining. And hands moved between thighs, teasing tender foreskins excitedly back and forth.

Still Mike had not seen the delicate sex he was caressing and rubbing with ever-increasing rapidity. With a swift movement he threw the duvet from their entwined bodies, rolled Naresh onto his back and began to kiss toward the erect cock. Naresh whimpered as the mouth moved lower.

Enthusiastically, Mike began descending the delightful torso, swirling his tongue over flat nipples which barely rose as they were tweaked and teased. Next the moist tongue darted into the navel. Naresh released a mouse-like squeal of delight as it searched and began to rub Mike's head, forcefully pushing it ever lower, desperate for the mouth to reach his swollen sex. Mike obliged, moving ever downward, anxious to reach it himself.

Just before reaching the solid, teenage sex, Mike raised his head. He wasn't disappointed. The cock was magnificent. A tuft of tight black curls were partly obscured by the rigid four inches which stood proud and upright against the brown satin tummy and lying in a puddle of pre-come. Mike licked away the pool and began worshipping the cock with passionate kisses. It felt as though his brain would exploded, such was the passion raging throughout his excited body.

He could only think how superb and succulent it looked as he allowed his eyes to momentarily feast upon it. In fact, he didn't know where to begin. Like he'd just been given a box of chocolates containing only his favourites centres. Naresh helped him choose, and with another forceful shove, sent Mike's mouth over the throbbing head and down to the bush of black curly hair.

Naresh thrust into the welcoming hot mouth, his small buttocks flexing furiously. Frantically he grasped Mike, pulling him into a sixty-nine position. Excitedly Mike shuffled his body around keen to oblige, his cock leaving a trail of pre-come on the sheet.

Like Naresh, he too had never had a blow-job before!

Naresh's cute mouth parted over the much larger sex, sucking it feverishly, his own young thighs wrapping tightly around Mike's head. Chest rubbed on tummy, tummy on chest as they devoured each other bud to the base. Their excitement increasing with every thrust, desperate to bring themselves off.

Hands glided tenderly over tightening buttocks and into the hollows of firming cheeks, then along backs and shoulders. Their movements synchronised as they thrust and withdrew.

It was Mike's cock which fired first, his balls rising inside the hairless sack, crazily shooting his come, unable to hold back the pleasurable pain any longer. Enthusiastically, Naresh swallowed the juice, lapping lustfully on the bulging head for the final remnants until Mike could take the sensitivity no longer. Mike worked ever faster on the young cock he was savouring, keen to swallow his own mouthful of come before his had been fully jettisoned. Naresh obliged, squealing uncontrollably as his thick cock pumped and pumped and pumped, filling Mike's mouth to capacity as it returned to the pubic bush.

Both lads were spent, their bodies glistening sweat. They rolled apart. Mike swung himself about bringing them face to face. Lovingly they embraced, locking their teenage bodies tightly together and began playing with tongues in mouths. Both smiled warmly and affectionately. Blissfully happy.

Exhausted and deeply in love, they eventually found sleep.

It was early morning when Mike awoke. His cock stiff and bursting. His arms wrapped Koala-like around his lover's body. Naresh's soft, firm bottom nestled in his lap. Quietly, he slipped from beneath the duvet and entered the bathroom. Desperately he wanted to fuck Naresh. Make love to him.

Mike always had condoms in his bathroom but wasn't too enlightened about gay sex. But he knew he would need something to make screwing easier. Sailors often joked about Vaseline and because of that he'd never plucked up the courage to buy any, thinking that they would discover he was queer. Searching the medical cabinet, he discovered a substance he thought might work, his mother's hand-lotion.

So excited he could barely breath, he slipped back beneath the duvet and locked his body onto the lad he loved. In anticipation of fucking Naresh, his cock immediately sprang to life.

Lovingly he began to caress Naresh's short sex, bringing it stiff. He wasn't sure if these were the roles that each should play, but he desperately wanted to be inside of him.

Mike rolled the condom over his stiffened cock, his heart beginning to take on an excited rhythm. He could feel Naresh's pounding in sympathy against his chest. Carefully exploring with a lotioned finger, he gently eased it into the virgin hole, delighting in the soft texture. Naresh wriggled excitedly backward. Mike probed deeper and deeper into the darkened depths.

Sensing the time was right, Mike lathered his cock excessively. A large quantity of lotion dribbled onto the sheet. Silently, he placed his cock between Naresh's virgin cheeks and began to push. Again Naresh didn't object and wriggled backward.

The head of the cock vanished. Naresh's legs twitched and trembled excitedly. Mike ceased movement but didn't withdraw, waiting for him to speak. Only a moan meandered from his mouth and his palm fell onto Mike's buttocks and pulled them toward his own. Realizing Naresh was comfortable and wanting him, Mike resumed his forward movement.

Naresh began sucking in gulps of air as he took more and more of the large cock and fought against the pain of losing his virginity. But still he didn't cry out, and continued to grip Mike's buttocks and pull them toward his own. With a little more patience and gentle persuasion, Mike's cock vanished! Almost immediately, his rhythm took on a more enthusiastic pace as both entered a state of euphoria. Soon he was thrusting hard and fast into Naresh's buttocks, the cheeks relaxing or contracting as the depth changed.

Whimpers of pleasure signalled that Naresh was in a state of indescribable bliss. It caused Mike to fuck him even more fiercely. Swiftly, he wrapped his palm around his young sailors cock, pumping it hard and fast.

It was Naresh who emptied his cock first, filling Mike's palm with come. Twisting his head around, he cried out, "I love you Mike. I love you so much." Pushing their mouths together and reaching back to pull Mike deeper.

Mike responded with his own words of love as he buried his cock lovingly into Naresh. Moments later, his own come filled the condom to overflowing, accompanied by ecstatic sighs and whimpers.

They completed their love-making as before, bringing themselves face to face; kissing, cuddling and embracing. Neither of them were in any doubt that they were hopelessly and dangerously in love. It had been carved for them in stone by some unknown spirit. Never to be broken!

And that was how it was to remain. Whenever possible the two of them would be making love together in Mike's flat. But when on board a healthy distance was always kept between them. As far as they knew, nobody ever suspected that they were inseparable boyfriends. So deeply in love!

TWELVE

Mike's automatic pilot turned us left toward a house and up a short flight of steps. Neither of us had noticed his tears during our walk, the heavy rain quickly washing them away. He fumbled a key into the lock of the door and let us in.

On a corner, some two hundred yards back, a solemn silhouetted figure stood silently watching.

The warmth of the flat was welcoming and made even more so when Mike threw some switches. "This way," he called, leading into the lounge.

"Nice pad," I admired.

"Sure is," Dave agreed.

"My folks," Mike informed us, and vanished into a bedroom.

I spotted the table's broken glass, small shards lying on its surface, and nodded to Dave. He acknowledged with a finger to lips, indicating I should not mention it.

Mike returned from the bedroom and tossed track-pants and T-shirts to both of us. "Here put these on. I'll stick your kit in the airing cupboard." It was a sensible gesture, we were soaked to our underpants.

Whilst we undressed, Mike went to fetch glasses for the rum. I couldn't help noticing Dave's body, after I'd dwelt momentarily on his dick, and what appeared to be long thin scratches and a couple of massive love-bites close to his cock. "I hope you keep her in a cage," I laughed.

Dave grinned back at me, pulling his track-pants up, his long cock hooking on the elastic waistband then flopping inside.

"Lucky her mouth didn't get to your cock," I laughed again, referring to the love-bites. "By the looks of things, she'd have sucked your bloody balls through the end of your dick." Dave didn't comment but continued to grin as his T-shirt came over his head.

For a brief moment I considered my track-pants. Dave's, I noticed, fitted him perfectly, obviously belonging to Mike. Mine, however, were even too short for my small self and obviously belonged to somebody else. I didn't comment upon it when Mike returned with glasses and ice, dressed in a dressing-gown. Anyway, he appeared to have brightened considerably since leaving the bar.

"Rums?" he offered.

There seemed little point in refusing, Mike would only have insisted until we accepted. "Sure," I agreed, "But just a smidgen." Dave requested a similar measure.

Three glasses were brim-filled and topped with ice. "Sorry, I don't have any optics," Mike laughed as the rum gurgled out. It was pleasing to see him cheerful again. "Is that a smidgen, Smudge?" he giggled again, passing me mine.

"Reckon it's spot on!" I accepted the quarter of a pint of Navy Neaters.

Dave took his and took a gulp, wandering over to the sideboard where he'd spotted a photograph of us lads. "Remember this, Smudge?" he asked, handing me the picture.

"Shit, yes. Look how pissed you are! And how come Danny's so tall?"

"Remember? We stood the little bugger on a beer crate. Said he didn't want to look the odd one out," Mike recalled, sinking almost half of his tot in a single gulp.

"Was that some run ashore!" Dave rubbed his forehead. "Four paralytic, virgin sailors."

Mike looked thoughtful for a moment. "Yeah, some run. To virgin sailors!" he brightened again, raising his glass.

"Virgin sailors!" we both saluted.

Mike zapped the CD and sent some love songs into the room. Dave moved around to the spare armchair and plonked himself down. I returned the picture to the sideboard and retook the other armchair. I could sense Dave wanted to ask Mike what the problem was but things had mellowed since we'd arrived, so he held back.

During the following quiet moment, I was tempted also to ask Mike what he'd been talking about when he told Danny about being inside some box. I also wanted to know what these signals were that Danny was supposed to have read. Again it seemed the wrong moment, so I sat silently with my own thoughts, leaving Mike and Dave to theirs.

The storm continued to zap lightening flashes around the flat, a close bolt causing each of us to jump. Mike topped his glass but continued to remain silent, the love songs taking him somewhere beyond our company. Dave spotted his watery eyes and decided to ask his inevitable question.

"So, what's going on, Mike?" he asked with a concerned smile.

Mike wrestled thoughtfully with his reply, turning his glass in his hand. He took a huge gulp, lowered his gaze and blurted, "I'm gay!"

I have to say, I was totally stunned. But a thrilled excitement zipped from my brain right down to my dick. My heart skipped excitedly as I wondered what I should reply with. The most honest thing to say was so was I. Momentarily, I scanned Dave's expression, giving him the opportunity to reply first.

"So what," Dave calmly responded. "It's no big deal. Is it, Smudge?"

"Not a problem for me," I supported but still too cowardly to reveal my own sexuality. But by the dejected look on Mike's face, I knew there was more to come.

Mike drew the back of his hand across his face and wiped away newly formed tears as he wrestled uncomfortably with his next piece of information.

Dave quickly slipped from his armchair and placed himself supportively beside him and rubbed his leg. "Look, Mike, there's loads of gays in the navy. It really isn't such a big deal. You've just got to be bloody careful, that's all."

Mike began to sob uncontrollably. His head sank shamefully lower and he dropped his glass between his thighs. "It is!" he spluttered.

The sight of Mike sobbing so, brought tears into my own eyes. I sensed there was a dynamite revelation about to explode in our faces, and my body tensed and braced itself.

Dave's arm went over Mike's shoulder and pulled him close. "Come on. Spill it," he encouraged.

Mike sat upright, threw his head back, sighed, laughed and cried even more.

"Don't do this to yourself, Mike. We're your mates. For Christ sake, I'm gay as well!" I came clean.

Dave shot a proud glance across at me. "And so am I," he stunned both of us. "And what's more, I'm a bloody rent-boy!" he laughed.

Mike erupted in confused giggles and rubbed his eyes. "Shit!" he laughed and cried.

"Right, then. Let's have the lot," Dave encouraged. "From the top."

Mike gave a sniff, dried his eyes more thoroughly, took a deep breath and began. "Danny was right. I was on Hunter. For about eight months. I met this lad, Naresh." Mike stood up and walked to the sideboard, pulled out a picture and handed it to me. In all honesty, all I wanted to say was what a gorgeous kid he was when I saw this most beautiful of guys staring back at me, but remained silent and passed the photo over to Dave.

Whilst Dave studied the teenager, Mike continued where he'd left off. "After about a month, I invited Naresh to stay for the weekend. It was the most wonderful weekend in my life." Tears began to stream down his sorrowful face. "Well, we fell in love. Madly in love! " he emphasised with a sigh. "It was real difficult to keep it secret. And even harder not to be all over one another when we were at sea."

Mike took another supportive gulp of rum, bracing himself for what I sensed would be something tragic. "Anyway, everything's going fine. Whenever we were both off watch, we would spend our time together over here," he took a deep breath. "Naresh was an orphan, you know? Never had anyone truly love him before. God, we were so happy!" Again the tears flooded his eyes. Dave embraced him tightly.

"Then it happened," Mike cried. "Everything fell to bits!"

I leant forward and filled my glass, barely able to listen to anymore and watch my friend in so much pain.

For what seemed and eternity, Mike sobbed helplessly into Dave's chest.

"Come on, Mike," Dave encouraged him, gently rubbing his head. "It'll feel better when it's all out."

Mike sniffed and attempted a smile to reassure us he was fine. "I got this draft to the Far East. It was a bolt out of the blue. It's funny, but we never thought that one day we'd get drafted and have to separate." He smiled at his own stupidity.

"Naresh asked me not to go," he continued. "Told me he'd die without me. Begged and begged for both of us to turn ourselves in and get booted out. But I loved the navy. And what would I do in civvy street?" Mike broke down again, the unbearable pain of recalling these events swamping him. "We didn't even have time to say goodbye," he sobbed. "One day I was with him, next day I was in Singapore."

I began to feel that we were over the worst of his story, and Naresh and himself had merely split. I began to feel better, realising it wasn't the end of the world for him, although obviously painful.

"I thought things weren't that bad," he continued, "because he sent me letters every week and I wrote back. But suddenly they stopped. I wrote and wrote but he never replied."

Another flood of tears rushed from his eyes and he buried his head into Dave's chest. "Oh, Dave, Dave," he wept.

I stood and walked into the bathroom, shamefully embarrassed by my own tears which were falling freely. Dave, too, was the most upset I'd ever seen him.

Mike had stopped speaking but restarted his depressing story once I'd returned.

"Next thing I know, I'm on a plane flying back to the UK. It was strange but I felt excited and happy. At last I'd be able to find out why Naresh hadn't written," he laughed nervously between sobs, again thinking how naive he'd been. "I couldn't believe it, but I was met at the airport by the Military Police. They escorted me to Pompey barracks and handed me over to some Special Branch guys."

Mike was shaking badly now and could barely lift his rum to his lips as he moved into the details of his Special Branch interrogation. "A bundle of my letters to Naresh and some damn photo of Naresh and myself kissing were tossed in front of me. They asked what they meant. There was nothing in the letters to say that we'd been having a relationship. We were careful about that. So I denied that anything was going on between us. But the damn photo said differently," he sobbed.

Mike took another slug of rum. "Then...." He stopped abruptly. His face as white as snow. It was as if he had just died. Dave gripped his trembling body tightly. I left my armchair and moved to his other side, wrapping my arms about him, sensing that we'd finally got there.

The dynamite was about to go off!

"Then this bastard shouts at me..." he sobbed hysterically. "'So why did Naresh kill himself!'"

"Oh, shit!" I cried as the lad's pretty face flashed before my eyes. "I'm sorry, Mike," I hugged him as tightly as I could, "I'm so sorry."

Mike plucked the Navy Neaters from the table and drank straight from the bottle. It slipped from his grip and crashed onto the glass, dividing it into three large sections which shattered when they hit the magazine rack below. Quite remarkably, I managed to catch the bottle before it met a similar fate.

"The fucking bastard!" Mike screamed and sobbed, slamming his fist down and sending blood spurting from a small gash as a shard of glass sank into his flesh. "They kicked me out for being gay. Couldn't give a fuck that I'd just discovered my boyfriend had killed himself!"

Dave didn't speak, he was sobbing uncontrollably, unable to take in the enormity of it all. With a most loving gesture, Mike momentarily overcame his own grief and began comforting him.

"Sorry, Mike," Dave finally composed himself. "I'm so very sorry."

Mike gently raised Dave's sorrowful face and wiped away the tears. For a moment they gazed into each other's eyes. Bending forward, Mike lovingly kissed him. Moments later, their mouths met more meaningfully. I wasn't sure if it was the right thing for each of them to be doing. Whether Mike was on some rebound thing. But I was in no doubt that some desire which they held for one-another in training had just been rekindled. To be quite honest, I found it a beautiful moment.

I decided the best thing to do was to leave them alone for awhile. Picking up the pieces of glass and placing them onto the magazine rack, I took the table into the kitchen and closed the door. Whilst I carefully wrapped the broken glass in old magazines and dropped them into a bin, it occurred to me who the track-pants I was wearing belonged too. An iced finger drew itself down my spine, and I shivered with the thought of wearing the dead lad's clothing.

Not really wanting to disturb Mike and Dave, I re-entered the lounge. They were embracing and kissing more passionately than before. Still I wasn't sure if it was a good thing, but the immense pain of loosing a boyfriend was one I really couldn't comprehend and therefore I had no right to be judgmental.

I think my doubts soon evaporated once I had retaken my armchair position. Mike had a new glow in his cheeks. A more vibrant 'I want to live' look about him. Dave, too, appeared as if he found the Golden Fleece.

"You boys okay?" I asked. Both beamed joyful smiles toward me and beckoned me join them. They kissed again as I walked over. Four arms hugged me into the triangle as I sat down. And a friendly kiss from each spoke volumes. I was sure Mike was not to be alone for much longer.

Mike had a new spring in his step as he went to make coffee. Lifting the picture of himself and Naresh, he kissed it once, opened the sideboard and laid it to rest.

"So your granny's a punter?" I laughed at Dave.

"A nice rich one," Dave laughed back.

"And she's got long nails and a wicked mouth," I teased.

"She's got a whip!" Dave grinned.

"Has she?" I said, wondering what it was like to be whipped and how much Dave was into that sort of thing. "Hurt, does it?" I asked.

"It's only play," he informed. "I'm not into heavy stuff. You got a boyfriend, Ken?"

I was pleased Dave wasn't into the heavy stuff, and again it was nice to have him use my name. "No. But I've had some fun."

"I bet you have," he grinned. "I've always suspected you were gay? Your eyes were always glued to Danny's dick."

Mike came in with coffees and a fresh bottle of booze, scotch this time. He retook his position beside Dave and immediately gave him a kiss, dropping his palm onto a thigh. I wanted to ask if they were going to get something going between them but thought it out of order. If I was wrong, then it would have been a pretty cruel assumption, Mike having recently lost his boyfriend.

For a good half hour we chatted like the old buddies we were. With every minute Mike's spirit was soaring higher and higher. He even told a few sordid stories and cracked a couple of sexy jokes, continuously topping our coffees with dashes of scotch. At last, the reunion I had been looking forward to was beginning to materialise, only trouble was Danny wasn't with us anymore.

THIRTEEN

The doorbell rang loudly, surrounding the flat in a constant buzz, the unknown visitor determined not to release it! Mike and Dave continued to be locked together in a cheerful embrace as I was detailed to answer the door.

"Who is it?" called Mike, somewhat disinterestedly.

I looked at the bedraggled figure before me. "Danny!" I called back. "Shall I let him in?"

Danny looked up at me decidedly alarmed. "Smudge," he pleaded.

"Not my flat," I told him rather cruelly.

A deliberating silence followed. "Well?" I asked again.

Dave voice thundered through the hallway. "Let the little sod in," he laughed.

Danny walked beside me, head bowed. I ushered him before his jury. Before he'd even gotten halfway through the lounge door he began apologising. It was a sorrowful sight to see him dejected so, and I knew he was truly sorry for his outburst. More honestly, he was probably worried that we now knew something about him which he hadn't told us.

I cannot say he fell to his knees before Mike and Dave, but it was humble enough. Mike responded to his pleas for forgiveness with instructions for me to fetch a glass and pour the soaked slime-ball a large scotch. I guess his remark was fair comment. Danny gulped heavily upon the large whiskey I'd poured and plonked himself in my armchair. Immediately, Mike told him to get up because he was sodden through. Danny jumped as if some officer had shot a command at him.

Again I was summoned to do a chore. I didn't mind being ordered about. This time it was into a immaculately clean bedroom, to bring shorts and T-shirt for Danny. I deliberately chose the smallest, tightest pair I could find! Most likely Naresh's.

Unconcerned, Mike and Dave continued to embrace and engage in the occasional kiss. I have no idea what Danny made of that, but I was more than happy with the developments.

Danny dropped his head into his hands, then looked back up. "I suppose Mike's told you?"

"Yes, he's told us," I replied briefly recalling that sad scene.

"Look guys. I wasn't being a hypocrite," he defended himself, taking a supportive gulp of scotch. "You see, I never realised I was gay. Mann got me that day and tied me to the wall-bars and gave me this blow-job. I had no idea I would like it, but I did!" he confessed.

Dave and myself remained silent, rivetted to his every word. For some reason Mike had a wry smile on his face, enjoying every utterance which was coming from Danny's humble lips.

"As you know, Mann then throws me over this vaulting box and fucks me senseless. It was amazing, I just loved it!" he excitedly told us. "Next thing I know, is my cock is being stuffed through one of the handgrips and Mike's sucking me. Course I didn't know it was him at the time."

Dave and I shot looks of disbelief at Mike, who's grin widened.

"Well, after that, I suddenly became confused. Still am. I didn't have sex with anyone again from that day. I thought the answer was to get hitched, so that's what I did." Danny sighed. "It was a fucking disaster. I just couldn't shag her. Straight away, on our honeymoon, she tells me I must be a queer. Course she was right, but I still couldn't accept it."

Danny looked up at the three of us for some support or sympathy. We remained silent.

"So, there you have it. I've been an absolute pratt, especially to Mike. Even you, Smudge. I'm really sorry. Truth is, I'm a bloody closet case!" Danny lowered his head in shame.

I started laughing first. Mike and Dave soon joined me. Heartlessly, we fell about in tears, unable to control ourselves.

"What the fuck's all this! I'm trying to say sorry here," Danny angered.

"Danny, you stupid little sod. That's not what Mike's been telling us," I collapsed in laughter and slapped Mike's thigh. "But it was sure interesting!"

For a brief moment Danny was stunned, then seeing the funny side of things he too erupted. "Oh, shit!" he laughed, sinking another gulp of his drink. "I think I've just hung myself by the balls!"

Mike picked up the scotch and re-filled our empty coffee mugs and Danny's glass. "The Buffer. The miserable bastard!" he toasted.

The three of us raised our glasses. "The Buffer!"

At last we had finally got there, we were having our friendly reunion. Each of our secrets of being gay were revealed to Danny moments later. We didn't delve into Mike's sad story, there would come a time for Danny to hear that later. And Mike was the happiest he'd been for a very long time to be upset again.

"So, Danny, has Mann got a really big cock or does he have a conga eel as a pet?" I asked.

Danny laughed loudly, relaxing by the minute. "You ain't seen nothing like it!" he informed, drawing his short body into his armchair and tucking his legs under his bum. "You joke about the size of my cock but you'd be speechless if you saw his. When he dies, I'm sure the thing will be able to survive on its own!"

As Danny imparted that thrilling vision and took a more comfortable pose, I was pleased I'd given him the tightest pair of shorts I could find, for I could see his enormous cock dancing around like some caged animal, growing and growling beneath them. Being a Friend of the Earth supporter, I knew I would be only too pleased to release it back into the wild.

"Do you give good head, Mike?" Dave nudged him and winked.

"Better ask Danny," Mike kissed him.

Danny blushed slightly, still slightly uncomfortable with the knowledge he'd imparted. "I don't think he heard me objecting," he replied, again shuffling in his armchair and pulling that tantalising cock tighter against the cotton shorts.

I decided to get Danny off the hook. I'd do my own fishing later. "How much do your punters pay?" I asked Dave.

Mike shot him an inquisitive glance.

"Depends what I'm giving them. If it's special stuff, then anything up to a couple."

"A couple of quid," Danny giggled, pleased no to be wriggling at the end of the line.

Mike laughed at that. "So what's the strangest thing you've had to do?" he asked.

"Christ, there's been so many it'd take all night. I've worn maid's gear and dusted a guy's flat whilst he tossed himself, and sometimes he'd make me wear Marigolds whilst I tossed him."

"Your pulling our dicks!" I challenged.

"That's worth a couple of quid," Danny kept his joke going.

"I guess the most bizarre was this guy who was into classical music. He made me shove a flute up his arse and play Green Sleeves whilst he wanked."

"Bollocks!" I spluttered, blowing fiery bubbles of scotch through my nose when he caught me in mid gulp.

"Believe it!" Dave insisted. "You'd be shocked to know what kind of sex guys want.

"Done any straight stuff?" Mike threw in. But I sensed he wasn't totally happy with Dave being a rent-boy. Even so, like Danny and myself, I could see he thought Dave was spinning stories just to make us laugh.

"Did this married couple once. Mostly for the guys benefit. You'd be surprised the amount of straights who like getting screwed. She gave me a blowjob afterwards. It was awful. Birds have no idea how to suck a cock."

"What about you, Mike? Done any good blowjobs lately?" Danny asked, now bringing he legs back over the front of the armchair and spreading them wide apart.

I had no doubt Danny was being turned on by this talk, his cock was well stiff and crammed against his leg. And if he had been telling the truth and hadn't had sex since Mann shagged him in the gym, he must have been on the brink of shooting his whack just listening to Dave. However, my priority of helping him with his dilemma was overruled by wanting to keep Mike from having to go through the Naresh thing again. I opened my mouth to intervene but Mike got in first.

"Not many," Mike surprised me, appearing unaffected. "But I'm hoping that will soon be remedied," he smiled, glancing affectionately and lovingly at Dave and giving him another gentle peck.

Danny subconsciously pulled his prick into a more comfortable position, becoming more aroused as he sussed what was going on between them. "Guess a blowjobs out of the question, then?" he grinned.

"Not necessarily," I cast my line.

Danny reached for the scotch and topped his glass. "And you, Smudge. You've been pretty quiet about what you've been up to."

"Me? I'm a good boy, I'll have you know."

"Yeah, right. I've always had a feeling that you like a cock or two."

"So, what's wrong with keeping parrots?"

I think that one went over Danny's head because he didn't laugh. "Come on," he urged. "Who have you shagged on your ship? Hang on, you better tell us who you haven't shagged because I ain't got all night."

"Careful, Danny. I don't want to get you so excited that you come in your nickers before we go to bed," I hinted. "I know what it's like with you once a year boys. I can't cope with pre-ejaculating pricks."

Danny's scotch was working wonders for him. "Yeah, you certainly wouldn't cope with this one," he boasted, gripping his mountain of meat.

"Come here and I'll show you. You little short arse," I tormented.

Danny jumped to his wobbly legs. My cock was supplied with an urgent rush of blood and sprang upward in my track-pants. Danny reached me, unzipping his flies as he climbed over me. Disappointingly, he didn't whip it out. I guess he wasn't quite ready. Instead, he thrust the hidden lethal weapon hard into my face. Its mustiness hit my nostrils and I happily sucked in the odour. Meanwhile, I gripped tightly on his firm arse, squeezed the cheeks tightly, and clamped my teeth gently over the massive head.

Danny giggled drunkenly, "Eat me you bitch!" he urged.

I reckon he must have known how desperately I'd always wanted to do that but with two mates sat close by, I felt that now wasn't quite the time. I pushed him jokingly off but swung him about and sat him on my own stiff cock. Danny wriggled delightfully upon it.

It was only at that point that I realised that Mike and Dave's silence had little to do with their shock at our sexual caper, but more to do with each of them with tongues buried down throats and hands exploring track-pants and beneath dressing gowns. Danny noticed also, and taking a lesson from both, smacked his glorious mouth upon mine and began exploring.

My insides ripped apart with delight and expectation that something great was about to take place. Never had I believed that I would be doing this with him. And it was obvious, due to the ferocity and passion with which he sucked upon my tongue and gripped my cock, that he too had been long awaiting sex with a guy since the day Mann and taken away his virginity.

Mike's face, flush from feasting, turned to face us. "I'm whacked, " he said. "Reckon it's time we crashed." Dave nodded in agreement.

"No. Dave's been whacked," I laughed.

"You can bunk with me, Dave. If you want?" Mike kissed him. Dave's expression went all puppy dog. "There's another bedroom in there, boys" Mike indicated. "It's got a double bed. Or one of you can crash on the sofa," he winked.

With that Mike and Dave vanished into the main bedroom. Seconds later, just as Danny began kissing me again, Mike opened the bedroom door, laughed, then advised "I'll think you'll find everything you need in the bedside cabinet. You know where the bathroom is. Night boys. Don't sleep too well," he winked again.

FOURTEEN

Whilst Danny and myself moved into the bedroom, stripped and jumped quite beneath the hot spray of the shower, Mike and Dave slipped beneath the warmth of a duvet and snuggled up.

It was Dave who spoke to Mike first, once again saying how sorry he was about the shit he'd been through, but not actually wanting to bring the matter up. Desperately, he wanted to make love to Mike, but felt that to hold him close and pour some love back into his unhappy body was the the most important thing.

There was a vulnerability about Mike which Dave quickly sensed. And although he'd never experienced anyone who had lost a boyfriend, he knew there might be danger in taking advantage of someone in such a susceptible position. He also suspected it might be a cruel thing to do, however much Mike may have thought he was in love again. Aroused as he was, he was determined he wouldn't fall into that trap.

Mike, however, had different plans. Although he too knew what dangers lie ahead if he allowed himself to be swept away by fantasies of replacing Naresh with another lover so soon, he couldn't help bringing their bodies so intimately close that he could have drained Dave of every ounce of love he possessed.

Lovingly, he caressed and searched every centimetre of Dave, fighting back the desire to tell him how much he loved him, thinking it would sound so uncaring toward Naresh so soon after his death. Deep inside, he knew he'd always wanted Dave as a lover, long before Naresh swept into his life. He hoped Dave knew this.

Satisfyingly his mouth searched Dave's smooth skin, lips surrounding bullet nipples, and tongue delving deep into musty, hairy armpits, ears and any other sensitive area which would arouse him. Dave reciprocated, working his mouth down the sensational brown skin of Mike's body. At one point, Mike's rigid cock was too wonderful to resist and Dave slurped around the swollen head and down to the base of the shaft and back. Mike held the working head tightly when the mouth reached his pubics, but Dave eventually pulled away and they returned to kisses and cuddles, embracing more affectionately than ever.

A tear did escape Mike's eyes, but went unnoticed.

The moon and clear skies had replaced the stormy weather, its cool light bathing both their nakedness as it shone through the bedroom window and rested on bare skin. Mike pulled Dave onto himself, chest on chest, the silver light now upon his back. He guessed with Dave's withdrawal from his dick that any passionate sex was unlikely this night. In fact, it was a strangely silent moment. In all honesty, Mike really didn't mind, still toying with whether it was right for him to be doing it. Although, the sensation of having another's body close to his own after such a long time was blissful in itself.

As they kissed and caressed, their gyrating rhythm increased - tummy against tummy, cock against cock. So did their breathing as the pleasure became more heightened, more sensitive and sensational. For Dave it was extra meaningful, extra special. Sex with punters never was a loving affair.

Carefully pulling open the bedside cabinet draw, Mike opened the lube and squeezed a generous dollop onto his palm. Desperately, he wished to place it between the hairless cheeks of Dave's arse which he'd been fondling whilst they rolled their cocks around each others. Instead, he slipped his hand between their firm stomachs and lathered both cocks. Dave gushed a moan of approval.

Frantic movements replaced the gentle gyrations. Both boys biting hard onto necks and forcing tongues deeper into throats as their excitement boiled.

The point of exploding passion came from both lads when Mike's moist fingers shot deep into Dave's hole, causing him to thrust ecstatically backward and forward; all the while jettisoning his juices over their slippery bodies. Mike's come soon followed, but not over tightened stomachs. Fired up so deliriously, Dave had dived upon his solid shaft, gratefully taking the load into his working mouth as Mike let it lose in lavish helpings.

Comforting cuddles and chat followed their love-making after they'd wiped their bodies clean. They would wash each other's bodies in the morning, the shower being occupied; the ecstatic cries emitting from it all too audible. Dave was looking forward to that. He was also wondering what fun was going on between Danny and myself. A couple of times they both giggled as their imaginations took over. And at one point they nearly crept in.

Eventually Mike drifted into slumber but Dave remained thoughtfully awake.

I cannot quite put my finger on it, but there was a sort of anger flashing between Danny and myself. Not a vicious anger. It was as if both of us had something we each wanted to get off our chests. Kindled, no doubt, in the pub. If nothing else, it would make for a raunchy, sex session!

Danny's body was still superb. He'd kept it fit and firm this past year. I expected gym visits were frequent for him, most likely laying into a punch bag and imagining it as Mann.

I took the shower-gel and squirted a lavish helping over his body. My cock was against my stomach and could climb no higher.

"Like that, Danny?" I asked as I lathered his back and strong biceps. He grunted an affirmative but seemed reluctant to admit that he was in heaven. Even his ten inch dick, that long thick dick, was lazy and only at seven. I quickly decided to change that and brought my soapy palm along its length several times. It jarred in my hand in appreciation.

I swung him about to kiss him lovingly, spotting a small tattoo of an eagle above a pierced nipple. Danny had other plans, less loving, and pulled my head firmly down onto the surgical ring. "Suck it!" he demanded.

I knew he was butch but I'd never suspected he was domineering as well. I obliged by nibbling the unpierced nipple whilst tugging gently on the ring of the other. I felt it wasn't painful enough. I've no idea why. So bit even harder. The nipple stud reddened and firmed with the attention. I bit hard again. In a strange kind of way, I was enjoying the pain I was inflicting.

Danny yelped loudly, grabbed what little hair I had and yanked my head upward. "Always thought you were a vicious bugger," he grinned.

Before I had time to reply, his mouth was on mine, sucking and slurping, teeth nipping at my tongue and lips. I felt his cock begin to rise and touch the underside of my balls. Mine had no rising problems, it was as high as it could possibly go, dripping bubbles and pre-come down the stiffened shaft.

With a sharp tug, less painful than I imagined, Danny grasped my balls and pulled them sharply down. Still he held my hair tightly around the fingers of the other hand, his mouth against my throat sucking a love bite in painful pleasurable sucks.

Not to be outdone in the dominating stakes, I drove him hard against the shower's mirrored wall, pulled myself away and sank my own teeth into his solid neck. "Wanna play rough, then?" I challenged.

Danny yanked ever harder on my cock and balls. "As rough as you like!" he said.

It hurt like fuck. But, shit, I wasn't about to complain. I'd waited a long time to have Danny in my grubby little fingers; which I'd quickly encircled around his massive cock whilst I continued to feed ferociously on his neck and shoulder. Meanwhile, excitement had finally made Danny's racing heart do its job and it had pumped the required amount of blood into his dick. At least four pints of the stuff, I reckon. Crammed against my tightening stomach muscles, I could feel a vein throbbing along the swollen shaft.

A cock in hand apiece, we began to pump more forcefully, mouths working on chests and nipple studs. Mine more so than Danny's, almost pulling my teeth out as I tugged ever harder on the silver ring.

With an unexpected stab between my buttocks, Danny parted the cheeks and rammed a couple of soapy fingers second knuckle deep. "Shit!" I yelped as they vanished into my hole.

"Too rough for you?" he smirked, delighting in my pain.

I pinched Danny's nipple hard. "I'll show you rough," I said, and twisted it sharply.

"Bitch!" Danny spat at me, gripping my hair and forcing me to my knees, and ramming his solid soapy dick between my lips. "Suck it!" he barked.

"Suck it yourself," I dampened his dominance, turning my head away.

Danny gripped my nose tightly to stop me breathing through it. I couldn't pull away and my mouth reluctantly opened as I gasped for air. Instantly his cock spread my lips wide. Forcing me against the mirrored wall, he shoved the whole thing home, his balls slapping the underside of my chin.

Now I really couldn't breath!

Desperately I gagged as he forced his dick deep then withdraw, then forced it deep again. Each time the head came back to my lips, I sucked in as much air as possible before it tore past my tonsils again. Deliriously Danny drove it hard and fast, releasing delighted shouts of "Take it all!" each time he sent it toward my stomach.

More comfortable now with the cock's girth and length, I eagerly awaited each downward thrust after it had been withdrawn; passionately glancing upward at Danny's ecstatic face and watching closely his every expression, waiting for his prick to spread my throat wide apart and begin pumping spunk.

Quite unexpectedly, just when I was relishing his ramming actions, Danny gripped my hair and began pulling me upward. Frantically, I fought him off and moved back upon his cock, begging him not to take it away; like some spoilt boy who was in danger of loosing his favourite toy. Again Danny pulled me upward, saying I didn't deserve it. Again I sank to my knees, begging and pleading, sucking and slurping along its length, worshipping his wonderful cock whilst I still had the chance. Christ, I'd almost come without even touching my own cock, so fantastic was it.

Then, without a word, Danny left the shower, treading wet footprints over the vinyl floor and onto the bedroom carpet.

My heart sank. What a master bitch! I thought. Mann must surely have sown something sadistic into his psyche for him to be turning someone on like that then buggering off. Sod him, was my next thought. And I began to soap my cock and pump it feverishly. Admittedly, my thoughts were mostly centred on what I'd just been lavishing so lustfully upon.

Moments later Danny re-entered the shower and grinned hurtfully, his sex still solid and standing proud. "Impatient, aren't we?" he wickedly laughed, pulling a rubber over his immense cock.

A mixture of stupidity, excitement and fear rushed throughout my body in tingling spasms. Stupidity, because how could I possibly think he'd get so worked up himself and not to finish the job. Excitement, because he'd returned. And fear, because he was stroking a rubber down a massive dick the likes of who's mammoth proportions I had never taken before!

"Just keeping things ticking over," I grinned back at him. "Thought I was wearing you out?"

"Boy, are you in for a shock!" he boasted, then grabbed me roughly and swung me around to face the mirrors.

I think I could have fought back. Should have fought back. I think he used something to make his entry less painful before he sank his dick in a single thrust into my arse, and his balls swung between my thighs and struck my own. I don't think I screamed. I know I did! It didn't just hurt. It fucking hurt! And my insides exploded in fire as the solid flesh tore against soft.

"Oh, God!" I cried as my cock went limp with the shock and my legs turned to jelly and folded beneath me.

Danny was unmoved and soon had a remedy for my disappointing dick, pumping it briskly up with a soaped palm, slam-dunking his cock into my basket with such ferocity, a tile cracked as I was buffeted against it.

He gripped a chunk of neck with his teeth, continuing to ram his cock into my arse with even more intensity. "Wore me out, eh!" he growled.

Truthfully, at that point all I wanted to say to him was that I was sorry. Very, very sorry. Or more truthful than that, that the sadistic, little bugger was killing me. But then, just before I screamed my submission, my head became delightfully dizzy, like I'd taken some euphoric drug. Immediately my buttocks relaxed and my cock bolted upright.

"Fuck me, Danny. Fuck me until you drop dead or it kills me!" I pleaded. "Give me all you've got you little runt!"

I guessed I'd thrown some secret switch because Danny was taken aback by my outburst and stopped fucking. Just as quickly as the rough stuff started, it stopped.

"You okay, Smudge? Not hurting you, am I?" he lovingly whispered.

"Don't stop you little sod," I yelled at him, shoving my arse with all of my might onto his dick. "I told you to fuck me hard. Fuck damn it. Fuck!"

Danny swiftly obliged and moved back through his gears. But this time there wasn't the aggressiveness. Instead, he gently lathered my body with gel, hair as well, and sensuously slid his palms around my willing buttocks.

Seductively, he rubbed his strong chest against my back and his hands on over every inch of my body. Come climbed inside my cock as he tormentingly teased and massaged it. But it was his massive cock constantly broadening my arse and breaking unknown barriers within which was doing me the most damage. No, not physically but to my brain which was being fed mind-blowing chemicals by some sex-maniac gremlin within my head.

If there was another planet which was devoted purely to sex, then I was definitely on it. I hardly knew where I was, let alone what day it was. And by the look on Danny's euphoric face, he was on the next flight.

"Oh, Danny," I gushed. "I've got to come. Soon. Now!"

"Yes. God, yes," he agreed with a rush of warm breath into my ear, turning our bodies side-on so we could watch his final thrusts duplicated in the steamed-up mirror tiles.

In a state of bliss I watched his handsome, boyish face pressed against my own as those luscious lips and tongue nibbled at my earlobes. Lower down, I could clearly see his mirrored buttocks flexing as they thrust back and forth, impaling me so joyously on that huge dick which was being withdrawn completely then plunged back into darkness.

And now, through ever dimming eyes, I helplessly witnessed him pumping my prick wildly as my body dissolved into his. The shadow was something new. I barely had the presence of mind to take it in. Danny's mind was gone, to where I do not know, so he didn't notice. He'd found his planet 'euphoria' and would probably never return.

I think it was Dave's face which peered through the misty steam and made some sort of apology about needing a pee. I think it was Dave's head I gripped tightly upon as the mouth sank over my cock, replacing Danny's hand, and sucked and sucked until I was senseless. Whoever it was, I didn't care. I only knew I filled a mouth to overflowing with a wealth of creamy come, shooting it in thick streams and ecstatic screams as Danny drove his dick deep into my arse and yelled, "I'm coming! Oh shit, I'm coming!"

FIFTEEN

A block of sunlight pushed my head against the pillow, bringing my eyes wide open and shut again into a squint. The clock had already ticked us past midday. Beside me lay Danny, slumbering like a baby, sucking his thumb. I would soon replace that with something more substantial.

I brought myself close to his hot body and cuddled up, wrapping my arms about his waist and gripping his dick, which stood proudly with its usual morning glory.

Danny stirred, rolled onto his back and opened one eye. For a moment it looked as though he was unsure where he was. "Smudge," he sighed. "What time is it?"

I kissed his mouth before I answered that it was closing on one and then began to bring my attention back to his dick.

Danny groaned disapproval and pushed my palm away. "Shit. It feels like I've got a dead donkey in my mouth."

"I had a pretty lively jockey in mine last night," I kissed him on the chest, again bringing my hand over his cock.

"Shit, I'm sorry, Smudge. Wasn't too rough was I? A bit pissed, I was."

"A bit pissed off, I reckon. I've only got one ball now and I think you could put a submarine up my arse and it wouldn't touch the sides," I teased.

Danny laughed then closed his eyes. He looked baby-face beautiful. A different lad than yesterday. "Fuck, my tit hurts," he told me, rubbing it and screwing up his face.

I bent and gave it a lick. It did look sore and I could see a bruise would form. "Yeah. Reckon I got a bit spiteful on that one. Sorry."

Danny embraced me, climbed on top of me and lovingly kissed. "The lads up yet?"

"Don't think so."

"You know last night?" he suddenly remembered.

For a minute I thought he was going to come out with some I'm not really gay thing. "What about it? You enjoyed it didn't you?" I challenged.

"Fuck, yeah! Thanks," he kissed again. "No, I was talking about after

I arrived and I thought Mike had told you about Mann. What was it he told you? I was wondering all night."

"Suppose I might as well tell you," I said. "He's been booted out."

"Thought he had. I guessed as soon as he didn't come in uniform that something funny was up. And those signals made me even more sure. Poor bugger, he loved the navy."

"That's not the worst of it. He got kicked out cos his boyfriend topped himself and they found all these letters and things."

"Jesus Christ! The poor sod. He must think I'm the son of bitches. Why the fuck didn't I keep my big mouth shut?"

"I wished I'd kept my big mouth shut last night," I made light of it, "then perhaps my throat wouldn't be killing me."

Danny laughed. "That was some blowjob!"

"It sure was," I agreed.

Danny looked concerned. "Is Mike okay?"

"I think so. I reckon he got most of it out of his system last night. Just thank God you weren't here. It wasn't pleasant. Anyway, he's got Dave now. He'll look after him. And I've got you, at least for awhile," I winked.

Danny kissed me again, more meaningful this time. But I knew I'd spoken the truth. Knew it was for only until he went back to his ship.

Our lips parted. I began to work my way down his body, licking and kissing over his defined pecks and muscled abdomen, then finally into the fuzz of hair and over his cock.

"Ah, yes," sighed Danny, as my mouth went deep on his dick.

The bedroom door burst open. Mike and Dave - trays in hand and wearing white briefs - barged in. They were greeted by a pregnant Danny with a blissfully happy face.

"Thought you might me hungry, Smudge," Mike giggled. "Looks like we're just in time."

Hastily, I scrambled from beneath the duvet and onto my side of the bed, my face crimson from the heat and the important work I'd been engaged in. "Don't you buggers ever knock?" I asked.

"Only when we come into a ladies room," Dave laughed.

"Well you should have knocked, then," Danny rubbed my head, grinning.

"Knock. Knock." said Dave.

"Who's there?" answered Danny.

"Izure," said Mike.

"Go on then," I said. "Izure who?"

"Izure breakfast," Dave and Mike spoke together, walking one either side of the bed and sitting down.

"Wow! Cremated toast, runny eggs and leather bacon. My favourite," I teased.

"Didn't know you've been in my ship's canteen," said Danny, pulling the tray with food toward himself.

"Hey, pig! It's for the four of us," Mike slapped his hand.

Whilst Danny and I held the trays, Dave and Mike slipped beneath the duvet at the other end of the bed; one of Mike's legs between Danny's and one of Dave's between mine. Some tickling of cocks and balls with feet followed, and both Danny and myself nearly dropped the breakfasts, giggling helplessly.

I cannot say we ate like pigs but we certainly pigged out. I for one was famished. Coffee followed that fantastic breakfast, accompanied by loads of friendly chat - nothing about Naresh and not too much navy stuff. There were a few digs about Mike's ability to cook and he had a few digs back at us, mostly sexual.

Meal over, the trays went to the floor and we continued to chat.

I suppose it was inevitable, mates in a bed together, and soon the four of us were under the duvet and playing games like scouts at camp. Tickles and wrestles, screams and yelps passed away an hour. Both Dave and Mike's briefs disappeared during that frolic. The duvet also did a flight across the room, along with the pillows.

It was Danny who momentarily dampened things by saying that he'd have to leave within a couple of hours. It wasn't his fault. I told Mike that I'd have to be off at the same time. It was a lie really. I just felt that Dave and Mike should spend some time alone

"Hug for old buddies," suggested Mike, stretching his arms wide.

We moved our bodies together, sitting cross-legged, me opposite Dave, Mike opposite Danny - a kind of square, rather than a circle. Arms went over shoulders, scrum-like, as we huddled even closer.

"I love you lads," whispered Mike. "Thanks for last night."

I gave him a huge hug and kiss. That was followed by both Danny and Dave's lips. Then each of us kissed Danny. Then Dave. And finally it was my turn. About nine kisses apiece. We seemed to enjoy that, so we began again. And whilst I kissed Mike, more lengthy this time, Dave kissed Danny with equal passion.

We swapped around several times and continued to kiss ever more passionately. Each embrace becoming more meaningful and sexual. There could be no hiding the four erections which had developed. I'm not sure who's hand moved first, but mine was around Mike's, Mike's around Dave's, Dave's around Danny's and Danny's around mine. Our other arms resting on shoulders.

We stayed that way for ages, caressing backs, kissing and licking bodies, gently rubbing cocks, breathing becoming more excited as our passion grew.

It was Mike who released Dave's cock first, bending over to release Dave's hand from Danny's dick. Of course he knew what that dick tasted like, but he sent his mouth smartly down, obviously keen to suck it again.

We each received the same treatment from Mike whilst we continued to reach whatever body or cock we desired, but careful not to bring ourselves off. No words were spoken as we kissed and savoured sexes, only whimpers of pleasure and satisfied sighs escaping our lips.

Danny went next, sucking furiously on each cock. Dave followed with just as much zeal. I followed him.

It wasn't a competition, but for myself Danny had the best mouth for sucking cock, or maybe it was just the biggest. I guess it didn't matter, each of us were brought to the brink many times but released at that vital moment.

There was no set plan. Nobody had choreographed it for us. Instinctively we knew what positions to take. Mike and Danny went head to tail and began slurping under balls and over bulging cock-heads. Dave and myself knelt against the small of their backs - one on either side - locked our mouths together, gripped cocks and began tossing above them.

A whimper from Danny and his palm reaching for my cock, told me to turn the page to the next act.

I gave Dave another lengthy kiss then pulled away. The bedside cabinet opened with a squeak but didn't disturb the sucking lads. I grabbed the necessary equipment and rolled Dave's condom over his dick whilst he did mine. We lubed each other's dicks and both of the lad's buttocks with lavish helpings. Silently Dave and myself took our respective places, our cocks stimulated and stiff.

It must have been a wondrous site for any onlooker. An adorable, edible sight. Three beautiful white bodies with a cute coffee-coloured one sandwiched in between. Like some exotic chocolate waiting to be devoured.

I had never thought it possible that I would be entering the sacred place I was about to enter. And to my surprise, Danny's arse, that sensational, firm, athletic arse accepted me willingly and without complaint. Dave and myself barely needed to move, Mike and Danny's buttocks doing the work as they pushed their pricks into eager mouths and backed onto even keener cocks. But we did. Oh, God we did!

Deliriously, I drove into Danny. Biting hungrily into his neck and back. More lovingly, Mike accepted all of Dave, in slower, more meaningful movements. Whimpers of delight escaped from all of us as hands explored bodies, whilst mouth pushed passionately over cocks and cocks pounded more forcefully into passages. Dave and I glimpsed each other as we fucked. I could see he was in love. I, unashamedly, was in lust.

More excitedly, now, we screwed and sucked, sucked and screwed, coming ever closer to climax, ever closer to our second meal of the day. To this end, Danny offered me Mike's brown dick. Greedily, I gulped it down, giving Danny deeper thrusts into his arse as reward. Mike squealed in thanks as I drove my mouth deep upon it!

It was Mike's body which was first to tremble with an uncontrollable excitement, the fire within about to ignite the rest of us. With a gasp from the deepest part of his belly, his stomach tightened, pulling in and defining a ripple of muscle. Quickly, I returned his cock to Danny, who went wild upon it, sucking it like it was the last cock he was ever going to suck. On seeing his excitement, I moved my face close to his, nibbling his ear, thrusting harder and faster into his arse.

Dave, sensing Mike's imminent eruption followed my lead and went from slow penetrations into powerful thrusts, moving his face closer to Danny's dick which was darting in and out of Mike's mouth.

A squeal of delight, a gasp and another squeal of delight saw Mike shudder from tip to toe as he launched his load into Danny's mouth.

Danny gulped hard and fast but the juice kept flowing. Swiftly, he withdrew, unable to swallow all of Mike's pumping cream. My mouth was on it in a flash, sucking and savouring. Instantly, my own ecstatic cry escaped from my throat as the taste of Mike's sweet spunk melted in my mouth and my cock exploded inside of Danny!

Danny, knowing that I'd come, arched backward, then quickly forward, then backward again. Locking his lips onto my mouth, swapping some of Mike's come from his into mine, he let loose his juice. Come gushed from his cock, filling Mike's mouth to overflowing, a large amount flooding over his lips and down Danny's rigid cock. Dave was there in seconds, driving down on the pumping cock, then licking wildly over Mike's face.

Dave had bravely held back until the last second. His balls had almost vanished, drawn painfully inside his abdomen. With a manly roar, so loud it made me jump, he locked his mouth onto Mike's, his balls rose another inch and his cock exploded!

"Jesus, fuck," was our joint viewpoint as we fell in an exhausted heap.

A fifteen minute rest was all we had, an urgency for Danny to return to ship taking over. We showered together whilst Dave and Mike took our places beneath the duvet and cuddled up.

"Fetch scotch and glasses," was Mike's command after we'd both got dressed. Danny went for them.

A triple scotch filled each of the four glasses.

"Friends!" Mike toasted.

"Friends!" we joyfully sang, sinking half a glass each.

"Gotta be off now, lads." A worried Danny glanced at his watch.

Danny and myself moved over to Mike and Dave and gave them a final kiss and hug.

"Take care of yourself, Mike. Dave, you take care of him. And yourself" I said, feeling quite sad.

Both nodded.

"Yeah. Take care, you lovely buggers," said Danny, tearfully.

"Cabin Boy. Same time next year. Right?" said Mike, a few tears slipping down his cheek.

"Cabin Boy!" we all agreed.

"The Buffer. The miserable bastard!" Mike raised his glass, sweeping away his tears with his other hand.

"The Buffer. The miserable bastard!" we hollered back at him, draining our glasses.

SIXTEEN

So that was our reunion. And now, a year on, once again I'm sat in the Cabin Boy waiting for the lads. As usual, it's packed to the bulkheads with drunken, jolly sailors. I had left Danny at the dockyard gate that afternoon and Mike and Dave in bed together. As far as I know everything is well with each of them. What I can tell you is that Danny got thrown out of the Navy, as did Dave. Danny had told me that he'd walked up to some Military Policeman, in his usual cocky manner, and told him that he'd love to shag him. He was immediately arrested and after a lengthy investigation was discharged. He's a rent-boy now, working the south coat between Devonport and Portsmouth. I guess he really did hate his ship.

Dave did it a little more subtle and requested an interview with his Divisional Officer. He informed him that he was gay and had a civilian boyfriend. He, too, went through the usual unnecessary interrogation and was discharged. He's no longer a rent-boy but is happily in love with Mike and living with him on some houseboat idling around the Norfolk Broads. Dave did the decent thing and passed most of his regular punters onto Danny, who were more than pleased for that!

I guess that's all the gossip I can tell you until the lads arrive.

What about me? Oh, I'm still in the navy.

Why? I guess I love shagging virgin sailors!

more sexy novels from

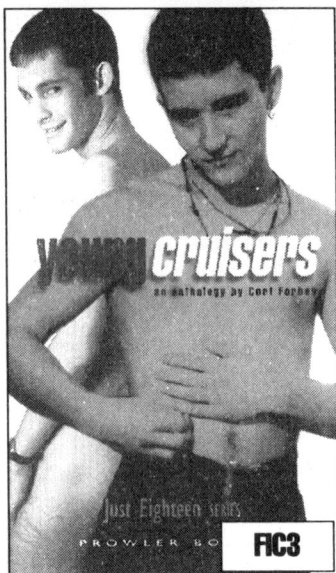

Corporal In Charge FIC4 £5.99

Twenty short stories of hot and sleazy sex. Fritscher details each story down to the last drop of cum. From teenage wank sessions to college locker room fun to hard sex in the army, this book covers every fantasy.

Young Cruisers FIC3 £5.99

The third novel to cum out of the Just Eighteen series is a tantalising selection of short stories on sleazy first time adventures. Black and Blue is a passionate story of how a young guy gets fucked for the first time by his fantasy man, a stud with a giant cock. Been There, Done That takes us into the world of hustlers where Ty unsatisfied with his tricks goes out and gets his fair share of hot spunky action.

PROWLER BOOKS

Slaves FIC2 £5.99

Slaves is the tale of Jack's sexual encounters which begin as he joins the mile high club. Cumming off the plane he falls headlong into one horny sexploit after another. Under cover as a journalist writing about the slave trade, Jack gets more than his fair share of native cock.

Diary Of A Hustler FIC1 £5.99

Follow the escapades of 18 year old Joey as he goes through his hot'n'horny training for his first hustling jobs. As muscular Thane shows Joey the ropes they soon realise that Joey's young blond boyish looks will be popular with a host of men looking for that ideal plaything.

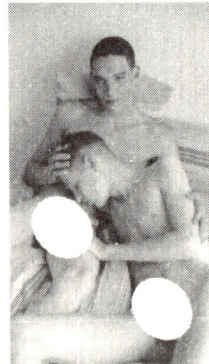

Young And In Love   JE7   £15.99

A beautifully shot voyeuristic & erotic film of young love.
Two young'n'cheeky English couples go on a hot'n'sleazy
holiday to Amsterdam. Let well endowed PJ and slim
Mark turn you on as their passionate clinches reach a
steamy climax. See Sean and big Brian's smooth, naked
bodies as they writhe in ecstasy. Good storyline & five
sexy boys who obviously enjoy one another as much as
you will. 75 MINS   BBFC CERT 18

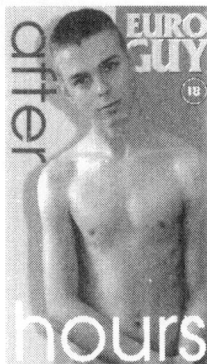

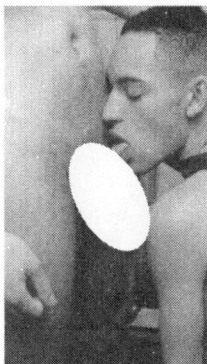

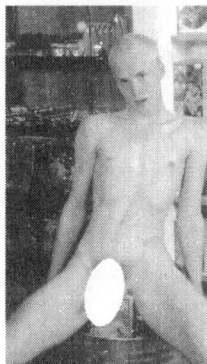

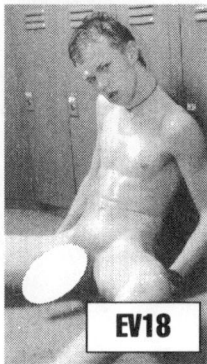

EuroGuy After Hours EV18 £15.99

Here's your chance to find out what really goes on in a shop after closing as five sexy boytoys let you in on their horny exploits. Slim smooth Dave shows what you really do with a penis pump. Discover cheeky Viper's intentions as he gets caught by blond Matthew for stealing. Cute, hung and ready for anything these guys are the best we have seen in ages. 60 MINS BBFC CERT 18